UNEQUAL JUSTICE

Beverly Lane Lorenz

iUniverse, Inc.
New York   Bloomington

iUniverse books may be ordered through booksellers or by contacting:

iUniverse
1663 Liberty Drive
Bloomington, IN 47403
www.iuniverse.com
1-800-Authors (1-800-288-4677)

Because of the dynamic nature of the Internet, any Web addresses or links contained in this book may have changed since publication and may no longer be valid. The views expressed in this work are solely those of the author and do not necessarily reflect the views of the publisher, and the publisher hereby disclaims any responsibility for them.

ISBN: 978-1-4401-1737-4 (sc)
ISBN: 978-1-4401-1738-1 (ebook)

Printed in the United States of America

iUniverse rev. date: 01/24/2009

CHAPTER 1

A S THE WHEELS OF the wide-bodied, jumbo jet gently touched down on the slippery, wet, runway at JFK International Airport, Evan William Judd peered out from his small, rain-splashed oval window into an ominous, cold, grey day. The scene was one of extreme contrast from that which he had left only three hours earlier in West Palm Beach. The sun had been shinning and it was 82 degrees. April in New York was uncertain at best. The weather could go either way. It could offer encouragement with an occasional warm day to accompany the ever optimistic signs of spring in shop windows. Or, as usually was the case, it could be harsh with cold winds and an occasional late season snow. Winter weather had a way of forcing its lingering, unwelcome presence upon city residents regardless of the date. If there was anything to dislike about the Northeast, it was winter that was determined not to let go.

Evan was glad his driver would be meeting him at the gate. He was uneasy about his meeting this afternoon and didn't need the unnecessary frustrations of public transportation. He could still remember what it was like to fend for oneself in a sea of irritated, sometimes hostile, travelers who were arriving from all over the world. It had been long ago, but still, in some ways, it seemed like only a few short years since he arrived at this same airport from Great Britain to begin a new life in America.

Clearly, he was unaware of it at this moment, but, in a way, it was not unlike today in that his life would never be the same again. As the plane slowly made its way to the gate, Evan's mind drifted back to that fateful day nearly forty years ago.

His parents had both been tragically killed in an auto accident in London. Evan's only sister, Elizabeth, was not in a position to take care of her 13 year old brother. She had just turned 17 at the time of her parents' deaths. Friends of the family had offered to let her share part of a small, meagerly furnished room with their daughter until she had completed her high school education and was able to manage on her own. But, the family was quite poor and unable to take both children into their small flat. So Evan was shipped off to begin a new life in America after a distant cousin of his mother's had been contacted and offered him a home.

He had been responsible for himself from the moment he stepped off the airplane at the New York airport that spring of 1953. Back then, there was no one to greet him at the gate, and, if it had not been for the caring stewardess who had flown over with him, he might have become lost forever in the mass of people hurrying in every direction. As it happened, she was spending her two day layover in Manhattan. It was she who helped him to get to Grand Central Station by taking him with her and making the necessary connections which eventually put him on the Laurentian, the train destined to Montreal through Upstate New York.

The passenger train lumbered north stopping along the way at every whistle-stop. The scenes changed from grey concrete to a richer, softer grey-green as it chugged along and dusk settled in over the lush Catskill Mountains. With his forehead and nose affixed to the window, Evan could feel excitement building and the weight of the past several weeks lifting. He reached back into his jacket pocket and pulled out the lone photo his mother's cousin had sent him of the family he was soon to meet.

He had studied the faces for weeks and knew them by heart. Marion Holden Wright was a short, small-framed woman with medium brown hair. The eyes of her unsmiling face seemed to be looking toward something at a distance when the picture was taken. Earl William Wright stood nearly a foot taller and expressionless next to his wife.

Their two children, Evie, ten, and Earl, Jr., four, stood directly in front of their parents.

Evan put the picture carefully back into his pocket and pressed his face against the window of the train once again. Darkness was moving in rapidly. Soon there was little left to see until the train pulled into a station. The paper he kept clutched in his left hand said that he was to get off the train when it stopped in a place called Mechanicville.

The train slowed once again. Evan pressed his face hard against the glass as lights began to twinkle at a distance. The Laurentian was approaching a large, well-lit station. The door to his car opened and Evan peered at the conductor with great expectations as he called out in a loud, clear voice, "All-been-ee, All-been-ee." When the conductor was in front of the young boy, he said, "This is Albany, son. Only one more stop to go."

The train took several minutes to unload and board new passengers in Albany. Soon it was bound for Mechanicville. The excitement and apprehension began to build. Evan Judd was nearly home.

The train pulled into the small Mechanicville station at 10:25 p.m. As the conductor came through the car, Evan had his small bag in hand. "Ma--can--ick--ville. Ma--can--ick--ville." Evan watched as the man approached. "This is it, son. This is Mechanicville. This is where you get off."

Evan gripped his bag and stepped down the two big steps from the train and onto the platform. He felt his body tighten in fear as his eyes searched for those faces he had grown to know through the photograph. With his body locked in place, his eyes looked first far right and then far left. He quickly repeated the action without budging an inch. He was about to dart back onto the train when a female voice called out to him. "Evan? Evan Judd. Is that you?"

Evan's eyes moved cautiously to a point about one hundred yards directly in front of him and there, just as if the picture had come to life, stood his new family. Marion, Earl, Evie, and young Earl. He stood there staring at them until Marion came up to him and put her arm around his shoulders to lead him away. Earl took his bag and the two children fell in directly behind the new family member.

The long ride home from the train station was uneventful with the exception of the attempts at conversation by his Mother's cousin.

Marion asked him several questions. Evan was polite in answering but brief. They fell quiet after a few simple answers. Emptiness suddenly consumed him. This was not home. England was home. And, he was a long way from home. He missed his mother and his father. He missed Elizabeth. He could feel tears welling up. The adventure was over and he was tired. He wanted to go home.

Evan was young enough that he soon adapted to the routine of his new household and was able to work into their lifestyle. But, it was a far cry from the life he would begin to envision for himself. So when he finished high school in the rural Upstate New York community, Evan set off on his own. His life had pretty much been his own responsibility since his arrival in the United States anyway.

The Wright family lived on a farm, and Evan had to shoulder many responsibilities to earn his keep. He had countless chores to do, including milking and feeding the dairy cows before going to school each morning. Cleaning the horse stable was his responsibility as well, but he rather enjoyed the close relationship he was establishing with the team of old work horses, Major and May. The horse barn was a rather pleasant building which housed not only the remaining two work horses, but the farm's first iron horse, Big Bertha, as it was called.

Although Evan shared a small bedroom with Earl Jr., he spent most of his spare time in an empty stall in the horse barn next to Major. Evan's imagination allowed him to envision the old horse more as a handsome stallion out of the old west rather than the worn-out plow-horse, ready for the glue factory, that it actually was. Evan cared for and groomed both horses. Eventually, he began riding Major bareback. The work horse responded to the special treatment, and the pair seemed to thrive on this special relationship.

The difficult experiences of his youth seemed to enhance Evan Judd's character rather than damage it. He soon developed a very outgoing personality which won him friends and compensated for the loss of the family he so desperately missed. He became very popular with his classmates who welcomed an intriguing international figure. Someone not born and raised in this part of the country was so rare at the time that his differences were acknowledged as unique and special. Simply being from England would have provided him some celebrity status, but his British accent seemed to command an added dimension of respect which especially pleased Evan Judd; and, he made the most of it.

Although he had been short for his age when he arrived in the Saratoga area, he was nearly 5'10" by the time he was halfway through his junior year in high school. He picked up the last two inches of his full adult height before he entered his senior year. Although somewhat gangly in his early teen years, this did not seem to pose much of a problem with young women his age. He received more than the customary number of invitations to sweet sixteen parties and was rarely left alone when he was not working.

The community where he lived was situated adjacent to the Hudson River and was also not far from the famous Saratoga Race track. The track brought life to that sleepy city during the summers. In the days when Evan was growing up, people earned their living in customary ways. People worked at nearby plants and paper mills; they farmed, they sold insurance, and a few made the long commute to neighboring towns for private enterprise such as the General Electric Company in nearby Schenectady. A few held civil service jobs with the State of New York in Albany and made the long commute each day. Evan, as did many folks in the community, spent summers earning extra money by working any number of jobs the August races created in the town of Saratoga.

The year Evan turned 16, he got himself a job at the track cleaning stalls and helping to feed the horses. The experience of a child being raised on a farm had paid off. Not just anyone would be hired to work the stables and his experience with the horses was what landed him the job. As a stable boy, he was in the midst of the real excitement.

Evan Judd had no idea when he took the job that circumstances would alter the direction of his life forever. That summer, Evan Judd encountered Alice Whitley of the famous Whitley Stables and nothing would ever be the same again.

Alice Whitley's family owned several race horses and kept a summer place in Saratoga. Alice often accompanied her Daddy, Brandon Harris Whitley, to the track in the early morning for time trials. As was his custom, Evan hurried to get the stalls cleaned so he could watch the end of the workouts before his horses were brought back for their rub-down and feeding.

One morning, the third week of July in 1956, Alice, who would turn 15 in August, discovered young Evan as he watched the morning work-outs. She had discreetly maneuvered away from her father who was engaged in a lengthy conversation with their trainer. Evan did not hear Alice quietly approach. He did, however, feel the wood quiver slightly as she pulled herself up onto the white, wooden fence where she pretended to become absorbed in the workouts. As he looked over his shoulder to his right, Evan Judd was awe struck as he encountered the greenest eyes he had ever seen and a smile that looked as if it had been cut from the latest Colgate toothpaste ad. He could not help but return the smile. They quickly turned away from each other and focused their eyes on the track, but Evan's attention was no longer on the horses and trainers. Alice's attention had not been on the track from the moment she had set eyes on this handsome, young man.

Alice's early morning visits to the training track with her father became very regular after that first encounter with young Evan. Evan, of course, could be found at the same post every morning, without fail, from then on. After a couple of weeks, they had become well enough acquainted that Alice, in her youthful exuberance, excitedly told Evan about her forthcoming birthday party. After carefully observing his reaction to the affair, she invited him. It was at the birthday celebration he became smitten with Alice--if not exactly Alice, with her family's lifestyle. From that day forward, nothing, absolutely nothing, would come between Evan and his love for a better life. He had been bitten by the "betterment bug." Evan Judd was going to be rich and nothing was going to stop him.

Evan was jolted back to the present as the plane came to a sudden, complete, stop in front of the gate. He unfastened his seat belt for deplaning from the first class cabin. There were only three others traveling first class, so he was able to move swiftly toward the waiting flight attendant who held his raincoat ready for him to put on. A few polite words were exchanged and he was soon on his way through the exit door.

He moved quickly through the waiting crowd at the gate into the concourse and on to the main door of the terminal where his car would be waiting. His long-time chauffeur, Harrington, was opening the rear door to the limousine as Evan Judd pulled his coat collar up around his neck. He advanced swiftly through the automatic exit doors of the American Airlines terminal toward the waiting vehicle.

"Welcome home, Mr. Judd," was the only exchange between the pair. Harrington knew that Mr. Judd wanted to head directly to his Madison Avenue office before going to his Greenwich, Connecticut home. Ms. Carlisle, Mr. Judd's personal secretary for twenty three years, had told him, "Mr. J. has an urgent meeting and needs to be driven directly to the office from the airport." It was Betty, Carlisle's assistant, who had told him that the FBI was insisting upon seeing Mr. Judd the moment he returned to New York. Evidently, it was pretty confidential business because Betty made him promise not to tell a soul. Not that he would, of course. Harrington was closed-mouthed about all of his boss's affairs.

While the car rolled over the slick, wet roads from Queens to Manhattan, the cold dampness of the day permeated the air and seeped into the vehicle. He felt a chill and shivered even though the heat was on in the car. As he starred blankly out the window at the dark, dreary day, Evan Judd could not help but welcome the memories of warmer, happier, more exciting days of the summer, 1957. As his mind drifted back, his body also began to respond to the barely conscious emotional and physical demands of that summer. He was not inclined to deny his sexual urges. So, without thinking, he lifted the car phone and selected number 5 on memory recall. The voice on the answering machine was familiar as was the message. He had installed a line for his personal use into the uptown apartment he kept for Tammi. The sexy young voice said, "I'm yours darlin'. Just tell me when."

The voice, of course, was that of Tammi Lee Trottman. She had waited on Evan when he was shopping for perfume as a gift. Tammi worked at Bloomingdale's "waiting for a big break," she had told him. She was an aspiring young dancer from Iowa, (in actuality, a topless dancer from Des Moines). When she turned 23, she had decided she was ready for New York, "the big time," she called it. She just needed one good break. Meanwhile, the cosmetic counter kept her from starving. That was until Evan Judd made his arrangement with her. Needless to say, she didn't need to learn the ropes. This arrangement was actually quite a break for her. From then on, she never had to worry about starving or anything else, for that matter. He provided her with an apartment and other creature comforts as long as she was available to him.

He responded to the recorded message, "seven this evening," and replaced the phone. Evan settled back into his seat as memories of the distant past flooded over him. His mind took him back to Alice and that critical summer so very long ago.

Alice had corresponded with him throughout the fall and winter of that first year. They had telephoned each other on several occasions at prearranged times. Evan had even made a trip to Albany to visit Alice. The family was tolerant (at best) of the gangly British stable boy while in the country during the summer, but inviting him into their home in town was quite another matter. Alice had pleaded with her mother to invite him to their home for dinner during the winter of 1956-1957, but Mrs. Whitley flatly refused. So, the second best thing that Alice could arrange was to have Evan secretly meet her at a friend's house. The meeting took weeks to plan, but the tryst was well worth the effort. It was at that secret meeting Alice received her first real kiss from Evan. It was a kiss she was not soon to forget.

Summer of 1957 prompted many secret meetings. Alice continued to accompany her father to the track for early morning time trials. But, as innocent as the encounters with the young Evan Judd may have seemed to others, the fires of desire and passion were kindling as the hot days of summer passed.

The couple met behind the stable each day. Eventually, they moved their rendezvous into the empty horse stalls where gentle touching gave way to groping as their passionate embraces intensified. Alice's father was too busy with his own business to miss his daughter for the intervals when she disappeared. As a matter of fact, it was a relief to have her up and out on her own--exploring the horse business. Brandon Harris Whitley had always wanted a son to take over his interests, but his first born, a son, had died shortly after birth. Alice became a combination of the son he lost and the daughter he idolized. She meant every thing to him.

So it was not unusual to see Alice continually accompanying her father. He adored her and enjoyed having her ride in the car next to him. Never did he dream his young daughter was being introduced to the passionate, physical desires and pleasures typical for most adolescents during those teenage years of experimentation and exploration.

Summer meetings between Alice and Evan became regular. They were becoming physically dependent upon each other for satisfaction and physical release. They each lived for their brief, but torrid encounters in the horse stall. Every day as she pressed herself against his amply developed, hard, male body, it became more and more difficult to keep the heavy petting under control.

When her sweet sixteen cotillion came around that August, Alice's mother flatly refused to allow a stable hand to come to this major social event of the season. The young lovers were distraught, and Evan was bitter with anger at Alice's mother. Well, maybe he couldn't go to the party, but Evan William Judd would give Alice Stanton Whitley a sweet sixteen present she would never forget.

Three days before the party, Alice and her father arrived at the track for the early morning workouts. Brandon Whitley had several arrangements to make before the afternoon races. It was not difficult for Alice to locate Evan once her father as out of sight. Evan had made certain that his stalls were clear so that he could bring his young love back to the deserted area. As they groped each other's bodies, Evan pulled Alice gently down onto the straw. Their full-mouth kisses became increasingly urgent. It was difficult to tell where one body began and the other left off. She helped him as he maneuvered the skin-tight skimpy white shorts from her body. His blue jeans seemed to magically disappear as he pressed his hard male organ into her warm, wet, and welcoming body. Passion had given way to any clear-headed thinking. They were young and they believed they were in love.

The cotillion went on without a hitch, and most certainly without Evan Judd. But, in a strange way, he was as big a part of that night as any other guest. Alice Stanton Whitley was carrying a part of Evan Judd that was not going to go away.

He did not enjoy the memories of the months that followed. Alice and her family returned to the city at the end of August. They had phone contact every couple of weeks and he began dating someone locally that fall who he adored and hoped to marry after they completed college. But those dreams came to a bitter end when in January of 1958, Alice's parents found out she was pregnant with Evan Judd's child.

He had nightmares for years of the events that followed. Needless to say, he had to marry Alice. Not that he didn't want to "do the right thing by her," but her father insisted. Perhaps it was the way he insisted. He could still remember the day that the chauffer-driven limousine pulled up in front of the old farm house and Brandon Whitley got out.

Evan didn't care to remember the exchange between the two of them that fateful day and was relieved when the Lincoln Towncar pulled up in front of the 416 Madison Avenue office building. A uniformed doorman hurried toward the car with a large, opened umbrella. He pulled the car door open and held the umbrella for Evan and accompanied him to the lobby.

An attendant stood ready to engage the penthouse elevator as he hurried across the marble and brass lobby. "Good afternoon, Mr. Judd," were the only words spoken as the two men stepped into the car and the doors silently closed behind them. The operator engaged the equipment and the elevator moved quietly to the 74th floor where Judd's private suite of offices was located. The elevator doors opened and Evan moved swiftly from the car not slowing his pace until he entered the door to his own office. Ms. Carlisle was just two paces behind him. She took his coat and briefcase before either spoke.

"Where is he?" asked Evan in a hushed, concerned tone.

"They."

"What?"

"They. Where are they," Edna Carlisle corrected him.

"They?"

"That's right. There are two of them."

"Two?"

"That's right."

"Why?"

"I don't know why, but there are two of them and THEY are waiting in the visitor's lobby," replied Edna Carlisle.

"Have THEY said what THEY want?" inquired Evan in an appalled tone of voice.

"Not a word," replied Carlisle. "They have indicated that they will speak only with you about their business."

"Bring them in then, Edna. Let's get this over with and find out what the hell they want."

As Edna Carlisle moved from the room, Evan walked behind his desk and stood looking out the window at nothing in particular. It was a familiar view--one which he coveted. But today, the magnificent skyline and the distant East River were unnoticeable to Evan Judd as he searched his mind in an attempt to determine why the FBI wanted to see him. He was apprehensive about this meeting, to say the least. With all the money he had pumped into attorney Frank Spector, it seemed as if he could have dragged his ass in for this meeting. Hell, with the money he got from Evan Judd and company, Frank Spector should have been willing to sit in the lobby and wait to be needed. "Too busy." BULLSHIT!

Evan Judd was pulled immediately back into the present when the heavy mahogany door to his prestigious corner office opened and Ms. Carlisle cautiously led two tall, well-built FBI Agents into the room. As Evan watched her approach, her movement seemed to click into exaggerated slow motion and her voice sounded hollow and distant as he heard her say, "And, I would like to present Mr. Evan Judd. Mr. Judd, this is Agent Gordon Swift and Agent Ian Cooper from the U. S. Department of Justice."

Trained in the old school of marketing success, Evan Judd exhibited his flamboyant, "salesman of the century" personality as he greeted Swift. "Happy to meet you Mr. Swift and, ah, Mr. Cooper, is it?"

"We prefer Agent. Agent Cooper and Agent Swift," barked the tall burley agent who went by the name of *Agent* Cooper.

"Ah, well then, very well, ah..ah *Agent Cooper*. And to what do I owe this, shall we say, unusual honor?"

"Could we discuss this in private, please, Mr. Judd."

"But I have no secrets from Ms. Carlisle. We have been together for some 25 years," said Judd.

"That certainly is admirable, Mr. Judd. But all the same, we prefer to discuss our business with you in private," replied Gordon Swift.

"Surely you can't object," Evan began but was quickly interrupted.

"Private, Mr. Judd," Agent Swift interjected with finality.

Evan shrugged his shoulders in a puzzled, uncertain gesture as he dismissed Edna Carlisle with a look of helpless annoyance. As she left the room, closing the solid wooden door behind her, Evan Judd felt very small in his massive, library paneled office. He also felt very alone, perhaps a bit frightened as he looked into the confident, determined faces of the two FBI agents.

CHAPTER 2

REGAINING HIS COMPOSURE, EVAN's showman personality once again took over. "Please, won't you have a seat," he gestured to the chairs in front of his desk. "You may as well be comfortable." He sat down in his large, black, leather swivel chair behind the desk trying to look as if he had a superior, 'home-team' edge.

"Mr. Judd," Gordon Swift addressed Evan in a formal voice, "We are conducting an investigation and we believe you can be of some help to us."

"Is that right?" an incredulous Evan Judd responded.

"You wouldn't mind helping us, now would you?" again inquired Gordon Swift.

"Well, certainly not. I would be happy to." Evan Judd felt the tension release from his stomach when he realized that the Agents were not presenting any serious charges. "Help the FBI boys? Why not?" he thought generously.

"Okay, good, Mr. Judd. Let's see, you have been in the insurance business approximately thirty years. Is that correct?" Gordon Swift looked at Evan.

"That is correct," Evan responded easily.

"You have been at this address for the past seven years?"

"That's correct."

"You were on Sixth Avenue before that?"

"Yes."

13

"And, let me see, we do have all of that, I believe, pretty much in order. Now, let's see..." Swift looked over some papers and then looked back to Evan as he continued. "Our investigation led us to the Hudson River Insurance Agency."

Evan Judd's face turned chalk white. They obviously knew that he had to know that agency. It had been the connection that put him into the high risk business he was in today. The two agents looked at each other and Gordon Swift continued. "The Hudson River Agency is important to our current investigation into the insurance industry."

Evan adjusted the knot in his tie. He was having difficulty breathing but said nothing.

"You are familiar with this agency aren't you Mr. Judd?" asked Gordon Swift.

Evan hesitated and then replied, "Not really, Mr. ah, er, Agent Swift, sir." He cleared his throat and tried to appear nonchalant.

"We have a record of you calling them on September 17th, 1963. You spoke with a Mr. John Hughes."

Beads of perspiration began to pop out on Evan Judd's upper lip. He rubbed is clammy hands together under his desk and then against the top of his pant legs to dry them before he spoke.

"Ah," he cleared his throat, "ehmm, ahem" he could not seem to find his voice. "Maybe I spoke with Hughes. I routinely call other agencies to gather market information," he concluded.

"But according to our information, you called John Hughes again the following day and arranged to meet with him at his office on the 25th."

"I don't recall. It was too long ago," Evan Judd responded in a guarded voice.

"Well, let's see if we can refresh your memory," Agent Cooper interjected.

"You met with John Hughes and Donald Seaman at the Hudson River Agency in Troy, New York, at 10:00 a.m. You were living in an apartment with your wife and two small children in Delmar, New York, so you probably left home around 9:00 a.m. that morning. Actually, one child was an infant. Does that help ring a bell, Mr. Judd?"

Evan Judd looked as if he was going to faint. His hands gripped the arms of his chair as he listened to Agent Cooper. "It could be. Yes, I suppose I could have." Evan Judd was frozen to the chair as he realized that someone knew so much about him. He was finding it more and more difficult to breathe.

"So then you do recall involvement with the Hudson River Agency, Mr. Judd. Is that correct?" inquired Gordon Swift once again.

"Well, I suppose so, I'm just not sure," stumbled Evan.

"That meeting lasted exactly two hours. The three of you lunched at Dominic's Restorante across the street from Frearer's Department Store. You had reservations for 12:30 p.m.," Swift continued.

Evan Judd's mouth dropped open.

"Do you recall, now, Judd?" Ian Cooper snapped.

Evan was beginning to feel very nervous. This was a part of the insurance business he was not willing to discuss. "I'm sorry gentlemen. I'm not going to answer any more questions. I'm going to have to call my attorney," Evan had become seriously shaken.

"Well, Mr. Judd, you are certainly free to contact your lawyer and have him present, but we are not charging you with anything. But if you think you need a lawyer, if you have done something wrong....."

Evan was quick to defend himself. "No, no, but..."

"But what, Mr. Judd?"

"But you are asking questions."

"Yes, it is the nature of our business Mr. Judd, but if you have done nothing wrong, I don't understand why you can't simply answer the questions."

He was trapped. "Slick," Evan thought to himself. He regained his composure. "Perhaps I was hasty," he responded. "I have done nothing wrong," he swallowed, took a deep breath and waited.

"Let's see, where was I?" continued Gordon Swift.

Agent Cooper jumped in. "Do you or do you not know the Hudson River Agency Mr. Judd?"

"Well, I do know of it. Yes. But it was a long time ago."

"I see. And could you tell us of the activity of this agency, Mr. Judd?"

"Ah well," Evan hesitated, "I really don't know very much about it."

"Is it, or is it not true that this particular agency engages in mostly high risk insurance?"

"Well, ah, perhaps they do. I'm not really sure fellas. After all, it was a long time ago."

"And, is it not also true that this agency is extremely negligent in paying off any of its claims?"

"Gentlemen, I'm really not sure."

"Mr. Judd. You do know of this agency, do you not?"

"Yes."

"What then do you know of this agency?"

"Ah...a...a...well maybe...ah...I've heard that they don't pay as well as they should."

"I see. And is that all, Mr. Judd?"

"Gee, ah well," Evan squirmed as he was now unsure just how much he was expected to know.

"Can you tell us more about this operation or any similar operations, Mr. Judd," Gordon Swift stepped back in.

"That's about it. Ah...I only know that I heard that there was a pay out problem with that agency. That's about it."

"Why did you become involved with this agency?"

"It was too long ago. I just don't remember. You've got to believe me, Evan pleaded.

"Let us help you." Agent Cooper began to provide a list of telephone calls between Evan and John Hughes. He also listed several meeting conducted at the Hudson River Agency where Evan Judd was present. Evan tried neither to deny or confirm any of the information, but it had to be pretty much on target. With the exception of the exact dates, Evan knew the information to be true.

Discussion of the Hudson River Agency lasted more than two hours. They had records of every phone call and every meeting that had transpired which involved him. Eventually, Evan had to admit that the information they had was indeed true. His clothing was ringing wet with nervous perspiration. The Hudson River Agency had launched his own high-risk insurance business. It provided the underpinnings for the high stakes business he operated today.

But the FBI Agents did not stop at the Hudson River Agency. No, they ran this merciless interrogation through every illegal enterprise Evan Judd had been engaged with or in.

"Can you tell us of any other agency involved in this kind of scam?"

Again, Evan was on the spot. He was uncertain just how much they knew and how much they were testing him with. He remained silent as he mulled this over.

The questioning continued. As each agent took his turn at the helm, he would get to his feet and pace as he took the lead with the comprehensive questioning. The other agent would sit with the record and provide dates and times that would confirm the activities which had been part and parcel of Evan's life.

At the end of the third hour, Evan had to get his jacket off. He got to his feet to remove it and both Agents jumped to their feet and reached for their handguns which were holstered close to their chest inside their jackets. Evan began to realize that they had misread his intention and quickly tried to explain his actions. "Ah, no, no, gentlemen. Please, please. Don't!"

"Put the guns away. I'm, ah, I'm just going to take my jacket off. I'm feeling warm. See?" Evan took off his jacket and threw it over the credenza out of his way. "There. That's more comfortable." He quickly sat back down in his chair. His heart felt as if it was going to leap from his chest. These boys obviously meant business.

The agents looked at each other, took annoyed deep breaths, and sat back down opposite their prey. The questioning was far from over. As a matter of fact, the worst was yet to come. Maybe it was good that Judd knew that they meant business.

"Mr. Judd. When you purchased your home in Loudonville, you withdrew funds from the State Bank of Albany. According to our records, monies in that account were receipts from your insurance business." The knot in Evan's stomach tightened as he realized the depth of their knowledge of his affairs. "Is this true?"

"I, ah, I don't recall." Evan responded flatly.

"Let's see, according to our records, you deposited your receipts from October 1 through March 30th into that account. Let's see, that would have been three years worth of premium payments. Do you recall that, Mr. Judd?"

Evan did recall. However, he knew better than to admit to anything of this nature. "I would have to talk with my accountant, gentlemen. I have no knowledge of this whatsoever."

Evan Judd could feel himself weakening under this grueling questioning. There was nothing about him that these men did not know. "If I could get my hands on that looser Frank Spector, I'd kill him with my bare hands," he thought as the noose around his own neck tightened.

The line of questioning moved back once again to insurance fraud.

"Mr. Judd. Can you tell us of any other agencies involved in this type of business who don't pay up?"

"Ah...no, no I don't believe I know of any others." As he responded, Evan carefully tested each word to be certain that it would be received without objection.

"None whatsoever?"

"No sir, none whatsoever," he repeated.

"I see." Agent Swift was quiet for a few moments as he thought. Cooper did not move. Evan Judd, on the other hand, tried to control his breathing for fear it would be too loud or interpreted in some way by the agents.

They had been at it for several hours. It was quarter to ten at night when Agent Swift moved slightly forward in the chair. "Well then, Mr. Judd, do you know of any other irregularities of this nature which might help our investigation?"

"No, I can't say that I do, Agent Swift." Evan began to feel that the agents were accepting his responses to the questions. God, he hoped they were. He didn't know how much longer he could continue. The pressure was grueling.

Swift looked at Cooper, "In that case," Agent Cooper, "I expect we have concluded our business with Mr. Judd." Evan Judd took a deep breath and breathed a quiet sigh of relief. He moved forward in his chair ready to get to his feet in conclusion of this living nightmare which had drained him and stripped him of his confidence.

Cooper looked first at Agent Swift, "I believe so, Gordon." He then dramatically turned toward Evan Judd. "Except for that mail and wire fraud charge we came to make."

"Indeed, Mr. Judd, the Bureau believes you to be guilty of mail fraud."

The bomb hit with such impact that Evan Judd literally hurled backward in his chair. "What?"

"Actually, we have enough evidence to send you away for a long time, Mr. Judd."

"What the hell are you talking about?"

"We have been sent here to formally charge you with mail and wire fraud. You have been conducting fraudulent business and using the United States Postal Service to conduct your business. The Bureau has asked that we advise you of these charges."

Unguarded, Evan responded, "Son of... ah, ah what the...what are you talking about? How serious are these charges?"

"Oh they are serious, Mr. Judd. Very serious. In fact, when convicted, you will probably die in prison."

Evan turned a strange color of grey and started to slump backward in his chair when Agent Swift continued. "But, you do seem willing to cooperate, Mr. Judd. And, as long as you cooperate, they won't be pressing charges. You are willing to cooperate thoroughly, aren't you Mr. Judd?" Swift looked intensely at Evan.

Evan Judd was just beginning to become aware of the web they had been spinning around him. He did not respond as he mentally tried to review the events leading to this charge.

Agent Cooper impatiently reiterated the question, "Are you willing to cooperate or not, Judd?"

"Ah, yes, yes, of course I'll cooperate," Evan answered as the impact of what they were saying really began to hit him. He no longer had choices. He virtually belonged to them. And, there was nothing else he could do.

"We believe we are going to need you in this investigation. As a matter of fact, you can count on it," Gordon Swift stated nonchalantly.

"Yes, Judd, it would be prudent if you planned to be available at all times. We know we will need you to take part in our investigation." The Agents were on their feet. They were obviously nearing the end of this meeting.

Evan got to his feet slowly and began to move from behind his desk in a state of total shock. "Certainly, gentlemen. If I can be of any assistance to you, please let me know."

"We were hoping you would say that, Mr. Judd," replied Agent Swift. "Actually, we do need you as part of our investigation in New Orleans."

"That's right, Judd." Again, Cooper was eager to contribute. "We need you at our headquarters there. Better make arrangements to get yourself on a flight to New Orleans sometime tomorrow afternoon." He reached into his pocket and pulled out a card. He handed it to Evan. "Get yourself a room at the Latin Arms. We'll meet you there."

The two men headed for the door. "You'll be hearing from us when you get there," Agent Cooper said in his brusque, intimidating manner.

As Swift and Cooper opened the door and walked out of his office, Evan did not budge from his position behind the desk where he stood holding the business card which Agent Cooper had given to him. For a couple of moments, he simply stared after the FBI agents. Eventually, he looked at the card he was holding which simply said, "Latin Arms, New Orleans, Louisiana." There was a phone number and a street address but it didn't register with him. He was stunned. His whole life had been changed with a few simple words thrown at him at the end of this torturous questioning.

"Mail fraud. How much did they know? Sonofa....mail fraud could land him in prison for the rest of his life. What the hell did they say? 'Cooperate and we won't press charges.' What else could he do?" He reached for the intercom and buzzed Edna Carlisle. As if by magic, she appeared in the doorway. "Are you alright, Mr. Judd?"

Evan Judd seemed to stare through Edna Carlisle as he ignored her query. They had to be on to something or they would not expect him to pick up and head for New Orleans. "What the hell was going on in New Orleans? What were they finding out from this investigation of theirs?"

In a steady, monotone voice, Evan Judd demanded, "Get me Frank Spector. Now. I don't give a damn what he is doing or where he is. I need to talk with him NOW. There could be some serious trouble."

Carlisle turned and hurried from his office. Before she could close the door to Evan Judd's office, he began to pace in the space behind his desk with quick, agitated steps. His mind was racing as he tried to figure out exactly what was really going on with the FBI. Sure, he had cut a few legal corners in his day. "Hell, everybody did it." But how much did they know about his operation? He had been careful.

The intercom buzzed suddenly interrupting his racing thoughts. "Frank, where the hell...."

"I'm sorry, Mr. Judd, but Mr. Spector is not at home. Would you like to speak..." was all Frank Spector's housekeeper could get out before Evan Judd interrupted in a loud, impatient voice, "Where is he?"

"I'm sorry, Mr. Judd, but Mr. Spector did not tell me where he was going. Would you..."

Before she could finish her sentence, Evan Judd had slammed the phone down and was signaling Edna Carlisle. She was in his office practically before his finger left the signal. "Frank Spector, be damned. Get me Jimmy Carotti."

Evan Judd was no stranger to the legal profession. He had been courting attorneys for years. Call it safety or insecurity. Or, simply call it a quirk in his personality, but he wanted to be known by the company he kept. And, in the insurance business, lawyers were the best company to keep. If he couldn't befriend the people he wanted to be associated with, he bought them. The irritating thing right now was that he had paid the highest price for Frank Spector and Spector didn't have the common decency to be available when he needed him most. The fact that Evan Judd had for years considered him to be his friend created an emotional pain that Evan did not care to even think about.

"Well, to hell with Frank Spector. TO HELL WITH HIM!" was all that Evan Judd could silently scream in his emotion-filled head. But in is heart, he could feel only pain. "WHY? Why was Frank Spector deserting him when he really needed him? They had been friends for years, played golf practically every Thursday afternoon at the Club for, hell, as long as he had lived in Greenwich."

He brought himself back. He couldn't dwell on that now. He needed to talk with someone who knew the laws. Or did he? The only thing he needed to do was keep a cool head and do what the agents told him. If he needed legal help, there was plenty of time. And, there were still plenty of lawyers. PLENTY! If need be, he could call them.

He had been very calculating in his courting of friends. Well, buying actually. Evan Judd learned long ago that if you wanted to insure friendship, you needed to pad it well with money. In his business, you couldn't have too many friends, and you sure as hell couldn't have too many lawyers. So Evan Judd bought (or cultivated, as he preferred to believe) as many lawyers as he felt necessary for his questionable business dealings as well as his insecure ego.

With a slightly renewed sense of confidence, Evan Judd returned to his desk and pressed the intercom. "Cancel that call to Jimmy Carotti," he said quietly.

Edna Carlisle responded. "Yes sir. Will there be anything else, Mr. Judd?"

"You can call for my car to be sent around, Edna. That will be all."

"Right away, Mr. Judd."

Evan Judd felt very tired as he reached into the closet to get his coat. It had been a long day, a very long day indeed. He crossed his richly carpeted office heading for the door when it impacted him that night had over taken the city and lights from hundreds of offices were lighting the dark Manhattan sky. He usually cherished the warm glow of the city's lights, but tonight, he didn't care. Nothing could distract him from the heaviness of his thoughts.

He was tired and felt very old for his fifty-three years. He was glad that he had made arrangements to see Tammi. An evening with her would help him to forget all of his troubles. Hell, an evening with Tammi could make you forget everything. "When had he told her he would be there?" Didn't matter, she would be waiting. He was distracted by his thoughts as he automatically went through the motions of saying goodnight to Edna then leaving the building. Harrington was waiting in front. As he got into the car, he told his driver to take him to his apartment uptown.

Harrington had a martini ready for Evan. He pushed himself back against the seat and reached for the tumbler. He poured the liquid into the glass and took a long pull. He could feel the liquid as it began to warm and relax him on its way down. "Man, I should have had a couple of these five or six hours ago." He sat looking out the window and sipping the martini as Harrington skillfully maneuvered the Lincoln through the crowded streets of Manhattan toward the apartment.

Suddenly, Evan was jolted back to attention as he remember he had not told Edna that he needed to book a reservation to New Orleans for tomorrow. He picked up the telephone next to him and pressed the speed-dial button for Edna Carlisle at home. The answering service picked up. She had not yet arrived at her apartment which was only five blocks from the office.

"Tell Edna I need to book a mid-day flight to New Orleans for tomorrow."

"Yes sir. I'll tell her as soon as she checks in."

Evan replaced the phone as the car pulled up in front of the apartment building. He reached for the large cocktail glass and finished off the drink. "I won't be long, Harrington, wait for me."

"Yessir, Mr. Judd." Harrington quickly got out of the car and opened the door for his passenger. Evan pulled his coat around him as he headed for the building. The doorman held the door as he entered the lobby and headed for the elevator. He got off on the eleventh floor and went directly to the apartment door. He turned the knob. The door was open.

"Is that you, love?" a voice came from the other room.

"It's me, sweetie." Evan stood in the entrance hall and began to remove his trench coat. Instantly, Tammi was in front of him. "What kept you so long? Here, let me help you with that, darling," Tammi volunteered as she reached for the belt on his coat.

She had on a short, black, filmy chemise that he had bought for her. The high healed slippers helped to make her legs look even longer on her 5' 8" body. She had a gorgeous body, that was for sure, and fortunately, her mind never interfered with their relationship which was one of strictly physical pleasure.

"Let me get you a drink, love," she said in the exaggerated breathy voice she used when she was with him.

"I don't have time for that tonight," he responded as he headed directly toward the bedroom of the apartment.

She was a little taken back by this since they usually had a few drinks and engaged in some heavy petting before they moved into the bedroom for the climax. But, she immediately followed him as he entered the bedroom where she had some soft music playing. She had some candles lighted and set in strategic places around the room. Some had burned out.

He sat down heavily on the edge of the bed and continued undressing. He stood up to remove his pants and she was there next to him. After he tossed the last of his clothing onto the nearby chair, he grabbed her roughly and threw her onto the bed. She responded positively to this treatment demonstrating control and aggressively sought pleasure from him. He covered her with his body and drove his tongue into her open mouth. She responded hungrily as she urgently pulled him into her moist warm body.

The harder he sought physical relief the less inclined his body was to cooperate. Tammi did everything in her power to help him achieve gratification, but it was to no avail. Exhausted and defeated, a dejected Evan Judd rolled over on his back and stared at the ceiling. Tammi leaned over him continuing to encourage him, but he could not look at her. He had failed not only to satisfy himself, but he was incapable of fulfilling her obvious needs. "Please, Tammi. I'm sorry. It is no use. I just can't tonight."

"But darling, let's have a little drink-y-pooh and I'm sure you'll be back to your old self."

"No Tammi, I'm sorry. I shouldn't have stopped by tonight at all. When I called you, I didn't realize what was going to happen this afternoon. I'm afraid I have too much on my mind right now."

"But love, you're here now. Let Tammi make you feel better." She maneuvered her large, voluptuous breasts up onto his face as she slowly moved her finger down his abdomen.

"Please Tammi. Stop. I'm not in the mood. I have to get dressed. Get out of my way." Evan sat up abruptly pushing her aside. He dressed quickly leaving her on the bed just looking at him. He went into the bathroom to check his appearance. He reached into his wallet and pulled out a hundred dollar bill and dropped it on the nightstand on his way out of the bedroom.

As soon as she heard the door to the apartment close behind him, Tammi reached over onto the nightstand and picked up the bill. When she saw that it was a hundred, she kissed it and rolled back over onto the bed with youthful glee. She joyously kicked her legs high into the air causing one of the garters to slip free from her black stockings and snap her back into the moment. The night was young and she had a hundred bucks. She rolled over on her side and reached for the phone and dialed.

"Hello Mark? It's Tammi Lee. Wanna do some weed? Yeah, I got some dough. I'll meet you at Yezzi's in about half an hour. I gotta get dressed."

Meanwhile, Evan Judd pulled his coat collar up and thrust his hands deep into his trench coat pockets as he exited the apartment building and headed toward the car. When Harrington saw him coming, he got out of the car and opened the door.

Judd got into the back seat and huddled against the corner where he sat shivering. "Where to, boss?"

"Let's go home, Harrington. Take us home."

The traffic was light as the car headed north out of Manhattan toward the Bronx River Parkway and onto the Interstate heading for Greenwich, Connecticut. Evan poured himself a drink and gulped it down. In a few minutes, he began to relax against the soft leather seat. His mind soon filled with thoughts of the meeting with the FBI agents earlier in the day.

"Mail fraud. What was it...? 'We are not pressing charges right now...' or just how did he say it?" Hmmm, let's see, it was Agent Cooper who reinforced, in so many words, what Agent Swift had said. "Cooperate, and we'll see if we can't keep you out of jail. No guarantees, of course, but you have a good shot if you cooperate."

What choice did he have, he thought. He forced himself to curtail the stream of thoughts which flooded his mind. All he had to do for now was fly to New Orleans tomorrow.

He poured another drink as the car sped along the Interstate. His thoughts turned to his wife and family. He hoped that someone would be at home when he arrived. Somehow, the thought of being alone tonight disturbed him. He had not been close to his family for several years now. He had been too busy or distracted with other things to really notice them much. Tonight, somehow, he expected (or, rather hoped) that the family of his memory would be there for him as he had so often fooled himself into believing he had been for them.

The Lincoln Towncar slowed as they reached the final approach to his estate off Beach Road. As the car eased gently to a full stop in front of the iron gates, Harrington waited for the electronic security to engage and move the iron post gate on the long asphalt pavement going toward the house. The gates opened inward and Harrington pulled the car through. Trees lined the drive for well over a quarter of a mile before the car pulled onto the cement and stone that would circle into the portico of the main house.

There were lights on in the house, but, then there were always lights on in the house at night. The house was fully staffed--his long-time housekeeper, a maid, a cook and a combination butler, gardener. The car rolled to a stop at the front of the house. Harrington got out and opened the door for his boss. As Evan got out of the car, the front door of the house opened and his housekeeper who had been alerted by gate security greeted him. "Good evening, Mr. Judd. Let me help you with that briefcase."

He handed her the briefcase as he passed through the front double doors. Evan took off his coat and walked into the large entry foyer. His eyes move up the large curved staircase as he searched in hope of seeing his wife at the top. But, of course, she was not there. She was never there anymore. Evan turned to Mrs. Hoffsteader handing her his coat. "Where is everyone?"

"Mrs. Judd is at the club, sir, and I don't know where the others are," Mrs. Hoffsteader quickly replied.

Evan made his way to his study and closed the door.

Alice Judd was always at the club, and his oldest daughter along with that good-for-nothing, no account, second husband of hers were usually involved in some worthless activity. Hell, he didn't even know them any more. His oldest son never married and chose to make a career out of testing Evan's patience. Evan, Jr. and Alice were made from the same cloth. For Christ's sake, it was Alice who had ruined Jr. First, she coddled the boy, and eventually, as Evan's business interests grew and he couldn't be at home as much, she gradually turned young Evan against him. Hell, she had turned all the children against him. Julie, Jennifer, even young Todd had been pawns in her sick games. He loved them. Damn it, he loved them all. But, he didn't have time to play her stupid games. He could still hear her telling the children the lies right from the time they were young.

"Daddy doesn't want to be with us. We're going to Grandpapa Whitley's summer place in Saratoga without him. Daddy doesn't want to go with us. He doesn't love us enough to come with us. We don't need him. We'll have our own fun. You'll see. We'll go swimming, we'll ride Grandpa's horses, we'll go to the races, we'll go to parties..."

Evan walked into his rich, library-paneled study and closed the heavy double doors behind him in a futile effort to close off his thoughts. The lights on the chandelier sparkled and he was comforted by his rich masculine surroundings. Evan removed his suit jacket and tie and settled into his favorite winged leather chair in front of the stone fireplace. The heat felt good as it warmed the cold that penetrated him clear through to his bones. Exhausted, he was soon fast asleep.

CHAPTER 3

THE NEW ORLEANS AIRPORT was crowded and hot as Evan Judd made his way through the terminal. He had all but convinced himself that his uneasy feeling of impending doom was little more than a healthy conscience working overtime. The agents had assured him there was nothing to worry about if he cooperated fully with the investigation. And, the investigation was not about him. However, even though he had reminded himself of this at least a dozen times since yesterday, why did he continue to have this constant fear of "being found out?"

Evan slowed his pace for a moment to wipe his face. As he moved toward the right side of the corridor, he noticed a bank of telephones. He decided he'd give his secretary a call. Maybe Frank Spector was trying to reach him. Spector still hadn't returned his calls and this insult angered him.

He entered the alcove and found the phones nearly all filled with business men trying to contact home offices and customers. As he selected an available instrument and lifted the receiver, a subtle scent of expensive perfume tweaked his olfactory senses as well as his greedy, womanizing imagination. He recognized the scent as being the same as that which one of his regular girls in Las Vegas wore all the time.

Evan quickly tried to dismissed his lusty thinking, and occupy himself with the business at hand. He had no sooner punched in the numbers when his thoughts were once again lured away by a female voice saying, "I'm telling you, Fred, this is bigger than we thought. They ..."

"Insurance International," a female voice sang on the other end of the line.

"This is Evan Judd. Where the hell is Edna Carlisle?"

"Oh, Mr. Judd, I am sorry, a rattled, high pitched voice replied."

"I know I should have said 'Mr. Judd's office' but I forgot..."

"Never mind that," Judd snapped as he withdrew his handkerchief from his pocket and began wiping his forehead and upper lip once again. "Where the hell is Edna?"

"Oh, Mr. Judd. Ms. Carlisle isn't here right..."

"I can tell that much," interrupted Evan as he thought, "Some of these air-heads are good for only one thing--a quick roll in the hay. Well, maybe not hay. The last roll in the hay he engaged in gave him a wife and baby..."

"Ms. Carlisle said she had to go out for a few minutes. I don't know..."

"Were there any calls from my attorney?"

"I'm sorry Mr. Judd. Ms. Carlisle didn't say..."

"Forget it. It's not important," a more subdued Evan Judd responded. He was suddenly overwhelmed with a disappointment he would never admit to. "Tell Edna I called." His attention was distracted by a set of beautiful legs moving away from under the phone stall opposite his. Again, another whiff of the perfume tweaked his memory and caused some familiar stirrings within him.

Evan returned the phone to its cradle and found his way back to the main corridor of the terminal. He joined the pace of the crowd of people leaving the gates. He looked for the signs directing him to the baggage area. He would have to claim his own bag and find a cab to take him to the hotel.

When he stepped outside the building, he was nearly overcome by the hot, heavy air. It had taken him longer than he expected to claim his bag and he was now anxious about getting to the hotel so that he could shower before meeting the FBI agent who would brief him concerning the investigation. Evan reached into his suit coat pocket and pulled out a paper as he moved toward the street with his bag. A cab was waiting at the curb. The taxi driver made no effort to get out and help with the baggage as Evan approached the cab. He just sat there with his arm over the back of the seat, smoking a cigarette watching Evan. His indifference toward his potential fare did little to improve Evan Judd's mood. Evan opened the door of the cab and threw his luggage across the seat and got in.

"Take me to the," he hesitated as he looked at the small piece of paper he held in his hand, "Latin Arms. I'm in somewhat of a hurry."

The cab driver made no effort to move the vehicle, but appeared to be in communion with his cigarette as he rolled it between his thumb and index finger and stared at the ashes which were slowly building on the end. He took one more slow, steady drag on it before tossing the butt out the window and turning slowly in his seat in order to start the engine. He didn't bother to check for on-coming traffic as he dropped the transmission into drive. The engine responded sluggishly as it jerked forward a couple of times before the transmission seemed fully engaged and the car moved in a forward direction.

As the vehicle pulled out into the traffic, the driver seemed to be impervious to other vehicles. The cabbie weaved in and out of the lanes with complete abandon causing several drivers to honk in anger with his blatant disregard for other vehicles. Just before they cleared the terminal area, one cab driver leaned out the window and yelled something in French at the driver of Evan's cab. The words must have been in good humor because they both laughed. The female passenger in the other cab seemed to be oblivious to the exchange.

Evan wished he had his own driver. He was uncomfortable with this reckless, unfamiliar behavior. The remainder of the ride was reasonably uneventful. The driver was no Harrington, but he miraculously didn't get them into a serious accident. Evan paid the taxi fare and went directly to the registration desk.

"Reservation for Evan Judd," he announced to a disinterested hotel clerk. "Judd. Evan Judd. Reservation for tonight."

The hotel clerk totally ignored Evan as he continued to be absorbed in the newspaper he was reading. "You say sump'in, mista?" drawled the black man from behind the counter.

"Indeed I did," replied Evan. "I have a reservation for a room for this evening. I'd like to check in now, if it isn't too much trouble," Evan responded immensely irritated.

"No trouble, Mister. Whatcha gettin so 'cited 'bout? You gotcha self all aftanoon to get youself checked in. Whatcha says yo name is?"

"Judd. Judd. Evan Judd from New York."

"Thank yasa."

Evan was frustrated and on edge. But the attitude of these people was something else.

"Ya wanna spell that for me?"

"Judd. J-u-d-d. Judd." Evan could hardly contain himself.

"That's a interestin' name, Mista Judd," the clerk responded. "You got yo-self some kindofa accent, ain'tcha?" That ain't a regular New York accent, is it Mister Judd?"

"Could we please get this taken care of?! I need to take a shower and change."

"Yes sir, Mister Judd. Jus tryin ta make a little conversation. Didn't mean ta upset ya, sir."

There was no bell boy to assist Evan to his room. With resolve, he headed for the antiquated elevator. There were only two elevators in the entire building, so by the time the elevator doors opened onto the lobby floor, Evan had to wait as several people got off. He was not alone getting on. The car was filled to capacity. There was a pungent smell of body order as the car stopped on the 7th floor for Evan to exit. He could not wait to take a bath and wash away the ugliness of the day.

He opened the door to his room. It was dark and smelled dank and musty. Evan fumbled for the light switch which seemed to elude him. He stepped further into the unlit room feeling less sure of himself as his hand swept the wall in search of the missing light switch. He gradually inched his way forward, one hand tightly clutching his wardrobe, the other, brushing the wall. Eventually his fingers felt a familiar protrusion and he clicked on the switch.

Evan found himself standing in a short entrance hallway. There was a small, bathroom with tub and commode on the left and a closet with a clothes bar on his right. Directly ahead, the room was dimly lighted by a small ceiling light fixture. As he walked forward, he saw that the main room contained one double bed covered by a well-worn, heavy red and black imitation velvet bedspread. Two Mediterranean-style night stands flanked either side of the bed, and, a matching double dresser was on the opposite wall. A heavy black wrought iron chair with worn gold, crushed velvet upholstery sat in the distant corner. A heavy, round wood and wrought iron table with two chairs, seats covered with cheap, cracking, plastic, sat in front of the heavily draped window. A Mediterranean style lamp with a red shade hung over the table. There was one small boudoir lamp and an ashtray with a matchbook cover identifying the Latin Arms next to the bed. A rotary dial telephone sat next to the television set on top of the double dresser. Evan Judd felt a shiver run down his spine. He dropped his wardrobe on the bed and threw his coat on the chair.

As he pulled the heavy drapes back, his nostrils recoiled from the smell of dust and stale smoke. Inside the heavy red drapes were dingy, sheer curtains grayed by years of dust and smoke. His hands held open the sheer curtains as he peered out the dirty window onto a back alley below. He looked into a sea of building walls and alley-ways. A very empty, tired feeling crept over him. He let the curtains drop and walked over to his suitcase and got out a fresh set of clothing. He went into the bathroom, turned on the water and prepared for his shower.

It was nearly 5 p.m. when he finished dressing. Agent Swift had told him that an agent would meet him in the lobby at the Latin Arms sometime after 5:00 p.m. Well, he was ready. Evan turned off the light, closed the door and headed toward the elevator.

The corridor of the 7th floor was dimly lighted. Just as well, the scrolled, patterned, fuzzy, velvety wallpaper on the walls was badly warn and an obvious magnet for dust and dirt. The carpet on the floor was patchy and warn as well. In actuality, the dim lighting was advantageous. "The less you can see of this God-forsaken hole, the better," Evan thought as he waited for the elevator to take him to the lobby.

As usual, the car was nearly filled when it stopped on the 7th floor. Evan, impeccably dressed in his Armani sports coat, matching trousers, white shirt, and tie squeezed into the car that smelled like a combination of the locker room at the downtown athletic club and the Cosmetic counter at R. H. Macy's. He would have liked to have waited, but God only knew how long it would take for another car to come along. As the various fragrances tweaked his nostrils, he became agitated as he began to think he could have been spending this evening squeezed between the legs of his kept girl. He may not have gotten it on last night, but sure as hell, he would have made up for it tonight. He never knew what to expect from the little tramp. But, whatever it was, he liked it. Hot oils, whipped...

The door opened onto a livelier scene than he had left about an hour ago. As he walked toward the sitting area in the center of the room, he heard music coming from a bar over to his right. He headed for the overstuffed sofa directly out from the registration desk and stood beside it. He looked around the room to see if he could recognize anyone. Well, that was pretty stupid. Of course, he wouldn't recognize anyone. "How many FBI agents do you know, you idiot!" he thought. In his business, getting too close to the law could be dangerous.

But, Evan continued to look anyway. As his eyes searched the lobby, he noticed a young woman using the public phone. He watched as she talked. He could not hear what she was saying, but she was reading from a pad as she spoke into the phone. He decided to move closer. As he did, he could hear, "..call you tomorrow, Fred. Take care."

She hung the phone on the hook and moved swiftly toward the bar. Evan found himself following. Something triggered a memory in the message center of his brain as he smelled the scent of that unique expensive perfume, what was it called...JOY. That was it! Yvonne in Vegas always wore JOY.

Before he gave it any thought, Evan Judd was in the hotel bar. The beautiful, well-dressed woman with the notebook had seated herself next to a man at the bar. There was no room next to them, so Evan opted for a seat on the opposite side of the horseshoe bar so that he could get a better look at this lovely creature.

"I'll have a Tangueray martini, rocks. Dry. Just pass the vermouth over it."

"Yessa."

As the bartender moved away to make his drink, Evan got a clear shot of the young woman across from him. Early thirties, he figured. Good life, at least she didn't look used or hardened. Her face conveyed an anticipatory excitement, her skin was radiant, healthy, and her beautiful, soft, blue-grey eyes expressed intensity. She was a thinker, no doubt. Her blonde hair was full, rich, soft, and fell naturally on her shoulders. She was deeply involved in conversation with a man next to her at the bar.

He was short, rather heavy set, and wore thick glasses. He was dressed very casually in blue jeans and a Ralph Lauren polo shirt. Both his hands held his drink as he brought it to his lips. He appeared to be quite a bit older than the woman. They spoke quietly to one another.

When the bartender brought his drink, Evan remembered that he needed to be in the lobby where the FBI agent could see him. He couldn't fathom how the agent would know him but Gordon Swift had assured him that it would be no problem. Evan paid the bartender leaving a generous tip behind and took his drink into the lobby. He sat in one of the upholstered chairs and waited.

It was nearly six thirty when Gordon Swift and Ian Cooper arrived at the Latin Arms. By now, Evan Judd was pacing back and forth across the lobby as the two men approached from behind. "Judd," Swift said in a rather clipped manner, "You remember Agent Cooper. We will be working with you during this investigation."

Now Evan understood why the New Orleans FBI agent would have no problem recognizing him. Swift and Cooper had come to New York just to see him. They weren't simply FBI agents who worked in the City. They were agents assigned to this investigation, perhaps assigned to him in particular. Evan's heart began to beat a little faster. He could feel his stomach tighten and beads of perspiration appear from nowhere above his upper lip.

"There's been some problems. They aren't going to be able to interview you tonight, but we will meet you here first thing tomorrow morning," said Gordon Swift.

Evan began to take issue with the delay, "But I have to be back in New..."

"Remember what I said back in New York," Cooper interjected. "There won't be any trouble if you cooperate. If that means staying on for a day or two in New Orleans, then that's what it takes."

"But..."

"Are you having difficulty hearing, Mr. Judd?" Agent Cooper intoned in a rather demeaning manner.

"I believe Mr. Judd understands. Don't you, sir?" inquired Swift.

"Yes." Evan spoke quietly with the resolve of a man who has suddenly realized how limited his options really are.

"Good. We'll swing by around 8:00 a.m. Good night." And that was all. The two agents walked quickly from the lobby and out the front door of the hotel.

Evan sat there starring after them. He was beginning to experience that ominous feeling that he had when he first learned that the FBI wanted to talk with him.

Screw it. Swift had told him that the investigation in no way involved him. It was Erlich they were hitting. If he cooperated, they could overlook his mail fraud. How bad could mail fraud be? He'd cooperate to the fullest. He sure as hell didn't need them looking into anything else. But. . . mail fraud, wasn't that a felony?

Evan Judd could feel the sweat running down the sides of his body from both of his arm pits. "Where in the hell is that good- for-nothing Frank Spector? Damn it to hell, I'm no attorney," he thought. That's why he kept Frank Spector on board. "Son of a . . . ," he hissed with teeth clenched.

He headed for the phones in the lobby and dialed Frank Spector at home. Spector's maid answered. "Spector's residence."

"This is Evan Judd. Get Frank on the line."

"I'm sorry, Mr. Judd. Mr. Spector's not in right now."

"Where the hell is he?"

"I'm sorry, Mr. Judd. Mr. Spector did not..."

"When do you expect him?" There was no immediate response. He repeated, "When do you expect him?"

"I'm sorry, I don't know, Mr. Judd. Nobody's here right now and I jus donno."

"Tell him I called," Evan said and slammed down the phone.

"Now what do I do?" he thought in frustration. He headed for the bar.

The blonde was gone but her male companion remained in the same place he had been an hour and a half ago. From his appearance, he had magically revived and was talking with several of what appeared to be his cronies. They all seemed to be familiar with each other.

There were no seats at the bar or at any of the adjacent tables so Evan eased his way to the bar through an opening some of the patrons helped make for him. He ordered a double Tangueray martini on the rocks. He paid for his drink and moved back from the bar to drink it. The nagging apprehension which plagued him began to ease. Evan tried to follow some of the conversations that were going on around him. It was difficult to focus his attention, but necessary, if he was to maintain any sense of equilibrium, he thought. He began to recognize that some of the men seemed to be talking politics. From the conversations, he gathered that they were reporters or perhaps writers. They seemed to enjoy arguing their opinions. Eventually, Evan found a table away from the group. He was too tired to try to follow their conversation any longer.

Evan Judd arrived in the lobby at ten minutes before eight the following morning. He had not slept well and was feeling a little jittery. He paced slowly around the seating area of the lobby trying to decide whether to sit or stand. He noticed a discarded copy of the Washington Post on a coffee table in front of the sofa and decided to take a seat and have a look at it. As he picked up the paper and began to sit down, he though he could distinguish a familiar scent. Without thinking, he looked for Yvonne. Damn, he was tired. Hell, he was losing it. He dismissed the smell and settled himself into the reading of the paper. The smell of printer's ink was still apparent on the two day old paper. "Some kind of imagination," he thought as we leafed through the paper. "Confusing printer's ink with perfume must mean it's been too long without having a woman," he thought to himself as he settled into reading the paper. He noticed a small piece toward the back of Section A which captured his attention. He stiffened as he read the caption, "FBI Investigation Gets Underway Today."

It was 8:27 a.m. when Gordon Swift and Ian Cooper entered the front door of the Latin Arms. Evan Judd was completely engaged in his reading and did not notice them. They were standing in front of him when Agent Swift said quietly, "Let's go, Judd." Without formality or even an offer of a handshake by either agent, Evan Judd got to his feet and followed the two men who were already heading out the front door into the street. There was an unmarked government vehicle parked several car lengths to the left of the space directly in front which the hotel reserved for cabs. When they got to the car, Swift motioned to Evan into get in the back seat where he soon joined him. Cooper took the empty passenger seat in the front.

Evan slid himself awkwardly across the upholstered seat. When he reached the outside, he looked toward the front of the car. Just before Agent Cooper entered the car, he had noticed the blonde woman who had intrigued him last night. She hurried out of the front door of the hotel and stepped into a waiting cab. The cab pulled away from the curb immediately.

Within seconds, the government sedan was also underway and it began to travel in the same direction as the cab, just two cars behind. He couldn't help but wonder what brought her to this distasteful and uninteresting part of town.

Both vehicles sped east making a sharp right two blocks from the hotel. The car seemed to be following the yellow cab for a while. No one in the vehicle said anything. Three blocks south, the car took a left and then a quick right and continued on without turning for a while. The cab had disappeared into the city and before Evan could once again concentrate on the direction of his vehicle, it was stopping mid block in front of an old office building. A yellow cab pulled away as the vehicle in which Evan was riding pulled to a complete stop.

The two Agents began moving to exit the vehicle as Evan looked for a lead from Swift. The agent obliged signaling with a simple head-nodding gesture. The three men moved swiftly into the building and headed for the elevator. Ian Cooper pushed the button. No one spoke. When the door opened, Cooper stepped in and Agent Swift motioned for Evan to follow.

The three got off at the ninth floor. There were several offices within sight of the elevator. People were milling around, going from office to office. Some were waiting on benches in the corridor. With Evan Judd in toe, Agents Swift and Cooper moved steadfastly down the corridor and turned right at the next corridor. At the end of the corridor, they turned right again and stopped in front of a set of double doors. "Hope you're in shape, Judd. We're climbing on foot from here."

The trio climbed five flights of stairs before Cooper and Swift led him through a doorway onto the 14th floor of the building. This floor was quiet compared to the lower one. The trio walked a few feet down the hallway. Agent Cooper opened a tall, solid, walnut door and held it for the other two to enter.

The room was huge. Evan nearly gasped as he saw what appeared to be a hundred men wearing guns in holsters strapped to their chests.

The escorting agents took Evan Judd to a hot, stuffy, grey waiting room and left him there. The décor was standard government issue steel grey metal chairs with plastic vinyl seats, grey metal desks, grey metal ash trays on pedestals all in a green-grey room with grey linoleum floors.

Time passed slowly. Occasionally, someone would come in and announce to Evan Judd that someone would be with him soon. Each time, Evan made an unsuccessful attempt to tell the messenger how important his time was, but the person simply walked away without comment. A one week old penny saver sat on the edge of a chair, but other than that, there was nothing to occupy his mind. All he could do was sit or pace and wipe the perspiration from his face.

There was no air in the room. Evan could barely breathe. He was dying of thirst. Finally, he stuck his head out of the door and asked the nearest clerk where he could get a drink of water. The woman pointed to a grey water fountain several feet down the hallway. Gratefully, Evan headed toward the fountain. As he leaned over the faucet, he was sickened by the thick wad of gum that lay in the drain. He pushed the metal handle down harder in an effort to force the water out. The warm water trickled from the fountain, not enough pressure to allow him to drink without putting his mouth on the valve.

Evan returned to the room and began to seriously consider the dusty vending machines in the waiting area. Fortunately, he had sufficient change with him to get a soda from the pop vending machine. He put seventy-five cents into the machine and made his selection. Nothing happened. He punched the selection again. Still nothing. He made another selection. Nothing. Finally, he punched every button on the machine including the coin return. NOTHING. Now he knew why people kicked vending machines. He gave it a good strong kick just as the latest messenger came to the door of the waiting room. He tried to explain to the young man that his change was in the machine but the guy just shook his head and walked away after he had delivered his message.

Another hour passed. He was getting very hungry. He hadn't eaten since lunch on the airplane yesterday. He reached into his pocket and pulled out the remaining change. He dropped fifty-five cents into the next vending machine and pulled the lever for corn chips. "Thank God," he said under his breath. He ripped open the small bag and began to hungrily devour the contents. Within seconds, he was spitting the so called food product back into the bag. "Rancid. Damn it to hell." The taste was putrid. Desperately, he plunged the last of his change into the vending machine once again to redeem the one lone candy bar that was left. It dropped to the floor of the open slot. He grabbed the parcel, removed, the paper, and bit into the small bar. It was hard and stale, but not rancid, "thank God."

The stale candy bar gave him enough energy to begin his pacing all over again. "Who the hell did they think they were?" Evan thought as he paced back and forth. "Don't they know how busy I am? I don't have time for this," he assured himself as he became more agitated.

It was nearly 5:30 p.m. when the two agents returned to the waiting room. Evan was furious. This was inexcusable.

"Mr. Judd. It doesn't look as if we are going to be able to get to you today after all."

"Listen fellas, I'm a busy man. I can't just hang around here all day. I have..."

"Mr. Judd. We are all busy."

"But, you don't understand, I..."

"Mr. Judd. There is nothing to understand."

"Listen."

"Now you listen, Judd." Agent Cooper could not take what he considered belly-aching. "We are trying to conduct an investigation here. You are part of that investigation."

"But I..."

"There are no buts. We didn't get to you."

"Okay. Okay. You didn't get to me. No problem." Evan looked at his watch as he reached for his suit jacket. "I have a 9:25 flight to catch back to New York."

Evan had his jacket on and was about to leave the waiting room when Gordon Swift moved directly in front him blocking his movement. "Better stay put, Judd. They're not sure when they're going to get to you, but they will get to you. You can bank on that. Probably tomorrow morning."

"But I have return reservations on the 9:25..." his voice trailed off.

"Mr. Judd, we are sorry that you are inconvenienced. However, you agreed to cooperate. I think you had better stay right here for now. I'll call you tomorrow. There's a car waiting for you downstairs. It will take you back to the Latin Arms."

With that, Gordon Swift turned and walked out of the waiting room, Ian Cooper just two steps behind him. As they crossed the large room, Evan watched them blend in with the other agents.

Evan Judd found his way down the several flights of stairs and boarded the elevator on the ninth floor which would take him to ground level. The offices were no longer buzzing with activity as he passed through the deserted corridors. Occasionally, he saw someone behind a counter or a figure moving behind an opaque glass window.

He was alone on the elevator. When he reached street level, he went out the front door of the building and looked for the car. As soon as his feet hit the bricks, a dark black sedan pulled up directly in front of the building. Evan approached the car. The driver signaled for him to get into the vehicle.

Before Evan could speak to the man behind the wheel of the car, the driver stepped on the accelerator and the vehicle lunged from the curb and into the street. Evan started to say, "Latin Arms," when he realized the driver knew exactly where he was going. Evan was beginning to realize that little was left to chance with the Department of Justice. He sat back in his seat as the car headed toward the hotel.

CHAPTER 4

E VAN STOPPED AT THE desk to check for messages before heading for his room. There had been four calls from Edna Carlisle, one call from a Ted Jensen, an associate of Frank Spector, and one from Frank Spector. "Well, it's about time," thought Evan. He decided to return the calls from his room. He went to the elevator and stood with the waiting crowd. At ten minutes before six, everyone was heading for their rooms to change before dinner. Evan squeezed on board with the others.

The air conditioner was inadequate for the room. It could have been the right size, but it lumbered with age and constant usage. Evan removed his jacket and threw it on the bed. He picked up the phone and dialed the desk. The desk placed the call to Frank Spector in New York. "This is really an antiquated system," thought Evan as the phone finally began ringing and sounding distant at the other end.

"Spector Enterprises," the voice on the other end of the line sang.

"Frank Spector. Evan Judd returning his call."

"Mr. Spector isn't here, Mr. Judd. Would you care to leave a message, sir?"

"Where the hell is he? I have been trying to reach him for days," an very annoyed Evan Judd said.

"I'm sorry. Mr. Spector is NOT here, sir. This is the answering service. The office is closed for the day. Would you care to leave a message?" the operator ignored both his attitude and inquiry.

"Listen lady, this is Evan Judd. Did he say where he could be reached?"

"I'm sorry, Mr. Judd. Mr. Spector did not say. Would you care to leave a message?"

"Tell Frank Spector I HAVE to talk with him. This is very important. No, damn it, this is *urgent*."

"I'll tell him, sir, just as soon as he checks in with us. Thank you for calling Spector Enterprises," the sickeningly sweet voice at the other end of the line sang. The line was disconnected before Evan could say anything further.

Evan slammed the phone down. He could not think of any other place to leave word for Spector to contact him. Edna had seen to all of the regular places.

"Edna. Why didn't I call her first," he suddenly thought. She probably knows where Spector is by now.

Evan Judd began dialing Edna's apartment. She would probably be home by now.

After a couple of rings, Edna Carlisle answered her phone. "Evan Judd, Edna."

"Oh, Mr. Judd, I'm so glad you called. I have been trying to reach you all day. I finally got a hold of Mr. Spector. He is on a ship in the Caribbean. He will be gone for several weeks. He said he was recommending you talk with a Mr. Ted Jensen. I didn't know if that would be acceptable to you or not, sir."

Evan Judd was quiet for a few moments as he thought about this disturbing news. "Was Spector bailing out on him? Was that what this was all about? How could Spector do this to him? Spector was the only one who had any inkling of the extent of the operation. It certainly was convenient to be in the middle of the Caribbean right now wasn't it?"

Well, the fact of the matter was, Evan Judd was getting nervous. He needed to check a few things with a lawyer. Hell, he didn't have to get into great detail. He did, however, need some legal advice.

"I'm not keen on the idea," he finally responded to Edna Carlisle with a deep sigh, "but it looks like I have no choice if I want some legal advice."

"Will you be returning tonight, Mr. Judd?" inquired Edna.

"Shall I have him come into the office tomorrow?"

"No Edna. It looks like I'll be staying over another night."

"Shall I tell him Friday?"

"Better find out where I can reach him, day or night, Edna. I may need to talk with him before I get back. I'm just not sure right now."

"As you wish, Mr. Judd."

"Give me a call here at the Latin Arms when you have his home number, Edna."

"Certainly, sir."

"I'll talk with you later," said Evan as he put the phone down.

He was exhausted as he stepped into the shower. He was also very hungry. He realized he had barely eaten in two days. The lousy, stale candy bar was all he had had all day. It made him sick to think about it. "How in the hell did they expect him to survive?"

The cool water felt good on his face. Maybe if he stood there long enough, the tension of the last few days would wash down the drain.

Wearing a freshly laundered shirt and yesterday's suit which he fortunately had the forethought to have sent out and pressed during the day, Evan Judd looked refreshed as he entered the hotel bar. He felt only slightly revitalized from his miserable day as he moved toward the empty seat at the bar. The bartender noticed him immediately, and approached,

"What will it be, Sir?"

"Give me a Tanqueray martini on the rocks with a twist. Make it a double."

"Ya got it, Mack."

Within a couple of minutes, the bartender returned with Evan's drink. He took a long, slow pull from the glass. The liquid felt warm and good as it ran down his throat. He could feel the warmth from the alcohol spread out over his neck, shoulders and chest. "Ah yes, that felt good."

As he drew his second mouthful from the glass, he noticed out of the corner of his eye someone moving closer to him from behind on his right side. As he began to set the glass back on the bar top, a quiet, voice asked, "Been a long day?"

Evan turned his head to the right and was pleasantly surprised to see the blonde woman who had been crossing his path for two days.

He smiled a genuine smile acknowledging his obvious pleasure in seeing her.

"I don't believe I've had the pleasure, Miss..."

"Powers. Jessica Powers."

"I'm Evan Judd."

"I know."

Jessica Powers was well proportioned for her five feet seven inches. She had more than ample breasts and legs that wouldn't quit. Her fair skin was flawless. Her demeanor was that of a person in charge of her own destiny. Evan Judd tried to maintain a dignified presence as he soaked in this gorgeous creature.

"How did you know who I am?" asked an honestly intrigued Evan Judd.

"I have sources," replied Powers.

And indeed she did. Jessica Powers' managing editor had put her on a flight out of Dulles Airport heading for New Orleans within minutes of the time Evan Judd was to leave JFK in New York. His source at the Bureau had told him that the Erlich investigation was being moved to New Orleans and that a lot of "shit," as the source put it, would soon be coming down. The source at the Bureau had told him that the insurance scam they were following at the Department was small potatoes compared to what was coming down in New Orleans.

"What kind of sources?" Evan inquired.

"That's really not important, Mr. Judd. What is important is what brings you to New Orleans."

"I'm just here on business."

"Is that so, Mr. Judd?"

By the tone of her voice, Evan Judd began immediately to get the sense that Jessica Powers was not only fishing for a more detailed response, but that she, in fact, knew a lot more than she was letting on. He tried to play it cagey.

"That is so, Miss Powers. That is so. Can I buy you a drink?"

"Chablis, please."

"A Chablis for the lady," Evan addressed the bartender who had taken notice of the pair and moved in for the order. "And, I'll have another one of these," he said picking up his glass and emptying the contents.

Just as Evan was offering Jessica his seat, the man who had been sitting on the adjacent bar stool got up and left. She slid onto the seat. She stowed her rather large shoulder bag on the floor near her feet and starred after the bartender who was selecting the wine.

Evan began to make small talk. "So, what brings your to New Orleans, Ms. Powers?" inquired Evan. It was obvious from the way in which she expressed herself that she was in no way from the south.

"Business," replied Jessica.

"And what type of business might that be, Ms. Powers," he continued.

"Why don't you just call me Jessica, Mr. Judd," she responded.

"Please, call me Evan," he responded warmly.

They were quiet as the bartender placed the drinks on the bar in front of them. "Shall I add these to your room tab?" asked the bartender. Evan nodded affirmatively.

Usually very business minded and personally distanced from her subjects and sources, Jessica Powers decided she might try a somewhat different strategy with this good-looking, middle-aged man. He could be her ticket to one hell of a story. She would have to play her cards carefully. She didn't know as much about Evan Judd as she wanted to know. Normally, she would not have been inclined to have a subject call her by her first name--at least not this early on. But this was not normal. She had been on this story for months, and was yet to get a real scoop.

Sure, she had been able to uncover somewhat superficial information even though the FBI boys were playing it cagy. But Jessica Powers was a damn good investigative journalist. One of the best. And, her sixth sense told her that there was more to these investigations that the Justice Department was secretly holding than met the eye. Nothing about this whole situation was normal, as far as Jessica was concerned. She had been covering some aspect of this story for 3 months, and this present situation, the investigation here in New Orleans, smelled of a cover-up. She had no hard evidence. But something fishy was going down. She felt it. And, Evan Judd, in some way, had to be a part of it. She didn't have facts to substantiate anything. But, she sure as hell would have them soon enough she decided.

"To a pleasant evening," Evan toasted as he raised his glass and nodded his head toward Jessica.

"To a pleasant evening," Jessica countered as she picked up her glass and took a sip.

"You were telling me what brings you to New Orleans," Evan began continuing the same line of conversation they had started earlier.

Jessica Powers was a seasoned staff reporter for the Washington Post. She had been covering government business for nearly as long as she cared to remember. She was single because her work kept her so busy flying around the globe that she didn't have time to establish many long-term relationships. She had some good friends, but never enough time or energy to devote to a marriage. She loved her work and that was fulfilling enough for now. Oh sure, one day she would like to get married, she guessed. But not now. Her career was everything to her. She had wanted to be a journalist since she had been in grade school. She had started a one page newspaper, to use the term liberally, when was in junior high school in Overland Park, Kansas. In high school, she worked on the school paper first as staff writer, then she became editor. She dropped the newspaper and became editor-in-chief of her high school yearbook. It was only natural that she would win a scholarship to Kansas University's School of Journalism and Mass Communications in Lawrence where she went directly from high school.

"I'm a writer," she responded simply.

"Then you are here writing a book?"

"Well, not exactly," responded Jessica as she continued to sip her white wine and decide how she wanted to respond to this conversation. She decided that if she were to tell him the truth, she might scare him off and she did not want to do that. She had been involved with the Justice Department and FBI investigations before. But this one was different. She had not uncovered anything specific that confirmed her suspicions, but something told her that there were too many unusual circumstances.

"What then?"

"Oh, I'm trying to write an article. I hope to get it published, ugh. . . in a news magazine, maybe in a paper--who knows, maybe even the New Times or the Washington Post, if its good enough," she said laughingly to evade the actual truth.

"What's the article about?" continued Evan.

"Oh, I'd rather not discuss it. I'm superstitious. I'm afraid if I talk about it, I won't get it published. Let's talk about you for a while," Jessica evaded. "Tell me about you."

"Let's see, what can I tell you about me. Well, for starters, I'm hungry. I haven't had anything decent to eat all day. How you would like to go somewhere and have some dinner?"

"Oh, I wasn't planning on..." she began to decline the invitation automatically.

"Have you had dinner?"

"Well, no, but I have work to do tonight."

"You have got to eat," he argued.

"I was just going to order in..."

"I promise to have you back in plenty of time to get several of hours in before you turn in for the night. Come on. Please. I hate to eat alone."

"Well..."

"You would be doing me a great favor. I've had a frightful day. If you would have dinner with me, I would chalk it off as worth it. What do you say? Please?"

"Well, alright." She did not want to let him go. She knew there was much more she might uncover with Evan Judd.

"I'd like that very much, Evan. Thank you."

The couple took the first available cab from in front of the hotel. "Take us to the best restaurant in town," Evan ordered the cabby.

"Yessa!" responded the driver.

They enjoyed a nice bottle of wine with dinner. By the time they were finished, Evan was more relaxed and in much better spirits. Hot and spicy food was not his favorite, but the company was tops. It was nearly midnight when they left the restaurant and headed back to the Latin Arms. Evan would have liked nothing better than to become intimate with this gorgeous young woman, but to approach her on that level was obviously inappropriate. Instead, he invited her into the hotel bar for a nightcap. Not surprisingly, Jessica declined. They said goodnight in the lobby of the hotel. Jessica Powers headed for the elevator; Evan Judd went into the bar.

Evan was invigorated. It had been a perfectly grand evening. Jessica Powers was a sophisticated and bright woman. She did not want to talk about her work, but had delighted him with stories about her youth in Kansas. He sipped his Courvoisier and forgot all about where he was-- that is until a small Jazz band returned from taking a break. The brassy sound coming from the trumpet quickly brought him back into this unfamiliar setting. He gulped down the last of the brandy, impounded the glass on the bar, and headed for the elevator. Suddenly, he was very, very tired.

Evan Judd jumped at the sound of the ring phone. It was nearly 10:30 the following morning. He expected the call to have come in by 8:00 a.m. When it didn't he had begun pacing back and forth in the small space at the foot of his bed until he was nearly dizzy from constantly turning. Well that, plus his mild hangover from the gin and brandy the night before.

"Hello," he yelled into the phone. "Yes. Okay."

He hung up and grabbed his jacket as he hurried out the door of his room. Ian Cooper had advised him that there was a car waiting for him in front of the hotel. As he walked out of the front door of the hotel, he automatically looked to the left where he recognized the government car, a black Ford Taurus sedan. It was the same car that had driven him back from the investigation the day before. He went directly to the back door and got in. The driver said nothing as he drove his passenger back to the FBI offices.

Evan Judd had been sitting in the steel grey government vintage waiting area for over two and a half hours when Agents Swift and Cooper appeared to take him to the conference room at the back. He was wet with perspiration. The conference room was an average sized room, about 20 feet wide by about 25 feet long. The walls were painted a sickly grey-green color and the badly warn black and white squares of linoleum on the floor were grey from wear and dirt. There were two men and one woman seated at the farthest end of the long, solid walnut conference table. They each had several file folders and legal pads in front of them. There were eight vacant wooden walnut chairs-- one at either end of the table and three on each side nearest them. Just off to the right at the farthest end of the table sat a legal secretary with a shorthand machine. As they entered, she was totally absorbed in her fingernails, studying each one as if it was new to her. She nonchalantly observed the trio as they entered the room and immediately resumed the study of her nails. As they ended what appeared to be a somewhat intense conversation, those already present did not acknowledge the newcomers as they entered the room.

"You sit here, Judd." Agent Swift indicated the vacant seat at the head of the table. Swift took the empty seat next to Evan on the right side as Cooper settled himself into the chair across the table from his partner. The room became quiet and what little noise there was came from the large office area outside the conference room.

Everyone in the room remained silent. No one said anything. Evan was beginning to feel very uncomfortable when a tall, imposing older man with grey hair came from behind him into the room and took the vacant seat at the far end of the table, closest to the court reporter. Evan Judd could feel the muscles in his stomach tighten. He felt a little sick to his stomach. "I'm gonna kill that Frank Spector with my bare hands when I get out of here."

His thinking was interrupted by the older man. "Mr. Judd, we are not going to beat around the bush. We know you are guilty of several counts of mail fraud. We also know that you not only know but have had business dealings with John P. Erlich, the subject of our investigation into insurance fraud. Now, Mr. Judd, we have enough to convict you and send you to prison for the rest of your life. But, we may not have to do that if you are willing to cooperate with us. Do you understand what I am saying, Mr. Judd?"

Evan Judd was stunned. He could feel the muscles in throat constrict as the man waited for his response.

"Do you understand what I said, Mr. Judd?"

Evan could hardly breath let alone speak, so he sat silent and nodded a "yes" to the person who was speaking.

"Good."

It was nearly 6:30 p.m. when the cab dropped Evan at the terminal. He was going to be able to get on the 7:05 to LaGuardia. He was lucky to get the flight. All of the earlier flights to New York had been booked. He went directly to the gate with his bag in hand. He did not want to take any chance of missing this plane and ending up staying another night in this "hell hole," as he had grown to think of the area.

The impact of the last several hours was beginning to settle in on Evan. He was badly unnerved. He hurried into the American Airlines Terminal and checked the flight board for a gate number. He raced down the corridor until he got to gate 4A feeling as if the weight of the world was in his wardrobe bag. He threw it onto a seat as he entered the waiting area. That was when he saw Jessica Powers, head down, reading a newspaper. She was sitting only three seats away from where he had thrown his bag. The sight of her jolted him momentarily, but nothing could take away the genuine fear that gripped him. She looked up when she heard the bag hit the seat. She smiled her recognition.

"Jessica, I didn't expect to see you here."

"Looks like we are on the same flight," she smiled back at him.

"I'll be right back, Jessica, I want to check in. I don't want anything to stop me from getting on this flight out of here."

Jessica folded her paper and shoved it into her bag. She had been reading her latest piece on the Justice Department. She was not ready to reveal any specifics about herself to Evan at this time, especially the fact that she was here in New Orleans to cover the FBI investigation of Erlich.

The plane to New York was not crowded and Evan easily arranged for Jessica to join him in first class. He was feeling empty and alone following the events of the afternoon.

"Can I get you something to drink?" inquired the flight attendant.

Jessica responded, "White wine."

Evan had his usual martini.

Evan was involved with his thoughts and was more quiet than the night before. Jessica inquired, "Is anything wrong? You seem to be preoccupied."

"I'm sorry Jessica," was his simple reply. He decided to change the conversation.

"You haven't told me why you are on this flight to New York, Jessica."

"I'm headed home for awhile," was her pensive response.

"Is your article finished?"

"No. I just need to get back and check on a few things."

Trying not to be too forward, but clearly wanting to know, Evan asked, "Do you live in the city?"

"Washington. This was the best connection I could make tonight. I'll catch a commuter to D.C."

For a moment, a flash of hope raced through Evan Judd's mind as he entertained the idea of perhaps spending some time with Jessica when the plane landed in New York.

The two settled into some easy conversation as the airplane settled into a comfortable altitude for its trip north. It was not difficult for Evan to convince Jessica to have dinner with him in the City. She would have no difficulty taking the train to Washington in the morning. As soon as they had deplaned, Evan made a reservation for her at the Plaza Hotel. With that small detail out of the way, Evan hailed a cab and they headed for Bici` in town.

Dinner conversation was light and relaxing. Evan Judd was in his own element once again, feeling confident, in control. He was also at ease and comfortable with Jessica, able to release some of the tensions created by his trip to New Orleans.

Following an absolutely delightful dinner, Evan got a cab to take them to the Plaza Hotel. The doorman knew Evan and greeted the couple as they got out of the cab. Evan, who was obviously pleased by the reception and recognition, generously tipped him as he signaled the bellman to take their bags and accompany them to the suite that is reserved for Mr. Judd. "This is a magnificent suite, Evan. Thank you so much," Jessica said as the bellman closed the door behind him. "Would you care for a nightcap?"

"Yes, indeed. Thank you, Jessica. Here, why don't you let me fix them?"

Jessica hung their coats in the closet as Evan removed his suit jacket and tie and poured them both a Bailey's. As he handed her the snifter, their hands touched and both felt something stir from within. Following an awkward moment, Jessica regained her composure. "For treating me to another super dinner, kind sir," she toasted.

They made themselves comfortable on the sofa as they sipped their drinks. Without saying anything, Evan had put his arm over her shoulders. It felt natural, good. He could feel the warmth of her body against his arm and side. Jessica was not oblivious to the feeling and felt herself longing to be closer to him. As she looked up into his eyes, she could feel his warm, sweet breath on her face. She melted into his soft, gentle kiss as he held her face with his other hand. She reached to his head to draw his face closer as he wrapped both arms around her in a passionate kiss and embrace. She shivered as she felt his hand slid up under her skirt and between her legs.

Although every ounce of her body physically desired this man, she pushed herself away from him. She could not allow intimacy. She did not know his role in the FBI investigation, and, he was, after all, her source. She excused the passionate exploration with "Evan, it's getting quite late."

"Oh, Jessica. I'm so sorry. I don't know what got into me. I should have known better. I'm sorry. Please forgive me."

Evan Judd felt more than his usual physical desires toward this woman. She was more than the usual "quick trick" as he so often thought of women. For some strange reason, he seemed to care about what she thought. Certainly, she was physically desirable. No question about that. But there was a certain quality about her that he was unable to put his finger on. Something about her intrigued him. She seemed to sense his emotions and appreciate his uneasiness without his mention of the situation he was in. She knew the right things to say.

That first kiss was as easy as breathing for both of them. The passion and desire that began burning instantly, was unexpected. "I believe we both felt something. I'm not blaming you for anything Evan. I just think we had better call it a night."

"Will I see you again, Jessica?"

"Perhaps, Evan. Perhaps. But I should get back to Washington. We'll have to see."

She walked him to the door. Just before leaving, he took her hand in his and kissed it lightly.

"Good night my lovely Jessica. Good night."

She closed the door and leaned up against it. "What is there about him?" She shook her head and pushed herself away from the door. It was time for a shower and a good night's sleep.

Jessica Powers was awakened by a knock at the door. She turned her head so that she could just read the red numerals on the clock radio which sat on the night table next to her bed. 9:00 o'clock!!! She jumped out of bed and began putting on the terry robe the hotel had left for her as she hurried out of the bedroom and through the sitting area. No one knew she was staying at the Plaza.

"Yes?" she inquired at the door.

"Delivery."

Jessica opened the door to a bellman ho was holding a dozen red roses. "Where would you like these, madam?" he asked as she stepped out of his way.

"Anywhere." Jessica went to the desk and reached into her handbag. "That's fine," she said as he placed the fragrant bouquet on the desk.

"Thank you, madam," he said as he took her tip and placed it in his pocket.

Jessica went to the bouquet and inhaled deeply as she reached for the card. She pulled the envelope from the bouquet. The card said simply, "I think I am falling in love. Evan."

Chapter 5

Evan had stayed at the Plaza overnight and called down to have the flowers sent to Jessica's room before she left the hotel. He was in the lobby early waiting for his car when the reality of his situation hit him once again. The doorman held the door as he walked out onto the street. "May I get a cab for you, Mr. Judd?" Evan Judd was not a stranger at the Plaza.

"No thanks. My driver should be here any moment," he told the doorman.

"Yes sir, Mr. Judd."

Harrington pulled in just as the two men were finishing their exchange. The doorman went to the rear door and opened it. Evan got into the back seat. "Take me to the office, Harrington."

The car maneuvered in and out of the early morning traffic as it headed for the Madison Avenue office building. Edna Carlisle was not in when Evan Judd got off the elevator on the 74th floor. He let himself into the suite moving quickly toward the door of his personal office. Once inside, he dropped his coat on the chair in front of his desk and moved quickly to the locked credenza behind his black leather swivel chair. He reached into his pocket and pulled out a key and began unlocking the file drawer. Evan immediately found exactly what he was looking for, and pulled the file from the hanging jacket. He closed the file drawer and settled back in his chair with the file.

It was 8:45 a.m. when Edna Carlisle arrived at the office. She turned on the office lights and hung her raincoat in the closet. As was her usual custom before doing anything else, she went to her boss's office to be sure that everything was in order for the day. She was startled when she opened the door and found Evan sitting behind his desk with the desk light on looking through some papers. As he looked up at her, she noticed his ashen color as well as the grim look on his face.

"Is there a problem, Mr. Judd?"

"Edna, I need your help. And, Edna, I need your confidence."

"Of course, Mr. Judd. That goes without saying."

"Edna, the FBI is accusing me of mail fraud," he began.

Edna Carlisle listened intently, hardly able to contain herself. At last, she could no longer restrain, "But, Mr. Judd, you..."

"Edna, please," he interrupted, "don't you see, I have no choice, I MUST cooperate with the FBI. I MUST do what ever they ask me to do or they will put me in jail."

"But, Mr. Judd," she lost her composure.

"Edna, oh Edna, please don't cry." He handed her his handkerchief. "Here. I need you to help hold us together."

"Oh, Mr. Judd. You know I will do anything."

"Good Edna. Just please try to do as I ask. They have told me I have no choice. Edna, I am scared. I can't stand the thought of being locked in prison."

"Oh dear Lord no, Mr. Judd. Not you in prison...." The color drained from Carlisle's face.

"I know what they told me Edna. Whether I want to or not, I have to cooperate with them."

"Alright, Mr. Judd. Whatever you say."

"So, Edna, I now need to go home tonight and talk with my wife and family. I need to prepare them. Would you please call my wife and have her assemble the family? I don't want to talk with her until then when I'm better prepared. There are some things I need to take care of today."

Feeling slightly relieved with having shared part of his burden with Edna Carlisle, Evan became more inclined, if not encouraged, about making the necessary arrangements in order to carry out the assignment given him by the FBI. After successfully setting up his meeting with

Henry Singer to take place at nine o'clock the following evening at the Cherry Hill Hyatt, Evan called FBI headquarters in New Orleans to advise them, as they had told him to do. He was completely unaware of the fact that Agents Swift and Cooper were waiting in Washington, D.C. for this information to be relayed to them.

The night was dark as Harrington slowly pulled the Lincoln Towncar to a gentle stop in front of the main entrance to the Judd home. As he carefully shifted from drive into park, he looked into his rear view mirror at his passenger. The lights coming from the portico cast grey shadows across Evan Judd's face making him look much older than his 54 years. "He looks as if he is aging before my very eyes," though Harrington as turned the engine off. He went around to the back door of the vehicle and opened it for his boss who made no attempt to get out.

"We're home, sir."

As if recovering from a deep trance, Evan Judd looked at his driver with a questioning frown. "We're home, Mr. Judd. Can I help you?"

"Thank you, Harrington."

Slowly, he handed the Moroccan leather briefcase to his driver and inched himself across the rich leather seat of his car. Harrington follow just in back of him as the housekeeper welcomed them at the door.

"Eve-nin," Mr. Judd. "They're all here, sir. They're all waiting for you in the parlor."

Evan handed Mrs. Hoffsteader his hat and coat, adjusted his tie in front of the huge mirror, and brushed at his jacket in a nervous gesture as he moved slowly across the grand foyer toward the living room. He could hear voices bickering back and forth at one another as he approached the arched doorway to the formal living room.

"I demand to know what this is all about!" was the greeting to first reach his ears as he entered the room.

Alice Whitley Judd had been demanding for years, so this was certainly not a new or unexpected challenge to Evan Judd.

"We have all had to cancel plans because of you. I demand to know what this is all about right this minute, Evan!"

As if on cue, the family chorus chimed in with their mother, "Yeah, I had a date..." "I'm supposed to be..." "What the hell is this all about? Do you know what I had to go through..."

Yes, he had been answering their demands for nearly all of his adult life. They were the reasons he was in this situation, and, they were the reasons why he would help the FBI. Sadly, he had sacrificed his entire life for this ungrateful family.

"This is serious," Evan interrupted the whining and the hostile remarks. "I did not ask you all to assemble here this evening so that I could interrupt your plans. You can be assured this is something that you have to know about, and I wanted to tell all of you the story since you are, indeed, the reason that we have this, ah, this well ah...we have this 'er... a..a..a... situation."

"What 'situation' are you talking about Evan? Tell us what on earth you are babbling about. Could you, *please,* get to the point?" Alice Judd said in her most caustic tone.

"Yes, Father, let's get on with it," repeated Evan Jr., as he deliberately made an issue of looking at the Rolex watch on his left wrist as he impatiently leaned back against the richly upholstered, winged-backed chair. His youngest sister sat staring at her restless feet which were playing with the shoes she had removed. Her annoyance with the meeting was evidenced in the constant restless movement of her left leg as she bounced it over her knee in an agitated fashion.

Surrounded by this family audience, Evan Judd became characteristically rejuvenated. He appeared to become almost animated in his delivery as he proceeded with his explanation for the "family gathering." Magically, as he progressed, he was able to take control with the charm he had counted on for years. Part of his charm stemmed from the fact that he is able to fool himself into believing he was completely innocent of any wrong doing himself. If he did do anything that was in fact perceived as wrong in the eyes of the law, it most certainly was done for his family. Not for himself. His family demanded the best. Evan's mind was whirling with self-pride. "And, they got the best," Evan justified. "If it weren't for them, he reasoned, I wouldn't be answering to any FBI right now. Never mind, I will do my patriotic duty, and be glad to do it. For heaven's sake, I haven't done a thing wrong except to give my family what they wanted. Doesn't everyone?"

He was ready. "First of all, have you not been well taken care of? Haven't you always had everything you ever wanted? Don't you have the very finest?"

No one responded. The lack of response evidenced to Evan that they no doubt did. It had been more of a rhetorical question anyway. He continued, "I have devoted my life to your comforts--giving you everything. You all went to the best schools, had the best clothes, belonged to the best clubs, had the best cars...you, my darlings, had everything money could buy. I saw to it that you did. I have always taken good care of all of you."

He paused as if to soak-up the unspoken gratitude he expected but did not receive from this formidable group. He continued, "There have been a few irregularities but they were absolutely necessary in order for me to make the profit necessary to support my family and treat them as they well ***should have and, in fact, demanded to be treated.***"

"Had it not been for you and the children, Alice, and the demands you put upon me--expecting to live in the lifestyle of your very own family..."

"But, Evan..."

"No buts, Alice. Your Father would not give us a penny. We had a child on the way...I had to handle the situation the best way I could. And, I did. Everyone will have to admit that we are quite well situated. Not one of you has ever wanted for a thing in your life." He could not help himself itemize for them once again. "You have been to the best schools, had the finest clothes, belonged to the best clubs, owned the most expensive cars. You have been well cared for indeed. Every personal luxury you ever wished for you got. There was no other way." His voice trailed off as he looked beyond the group and off into the magnificent foyer and the winding staircase that led to the floors above.

Evan stood quietly for a moment, obviously pleased by the attention he was getting from the family. It was certainly a rarity these days and he was enjoying it. The silence caught his attention, and he knew he had to fill it. He prepared to continue in a style of high drama in order to keep this attention he enjoyed so much. "The FBI is investigating. They just made me spend several days in New Orleans under investigation."

A low audible gasp was shared by several of the family members and Evan, Jr., first to speak, mouthed the words for the entire group. "FBI! Hol-y Crap!!!" Junior's voice echoed in the stillness. "What are they charging you with, Father?"

"Oh, for crying out loud, what have you done to us Dad?"

In her inimitable way, Alice Judd stepped in to handle trauma from her perspective. "No one must know of this. We must keep this amongst ourselves. Don't breathe a word of this to anyone. How will I ever show my face at the Club if this gets out? Oh my God, Evan, will Daddy ever find out? I can't believe this is happening.....Oh, dear God, what are YOU going to do, Evan? HOW COULD YOU?!!!"

Evan Judd was truly enjoying this attention. But, he was not going to take blame for that which he clearly knew to be their fault. "Now Alice, I have told you there was no choice. You certainly weren't naive enough to believe that a simple insurance agency would ever have produced the funds necessary for us to live this kind of a life, were you? Of course not," he answered his own question. "I had no choice. You wanted the best, and I wanted you to have the best. I did it all for you. Now, ..." he hesitated deciding just how much he was going to tell them.

"Now, what Daddy? Is someone going to take our money? Will we have to move?" Fear had gripped Jennifer, the youngest daughter.

"That's stupid, Jenny..." Evan Jr. piped in.

"Sweethear..." Evan made an attempt to console his youngest daughter.

"What the hell are they charging you with Dad? Are you going to jail?" Evan Jr. paused as his mind raced through the possibilities as he saw them. "How humiliating. Oh my God, mother, what will we do?"

Hysterical by now, Julie began sobbing. "We'll be ruined. What will they say.? Dad, how could you?!!!"

"Will everyone just SHUT THE HELL UP! What did you do, father? What are the damn charges?" Being the oldest of the children, Evan Jr. had no trouble believing he was the person to take control of the situation.

"It may not be easy, but I am going to try to get us out of this. The FBI has cut me a deal," Evan continued.

"FBI? Cut a deal? What in the name of hell have you gotten into, Father?" Suddenly, Todd was on his feet and red in the face as he yelled at this father.

Evan, Jr. looked as if he was about to pounce on Evan.

"Tell us! Tell us! I demand that you tell us right now!!!"

"Look, I have taken care of you all your lives. You are my priority. Always have been. If it weren't for my family, there never would have been a problem. But, you all wanted the best of the best and I made it my life's work to give it to you. I want *you to listen for once in your lives.*"

He waited. "Now, that's better. The FBI has assured me that *if* I cooperate with them, there will be no charges filed against us. So, that is what I am going to do. I am going to do some work for them." He continued to build on this theme as he continued. "It will be fine. I don't mind working for this country. America is a fine country, and if I can do a little work for the United States Department of Justice, I'll be happy to do so. So long as they don't bother my family."

"Now, I don't want any of you talking about any of this to anyone. Do you understand me? We are to keep this to ourselves. No telling who may be looking us over. I'll do my best to protect you, but you are going to have to mind your Ps and Qs. No talking about money or anything to anyone."

"So that's it? Nothing is going to change?"

"That's it."

Within minutes the room cleared--except for Evan and Alice. She was pouring another drink when he came up behind her. The years had hardened her, but she still had a gorgeous figure. She was wearing a tight, black jumpsuit trimmed with sequins. He put his arm around her shoulder. She was surprised by his touch and turned toward him. The deep neckline accented full breasts. He took the drink from her hand and pulled her to him. Their lips met and they shared an urgency which neither had experienced toward the other in a long time.

"I thought I would have Cook prepare a light supper. Are you free to join me?"

"I'd like to take a nice hot bath first."

"Why don't you do that and I'll see about supper."

When Evan entered the master suite, soft music was playing in the background. The lights were dimmed but he could see candles lighting the bathroom where Alice was luxuriating in the huge sunken tub. Quietly, he began removing his clothing and slipped into his robe. As he entered the bath area, she motioned for him to sit at the edge of the tub. "Do you remember how to wash my back?"

Evan took the soft, soap-filled sponge. He slowly applied the warm, soapy water to her back. As she leaned back toward him in total relaxation, he gently began rubbing her generous breasts with the soapy sponge. Alice closed her eyes and breathed deeply, enjoying the physical desires which were taunting her. She pulled his hand under the water and cried out as he touched her.

No words were spoken as he helped her out of the water, wrapped her in the large bath towel and began kissing her neck as he walked her to their bed. Somehow the passions of their youth were magically rekindled for one evening. Their tensions were released and neither thought about supper again that night.

Evan Judd was at his desk by 8:00 a.m. the following morning. He had awakened early thinking about the meeting he had arranged with the manager of Erlich's agency in Marlton, New Jersey. Weeks earlier, Erlich had put out feelers, as was his custom, to let Evan and some of his other associates know that it was time for him to cut a deal for the agency. The FBI had somehow found out, and this was what they decided Evan Judd would do as part of his cooperative effort--cut the deal and buy Erlich out of this "hot" agency.

By the time Edna Carlisle came into work at 8:30, Evan had paced miles around his own office. He was too anxious to sit still. "Mr. Judd, you surprise me again this morning." Although there was no one else in the vicinity, Edna lowered her voice into a near whisper as if to prevent anyone from overhearing their conversation, "Is everything, you know, alright?"

"It's so-so, Edna."

"The family? How'd Mrs. Judd take the.. ah, you know?"

"Let's just say no one was particularly happy with what I told them. But, really Edna, whatever I did, I did for them. And I told them that. You know that Edna, I have always done everything for my family."

"Yes sir, Mr. Judd. I know how hard you have worked to make them happy."

"I have bought them everything they ever wanted."

"I know."

"The kids went to the best schools, had the best clothes, cars, clubs--everything."

"The best, yes sir. You really provided for them, Mr. Judd."

"That's right Edna. Now? Look what happens to a guy who just tries like hell to give his family a good life. They threaten to send him to prison."

"I know, Mr. Judd."

"It just isn't right, Edna. It's just not fair."

"No sir. Not fair at all."

"I don't know, I just don't understand."

"No sir. Me neither."

"Well, I will do as they ask. Hell, I don't mind helping them with the investigation. I don't like risking my neck, but, I have no choice as I see it."

"Whatever you need, you just let me know, Mr. Judd."

"Thank you, Edna. I do appreciate it. As a matter of fact, I do want you to do something right now. I want to talk with Frank Spector. I've decided I don't want to talk to one of his damn flunkies. I pay Spector enough money so when I want to talk to him, I expect to talk to him."

"But he's in the Caribbean, Mr. Judd."

"I know, Edna, but I want you to get a call to him on that ship. He can use the ship to shore."

"Yessir."

"You can start working on that right now Edna. I want to talk with him BEFORE I go to my meeting in New Jersey this afternoon."

"I'll do my best, sir."

"I have to talk with him Edna. This is urgent."

"Yessir. I'll get right on it."

"Thank you, Edna.

Edna Carlisle sprung off the edge of the chair in which she was sitting and hurried to her office just outside Evan's door to begin her pursuit of Frank Spector--vacationing somewhere in the Caribbean.

Evan kept himself busy all morning making phone calls and checking information repeatedly in his confidential files. He arranged a luncheon date with his banker and was back at his desk by quarter of two. Evan inquired as he passed her desk, "Have you reached Spector yet?" She had been periodically keeping him posted as to her progress with the call to the attorney.

"They have been weighing anchor off the coast of Antigua, sir. He will call you from the Island. I expect him to call any minute."

Evan went into his office and began preparing for his drive to New Jersey late in the afternoon. The intercom interrupted him. "Yes Edna?"

"Mr. Spector is on your line, sir."

"Frank, damn it all. . . I need you, buddy."

"Evan. What is going on?" a cool Frank Spector replied.

"Frank, the FBI is investigating insurance fraud."

"Yes? So?"

"**Frank!** They have been here to see me. They had me go to New Orleans. Damn it all, Frank, they could send me to prison. Frank, I have..."

"Woooooooo, hold on, back up."

"The FBI, Frank, is charging me with mail fraud."

"Let me get this straight, you are telling me you have been indicted, and charged with mail fraud?"

"No, no, I'm telling you they CAN charge me with mail fraud if I don't cooperate."

"So, what you are saying is that they haven't charged you?"

"But, Frank, they can. They can and they will if I don't cooperate with them."

"What do they want you to do?"

"They want me to set up a deal to buy out one of Erlich's agencies."

"I see."

"Erlich has a hot agency in Marlton, New Jersey. They want me to make an offer."

"I see."

"So, I have a meeting set up with a Henry Singer, his man there, for tonight."

"What are you planning to do?"

"I am planning to make him the initial offer like they told me to do."

"Don't do it, Evan."

"What?"

"I said, don't do it."

"What are you talking about, Frank?"

"Don't be a part of this, Evan. You can get yourself in serious trouble. Don't do it."

"Frank! Frank! Frank! You don't understand. I don't have a choice."

"You have a choice, Evan. Don't do it."

"Damn it all, Frank, I have to."

"Evan, if you won't listen to me, get advice from other counsel, but don't jump in and do it. I'm telling you."

"Damn it Frank, I pay you good money to be here to support me and you're off in some friggin island half way around the world when I need you telling me not to do what the Justice Department has told me I have to do if I am going to stay out of prison. Frank, I'm telling you I don't have a choice."

"Evan. For the last time, I'm telling you to get advice from some other legal counsel. Don't do this. You can get into some serious trouble."

"Thanks for your support, Mr. Spector. Have a nice vacation. Don't get too much sun. I hear it can age a guy."

Without waiting for a reply, Evan hung up the telephone receiver. He shook his head in a disgusted disbelieving fashion. "So much for Frank Spector."

Evan turned in his swivel chair and starred out into the city. He thought about the events of the last several days. He was going to do what the FBI asked. "I don't need to get more legal counsel. I know what they told me. Damn it to hell, I'm not going to prison. I am going to cooperate. I'm no freaking idiot. I know what I'm doing. Damn it! Look what I have accomplished. Frank Spector, be damned and go to hell."

CHAPTER 6

IT WAS NEARLY EIGHT in the evening when the Lincoln Towncar pulled in front of the Cherry Hill Hyatt Hotel which was just East of the Marlton agency on Route 70 in Cherry Hill, New Jersey. Harrington parked the car and went to the back door to open it for his passenger. Evan Judd got out of the vehicle with his briefcase and small, overnight bag which he took with him into the lobby of the hotel. After looking around in an effort to see if he recognized anyone, he went to the registration desk to check into the room he had reserved for himself. One of the clerks behind the desk looked up as he approached the counter. "Can I help you, sir?"

"Yes. I have a reservation for tonight. Evan Judd."

"Let me check, sir."

Evan stood quietly looking at the clerk as he punched the keys of his computer. "Yes sir. I have it right here."

"Good."

"How do you wish to pay for this, Mr. Judd?"

"Credit card."

"Very good sir. May I see the card please?

Evan reached into his jacket pocket and retrieved the card from his wallet. He placed it on the counter for the clerk.

The clerk made the necessary arrangements to have the room and any other charges put on his credit card and returned the card to Evan. "Here is your card and let me get your room key. Let's see, the key to your suite is right here. Room 1103. Shall I have the bell captain take your bag up to your suite sir?"

"Please. Oh, by the way, I am expecting someone."

"Very good,   sir. We will ring your room when the party gets here."

The bell captain led the way to the elevators at the far end of the lobby near the main entrance. He stood aside for Evan to board the elevator. They rode in silence to the eleventh floor. The bell captain led the way to the suite reserved for him and opened the door. The bell captain went ahead and turned on the lights and opened the window drapery.

When the bell captain left with is tip, Evan went to the window to look out. His room overlooked the Cooper River and the Philadelphia skyline. He was glad to be a little early.   He wanted to freshen up before Henry Singer arrived. He took off his jacket, tie and shirt and put them on a hanger then went into the bathroom to wash up.

Before he could change into a fresh white shirt, the phone rang. "Yes?"

"Mr. Judd, there are two gentlemen in the lobby asking for you. I will put one of them on the house phone."

"Damn," he thought, "he's early."

"Judd?"

"Yes."

"This is Henry Singer."

"Henry, I'm in suite 1103. Come on up."

That was the end of the conversation. Evan returned to putting on his tie and jacket. He was checking his appearance in the full-length mirror when the knock came at the door. "Just a minute."

Evan crossed the suite and opened the door to his room. "Henry. Good to see you." He offered his hand and Henry Singer mechanically shook it. "Come in."

Henry Singer entered the suite and another man, considerably taller and certainly much more muscular, followed directly behind him. Henry spoke, "Judd, this here is Harold Turner."

Evan offered his hand, but Harold made no effort to acknowledge Evan. Evan felt uncomfortable but refused to let on. Deep inside, he remained aware of the fact that the whole meeting was a set up. "If I ever get caught…." He refused to think about it.

"I see, well okay," he awkwardly put his hand away when Turner ignored it. "Yes, please come in. Have a seat."

Singer spoke. "I assume you want to take a look at the figures, Judd."

"Yes I do, Henry."

Henry pulled up his briefcase and began opening it on the coffee table. He pulled out a file folder. "Take a look at this."

Evan Judd, sitting in a chair opposite Singer and Turner, reached for the file and opened it. He leaned forward and he began to study the information given him. He waited an appropriate amount of time before saying anything. Finally, Evan looked up from the papers and leaned back in his chair. "Some nice looking figures here, Henry."

"Yeah. The boss thought you'd like 'em," Harold managed to come to life as he interjected his two cents from the other side of the room. He had gotten up and was looking around the room.

"Well, he was right," responded Evan.

"Then we can assume you are willing to deal?"

"I am willing to deal."

Henry Singer quickly put his papers away and got to his feet. "We'll tell the boss," he said as he headed for the door. Harold Turner fell in behind him.

Evan Judd followed. He threw out one last remark before Singer opened the door. "Forty-nine percent?"

Singer did not respond immediately and was out the door with Turner at his heals. Turner spoke over his shoulder on his way to the elevator, "You know the routine, Judd."

Meanwhile on the other side of the wall in room 1101, Agents Swift and Cooper had been listening carefully. There instructions were not only to monitor his business, but also gather information on how the operation worked. This knowledge would not only help the FBI with the major investigation, but it would serve to lock Evan Judd into their system.

"Damn!" said Cooper pulling the earphones from his head as he got to his feet. "We really didn't get any solid information. We're going to have to run with Plan B."

"Let's go," responded Agent Swift."

"Hurry. We'll scare the devil out of him."

Agents Cooper and Swift quickly put on their jackets and waited with the door to room 1101 open just a crack to be certain that Singer and Turner were safely out of sight and on the elevator before they made their move.

Evan Judd, pleased as punch with himself, decided to celebrate. He pulled a bottle of Red Label Scotch from the mini bar in his room. He put some ice in his glass and decided to take off his jacket and loosen his tie. "Might as well get comfortable," he said out loud as he snapped on the TV with the remote.

He was startled by loud pounding at the door to his suite. He yanked his tie off and hurried to open the door. Swift and Cooper pushed open the door and forced themselves into the room, while a surprised Evan Judd nearly lost his balance.

"We don't know what you are trying to pull, Judd, but you are in serious trouble now."   Agent Cooper swung into full gear.

"I...ah, I...but I...don't understand," a shaken Evan Judd responded.

"We tried to help you, Judd. We could have put you in prison and thrown away the key. But, no, we gave you a chance to redeem yourself, to cooperate," Agent Swift reasoned.

"But, but I *am* cooperating..."

"You call that cooperating?" Cooper showed no mercy.

"I did what you wanted..."

"Judd, Judd. Don't screw with us," Cooper scolded.

"But I'm not..."

"Shut up, Judd. We weren't born yesterday. We've been in the business a long time. Get your things together; we're haulin' ass back to New Orleans."

"What?" Evan froze.

"Get that driver of yours to get the car around front. We are heading back to New Orleans tonight. We'll take the red-eye," continued Cooper. "Gordon, you get our things and I'll keep Judd here company.

Moments later, the trio left the Cherry Hill Hyatt in the Lincoln Towncar with Harrington at the wheel headed for Philadelphia International Airport. No one spoke.

When they got into the terminal, they went to the ticket window where three tickets had been reserved. They used Evan's credit card to pay for their airfare. They boarded the plane a few minutes later. The flight was not crowded, but whether it was for protocol or effect, the three sat shoulder to shoulder all the way to New Orleans. Evan Judd sat uncomfortably between the two agents. Not surprisingly, it was Evan Judd who paid the cab fare to the Latin Arms for the three of them. This is where the trio finally parted company.

"Okay, Judd. We're going to leave you, but you damn well better not tell a soul you are here. We mean it. We don't want you to call or contact anyone. Do you understand me, Judd? Do I make myself clear?" Agent Cooper yelled in a strained whisper directly into Evan's face.

"Yes. I hear you," a frightened and shaken Evan Judd responded.

"We'll get back to you."

The two Agents turned and walked out lobby of the Latin Arms.

There was a car waiting for them down the street from the hotel. "How'd you make out?" inquired the inspector.

"Like a charm, boss," replied Cooper.

"Good."

"Now we've got him hooked into the system," added Swift.

"Did you see how nervous that little turd looked when we said 'don't tell a soul you are here. Do you understand, Judd?'" laughed Cooper. "This is gonna be like taking candy from a baby, boss."

The black government sedan sped off into the night and Evan Judd lumbered into the hotel bar to console himself with drinks. "What'll it be, sir?"

"Scotch, rocks. Make it a double."

As soon as the bartender placed the glass on the bar in front of Evan, he grabbed it and gulped the down the liquid and shoved the glass back toward the bartender.

"You feelin' a little down tonight, buddy?" the bartender filled the glass again.

"Life! Ya work hard, ya think you are doing the right thing...I'll have another!"

Evan quickly finished the second glass before he began to get a sense of the tension leaving his body. As he ordered his next drink, he decided to make himself comfortable at the bar. He had no intention of going to his room. He climbed up on the bar stool and settled in.

With plenty of cash on the bar, no one bothered to keep track of how many doubles he was consuming. At some point, Evan's words begin to slur as he tried to continue to engage the bartender in conversation. It was not long before he wasn't sure who he is talking with. A familiar voice said, "Evan, I think you need some sleep. Let me help you to your room."

Unable to reason, Evan Judd willingly allowed Jessica Powers to help him to his room where she guided him into bed.

It was nearly 7:45 a.m. before Evan Judd awoke--with a hangover the size of Texas. The window drapery had been left wide open, and, as the warm sun began to shine into the room, he felt excruciating pain as he tried to open his eyes. He recoiled from the direct encounter with the sunshine and quickly turned his head away from the light coming in the window. "Oh no, big mistake," he realized a second too late. His head began to throb in response to this sudden movement. For a few moments, he was content to stay put, head completely still, eyes closed. But he knew instinctively that this inactivity alone would not get rid of his headache. He would have to muster up some courage and take action.

Slowly, he inched himself to the side of the bed and slid his legs over the edge. Carefully, he tried to arrange his feet for balance. He avoided the sunlight as he got to his feet. Next thing to figure out was where the bathroom was. His surroundings look somewhat familiar, but, he remained uncertain of his whereabouts. At this point, he really didn't care.

Evan held the wall as he inched to the bathroom. As he opened the door to the medicine cabinet which was above the bathroom sink, he saw that it was completely empty. He moaned, "Now what. . ."

Evan worked his way cautiously back to the bedroom and searched out the phone. Obviously, he was in a hotel. He would call the desk and have some aspirin sent to the room. As he reached for the phone, he noticed a small piece of paper tucked under the receiver. He opened it and read aloud, "Room 624 - Jessica."

Evan sat carefully down on the edge of the bed and tried to remember the night before. As some of the fog lifted from his hangover, he was mindful of the fact that he was at the Latin Arms in New Orleans, but, how...?

The activities of the day before came rushing back to his mind. Fear began to grip his stomach. He remembered landing in New Orleans and coming to the hotel with the FBI agents. They dropped him off and then left the hotel. He had gone straight to the bar. "Jessica...?" Evan Judd did not remember seeing her. He reached for the phone once again. "Give me room 624."

The phone was ringing as Jessica Powers turned off the shower. She grabbed the bath towel and tied it around her as she moved toward the phone. "Hello?"

"Jessica. Evan Judd, here. I found your note."

"Good morning, Evan. How are you?"

"I have one hell of a headache. Do you have any aspirin?"

"I believe I do, Evan."

Jessica Powers began rummaging through her large purse. "Here they are..."

"Do you mind if I come down and get a couple?"

"Not at all., Evan," she responded gently into the phone.

"I'll be right there."

Jessica returned the phone to its cradle. She made a turban of her towel and reached to the back of the bathroom door for her robe.

At the sound of the first knock at the door, Jessica peaked through the tiny peep hole as she completed tying the belt around her waist. She opened the door. "Please come in Evan."

She motioned him to the chair on the other side of the bed. "Please, have a seat. I'll get you some water."

She began running the tap water in an attempt to cool it as she removed the top from the small container of aspirin. She retrieved two of the tablets and replaced the lid. She carefully placed a glass under the faucet and filled it with cool liquid. Jessica handed the two tablets to Evan. "Here." She held out the water and he took it. He washed the tablets down with the water and returned the empty glass to her.

"I am surprised to see you back in New Orleans, Evan."

"I'm grateful to see you." He was sheepishly quiet as he looked up into her eyes. "Thank you for helping me to my room last night, Jess."

She sat down on the edge of the bed and looked deep into his troubled eyes. "You were not in very good shape last night."

"No, I'm afraid not." He did not have the energy to evade the issue.

"When I helped you to your room, you kept begging me not to let them put you in jail. Evan, who on earth would put you in jail? What have you done?"

"Oh Jessica, I'm in such a mess. I never meant to have things turn out this way."

"What way, Evan?"

"Trouble with the Feds."

"Feds?"

"I was just trying to take care of my family the best way I knew how. Alice was accustomed to having everything. She comes from enormous money, you know. Her family was so against our marriage. Then when she got pregnant, there was no choice. They are Catholic and we had to get married."

"I'm afraid I still don't understand..."

"Well, her father was so enraged, he refused to have anything to do with me in the beginning. So I went into business for myself. I guess I made some poor business choices."

"Poor business choices do not mean trouble with the government that will send you to jail."

"My choices do..."

"How so?"

"I had no money, so I had to work some deals. The people I dealt with weren't exactly legit."

"Erlich?"

"Erlich."

"It started innocent enough. I had a few bucks. I wanted to buy him out. He sold me my first agency. Hell, he offered to finance the deal for me. He even supplied my first agency manager to get me going in the car insurance business. Hell, I remember old Stevie as if it was yesterday."

"I don't see a problem with that."

"Well, as it turned out, he only sold me 49 percent. He kept 51 percent himself."

"Why did Erlich keep the 51 percent? Didn't you want controlling interest?"

"Well, at first, I didn't care. I needed some good money, and Erlich promised me I would have plenty. That was all I cared about at the time. Hell, I didn't know that much about the business...why would I want control?"

"I suppose..."

"So, I took what I could get. I had a unhappy new wife and a kid to support."

"I forgot."

"Believe me, I couldn't. I did what I had to do."

"So what was wrong with the business?"

"Well, old Stevie had some agents. We wrote plenty of business. We took in a considerable bit of money. We hired a good attorney. We never paid off a claim."

"Never paid off a claim?"

"Well not one of any substantial consequence."

"How did you manage that?"

"Well, any sizable claims we took to court. We sold that agency before we lost any cases."

"I don't understand."

"It's quite simple, actually. You get to town, right? Get a good lawyer who knows the system. The legal system gets so screwed up you tie knots in the plaintiff. Interrogatories, depositions, requests for admissions, requests for non-binding arbitration and continuances. By taking them to court, we could keep them tied up for a long period of time."

"Oh Evan..."

"But Jessica, I never really meant anyone any harm. I was young and foolish and I needed to provide for my family. I HAD to provide for my family. I sure as hell wasn't going to get any help from Alice's family, and mine was dead."

"Evan, I suspect they aren't out to get you. I don't know."

"Jessica, you have got to believe me. I never meant anyone any harm. My family needed to be cared for, and I had no choice. Anything I did, I did strictly for them. I would never have done this otherwise."

"What now?"

"They want me to cooperate, and they won't put me in prison, they say. But, I was doing what they asked, and they yanked me onto a plane last night in Philadelphia and told me not to let anyone know that I am here."

"I see."

"I was doing exactly what they wanted me to do, but somehow they listened in and didn't like what I did. The next thing I knew, they were hauling me back here. They said not to let anyone know that I am here."

"What next?"

"Oh Jessica, I don't know. I expect they will call or come for me shortly. I'd better get back to my room. I don't want them to know that I have said anything to you. Oh Jessica, I feel like I'm going crazy."

"Better get back to your room. I won't say anything Evan. We'll talk later."

Evan was on his feet and heading out the door. "Thanks for the aspirin, Jess."

CHAPTER 7

ALTHOUGH HE WAS EXPECTING the call, Evan Judd was startled when the phone rang in his room at 10:30 a.m. His headache had subsided, but his nerves remained jangled.

"Judd, here."

It was Agent Cooper who responded. "I'm at headquarters. How soon can you get yourself here?"

"I'll get a cab and be there within the half hour."

"Make it sooner," Cooper growled. Evan Judd pulled the phone away from his ear as Cooper slammed the receiver down.

Before he hung-up the phone, Evan rang the bell captain to request a cab. "This is Evan Judd. Get me a cab. I'll be there directly."

He thought of Jessica as he rode the elevator down to the lobby. He was glad he had told her what was going on. He was comfortable with her. He trusted her. The elevator doors opened. The heat was oppressive as he stepped out of the car. Summer had moved into New Orleans with full force. It was hot. Very hot. Evan Judd looked out of place in a suit and tie as he hurried across main lobby to the bell captain.

"Here's your cab, Mister Judd." Evan Judd pressed a five dollar bill into the man's hand. "Thank you, sir," the captain said as he held the cab door for Evan.

Evan gave the address to the cabbie as the car pulled away from the curb. "Would you mind putting on the air conditioning?" Evan said to the driver.

"It broke. Ain't had none since summer 'fore last," replied the cabbie. "Not so bad ta-day. You all should see it 'bout July here in New Orl'in."

Evan pulled the white handkerchief from the back pocket of his trousers and wiped the perspiration from his face. Before returning it to the pocket, he removed his suit jacket. His shirt was wet from perspiration already. "They could keep this God-forsaken hole. If this place wasn't hell, it would be a relief to get there," Evan thought as the cab moved slowly through the narrow side streets.

Evan Judd felt as if he had put in a full day as the cab pulled up in front of the government building. He paid the driver and hurried in. He knew the routine of getting to the headquarters office well enough by now and was soon on the 14th floor. Agent Cooper met him just moments after he entered the FBI office doors.

"They're waiting for us in the conference room right now. We'd better move it, Judd."

Evan Judd stepped in directly behind Cooper as he followed a familiar pathway between the office cubicles to the conference room in the back. As they entered the room, Cooper pointed to the vacant chair at the head of the table. "Sit over there," he said curtly.

Evan obeyed. Still hot from the ride, Evan Judd sat down in the empty chair keeping his suit jacket on as he would normally do at any business meeting. He was anxious, but determined not to let on to this audience. He leaned back in the chair after nodding and smiling to the group which consisted of Agents Swift and Kowalski as well as yet a fourth man who was new to Evan. This fourth man seemed to be the person in charge. He closed the file he was reading, pushed his chair back from the conference table and said, "I'll get Maloney." He left the room closing the door behind him.

The room fell quiet. None of the Agents made any effort to cover the guns they had strapped to there chest. Although he knew they carried them, just seeing the guns made Evan even more apprehensive. No one said anything. There was no air moving in the room, or so it seemed. He reached for his handkerchief to wipe the sweat that was accumulating over his upper lip. The handkerchief was not there. Evan began to check his other pockets. As he squirmed around in his chair, all eyes in the room turned in his direction.

"Can't seem to find my handkerchief," Evan awkwardly volunteered. The agents continued to watch as he resorted to using the back of his hand to wipe his upper lip. Five minutes passed. It seemed longer. Now the beads of sweat on his forehead grew heavier and began to slide down through his eyebrows into his eyes. The salt made them sting and Evan squinted uncomfortably. Again, he resorted to his hand to attempt to clear his face and forehead.

Another few minutes passed. No one moved. Suddenly, the conference room door burst open and a big muscular man hurried into the room. He was followed by the agent who went for Maloney.

"This must be Maloney," Evan thought as he again made an attempt to remove the perspiration from his face.

"Okay, let's get on with this," Maloney said as he moved to the far end of the room sitting at the head of the long conference table opposite where Evan was sitting. "Tony, what have we got?" he asked the agent who came in with him and sat two chairs to his left.

"Pat, as you know, we have been trying to work with Mr. Judd here to further our investigation of John Philip Erlich." The agent nodded his head in the direction of Evan as he referred to him. However, it would seem that Mr. Judd is not being forthright. He is holding back..."

"I'm not holding back anything," Evan blurted out nervously interrupting Inspector Tony Tancreddi.

Everyone immediately looked at Evan. "I've no reason to withhold anything from you," Evan said regaining his composure. "I'm more than happy to help you guys out. I consider it my patriotic privilege." He was beginning to turn on the Judd charm.

His last words seemed to echo in the large conference room as everyone waited quietly for him to conclude. The silence became deafening. Evan nervously cleared his throat.

"What is it that you want to know?"

Again, everyone continued to look at him.

"I'll do anything you ask."

With that last remark, Tony Tancreddi looked back toward Maloney and began to speak. "As I was saying Pat, we think Mr. Judd would be of better service to us if he continued the Marlton Agency buyout wearing a wire."

Evan listened nervously, but intently. Maloney was leaning forward, hands relaxed on the table. He was quiet. "We think this could help move the investigation along a little faster."

Maloney immediately responded. "Well, let's do it then, boys. I assume you have no problem with this, Mr. Judd. "It was more a statement than a question. "You make whatever arrangements are necessary, and I'll notify Northeast. Is that it?"

"That's all, boss. We can take it from here."

Everyone was on his feet before Evan realized the meeting was over. He pushed his chair from the table and got to his feet awkwardly not knowing what to do next. As the others left the room, Agent Cooper stayed back.

"Well, Judd, guess you'd better set up another meeting with the folks at the Marlton agency. When you get the date and time, give me a call right away. We will make the necessary arrangements for you to wear the wire for the deal."

"But how…"

"Look Judd, all you have to do is set up the meeting and contact me. Got that? Just do what we tell you. Do you understand? We will handle the rest. Now get your ass back to New York and let's get this show on the road. We've lost enough time. You know your way out," Cooper said as he left Evan standing alone in the conference room.

Evan Judd stood in the conference room for several moments before he gained the wherewithal to leave the Government building. Although there was no direct reference to jail made today, Evan Judd knew that he had no choice but to wear the wire or they would send him to prison. As he rode back in the cab to the Latin Arms, he knew beyond a shadow of a doubt that if he wanted to remain a free man, he would have to do anything these guys wanted him to do.

On the other hand, Erlich was no one to mess with either. If he even suspected Judd was working for the Department of Justice, life as he knew it would no longer exist. He really didn't know exactly how it would be arranged or exactly what would happen to him, but he knew better than to ever test it. Erlich was a powerful man with powerful connections. Evan Judd's stomach churned as he allowed his mind to wander through some unacceptable possibilities.

"How the hell am I going to get myself through this without getting nailed," he thought as his cab pulled up in front of the Latin Arms. He pulled out a twenty and handed it to the driver. "Keep the change." He was grateful for the air conditioning.

"Thanks mister!"

The bell captain opened the door as Evan got out of the cab. It was like stepping into an inferno. He quickly made his way into the hotel lobby where he immediately went to a house phone and dialed Jessica's room. There was no answer.

It wasn't long before he found himself in the hotel bar. "Give me a bloody Mary." A little hair of the dog never hurt anyone, thought Evan as he sat himself down in these now familiar surroundings. The bar not only had air conditioning, but a ceiling fan hummed quietly above his head. Before he could get his jacket off, the drink was in front of him. He pulled a fifty from his pocket and laid it down on the bar. He took the cool glass and touched it to his forehead before taking a sip from the glass. "Damn, that tastes good."

A familiar smell engaged his senses. He turned slowly to face a very concerned Jessica Powers. "How did it go?" she inquired.

"Let me get you a drink. This may take awhile. What can I get you?"

"Oh, I'll have a tonic water with a twist, thanks."

The bartender filled the tall frosty glass and gently squeezed a lime wedge into the bubbling liquid. He touched a straw to the side of the glass where it automatically clung. Evan picked up both glasses and carried them to a small table in a secluded corner of the room.

"Oh God, Jess," he said as he placed the drink in front of her and sat down at the small table. "I have to do what they ask. I can't risk going to jail." He studied his glass. "I would die in jail. Jess, I don't want to go to jail."

"Evan, Evan. Get a hold of yourself. You are not going to jail. Can you tell me what happened this morning?"

Evan Judd looked around the immediate vicinity of their table suspiciously. He did not want to risk having someone eavesdrop on their conversation. "They want me to wear a wire for this deal with the Marlton agency," he whispered.

"A wire?" she leaned toward him.

"That's right. They want me to tape the whole deal."

"Isn't that dangerous?"

"I sure as hell wouldn't want to get caught with it on," he responded in a hushed, nervous voice.

"They can't make you do that."

"What the hell choice do I have, Jess?"

"I think you can say no."

"Jess. I can't say no. If I don't cooperate, then they can nail me. I can't say no. I have to do it."

They were quiet. He was sweating again. He wiped the perspiration from his forehead with the napkin which had been under his drink."

"So what happens next?" inquired Jessica.

He took a long pull emptying the glass. "Hang on, I want to get another."

Evan walked back to the bar and ordered his favorite double martini on the rocks. He returned to the table and sat down.

"I have to set up the deal again and call Cooper when I have the time and date."

"When are you going to set up the deal?"

"I think I had better wait until I get back to New York. I sure as hell don't want anyone to know that I am in New Orleans, that I am part of this investigation. I know there is no way they should be able to know, but just the same, I'd feel a whole lot safer if I was making the arrangements from my Manhattan office."

"I think you are smart there."

"Oh Jessica. Why did it all have to happen? I don't deserve this. I haven't done anything that bad. I was just making a living, supporting a family..." his voice trailed off as he rationalized his activities. "Should I have to go to prison for that?"

"Oh Evan, it does seem harsh."

"I'm so frightened, Jessica. I feel so alone in this."

"I'll go back to New York with you. Would that help?"

Her offer took him by surprise. "You'd do that?"

"I'd do that."

"What about your writing?"

"I want to tell you about that. But first, let's see if we can get a flight out of here this afternoon. Let me call."

Jessica got up from the table and headed back into the lobby to the bank of telephones long the wall. She called the airport and got them both seats on the 2:15 p.m. flight to Kennedy International.

She returned to the table. "We're booked on the 2:l5 to New York. We better hurry. Do you need to get your things from your room?"

Evan nodded a positive response as he left a tip on the table and returned the handful of bills to his pocket. "We have very little time to spare," Jessica continued as they both headed for the elevator.

The ride to the airport seemed to take forever. Evan encouraged the driver to hurry by offering him a fifty dollar tip which seemed to grease the wheels. They were at the American terminal at exactly 2:00 p.m. They hurried through the terminal doors and quickly picked up their tickets at the ticket counter. Without stopping again, they were at the metal detector, then quickly through security and running through the terminal corridor. The plane to New York was all but boarded when they arrived at the gate.

"Final call for flight 422 to John F. Kennedy International Airport." Evan handed their tickets to the gate attendant. He tore off part of the tickets and returned the envelopes. "Better hurry," he said as Evan grabbed Jessica's hand and started running down the runway.

As soon as the couple had put their feet inside the cabin, the flight crew began closing the door in preparation for take off. The flight attendant welcomed them to first class and helped them with their bags before showing them to their seats. No sooner were they comfortably situated when the attendant was back offering them a drink. Jessica decided to relax with a glass of white wine and Evan ordered Scotch. As the plane started moving slowly toward the runway for takeoff, they both took a deep breath and settled back into the comfortable seats.

Jessica had made up her mind to level with Evan about her job at the Post. "There's something I want to tell you, Evan."

"What's that, Jessica?" he said taking her hand in his.

"It's about my writing."

There was a brief silence. "I thought you preferred not to talk about your work?"

"Well, I feel that I need to tell you."

Again, there was a silence which sort of hung in the air.

"Jess, I would hope that by now you know you can tell me anything. I care for you very much."

Jessica moved in closer to Evan and spoke very softly. "That's why I need to tell you that I am a reporter. I work for the Washington Post."

This time the silence was one of shock. "I wanted to tell you sooner. I do a lot of investigative reporting; and, as a long standing rule, I usually keep my business separated from my personal life. This time, however, I'm afraid there is no way to separate the two."

Evan let go of her hand and sat up, "Oh, my God Jessica. Oh no, Jessica. You're going to use me for a..a.. story. I'll be a...no, oh no, Jessica. How could..."

"Evan. Evan. Shhhhsh. Please stop. No. I could never do that and live with myself. I care for you, too. I care very much."

"But, but ...what..."

"Evan!" Jessica continued in a hushed voice. "I feel you also need to know what I am writing about. Please, Evan. I am not using you."

Evan was still in a state of shock, disbelief as she continued to reassure him. "Evan, please, I'm not going to hurt you. Please try to listen to me. Hear me out. Evan, I care for you very, very much."

"Oh Jessica, I am so ..."

"Shhh...I know."

"It's just that so much is happening to me all at once."

"I know that Evan. I didn't want to upset you. Believe me. I won't hurt you."

"It's just that I am so afraid...I couldn't stand going to jail. Jess, I am scar..."

"Evan. It's okay. We are going to get through this."

"Please, Jessica. Tell me, what then are you writing about. I have to know."

"I've been doing an investigative piece on the corruptive aspect of the Justice Department."

"Corrupt?"

"Yes. Some irregularities at the FBI have come to our attention. That's why I have been working out of New Orleans, following the Bureau's present investigation of which you are now apparently a very large part."

"But what...?"

"I had been involved in the general, overall Justice Department funding when something led me to the FBI. I had been following the FBI paper trail in Washington when I got a lead which took me to New Orleans."

"What was the lead?"

"It's not necessary that we discuss the specifics of the lead, but the case that I had to follow was the insurance one in which you have become a player."

"What do you know, Jessica?"

"Not much more than you do right now, Evan." She leaned closer to him and spoke very cautiously. "They could have someone tailing you," she said softly. "You can't be sure. From what I have uncovered, this scheme is gargantuan."

"Oh my God, Jess. I can't believe..."

The two fell into silence for a few moments as they thought of the ramifications of the situation. There was no limit to the possible enormity of this explosive plot.

Whether paranoid, or perhaps even smart, the couple decided not to continue this line of conversation during the remainder of the flight. They engaged in small talk and looked at magazines.

The fasten seat belt sign dinged on as the plane neared JFK. The flight attendant paused for a moment smiling as she noted the couple holding hands as they dozed. They had been no trouble at all to her during the flight. After the first drink, they had been so intense in their conversations, she had interrupted them only once and they rejected her offer of a snack. They were fast asleep, leaning against each other for support. She bent down toward them and spoke softly. "Excuse me." Gently she nudged Evan at the shoulder. "Excuse me, sir. We will be landing in a few minutes. Would you and your companion please engage your seat belts and put your seats in the upright position?"

Evan touched Jessica's face gently. His touch awakened her immediately. "Darling, we are about to land. It's time to buckle up." He helped her find the ends and lock the two pieces of metal together."

"Can I talk you in to staying over and catching the train in the morning, Jess?"

"I'm sorry, Evan. I'd like very much to do so, but, I have to get to the office. There is something I need to check on. But let me give you this..."

Without further explanation, Jessica reached for her large purse and pulled out a pad of paper which she always carried with her. "Let me give you my home phone number."

Jessica wrote several numbers on a piece of paper and tore it out of the notebook handing it to Evan. "My office number is there at the top."

Evan took the paper and carefully folded it so that it would fit in his shirt pocket.

"I want you to call me as soon as you have the meeting set in New Jersey."

"Not before then?" Evan managed to be light-hearted for a moment.

"Oh, Evan. You may call me any time."

"Are you certain I can't talk you into staying for the night?"

"I'm afraid not, but it isn't because I wouldn't like to."

The plane hit the runway with a bump and taxied into the terminal. Evan hadn't, of course, called Harrington before departing New Orleans.

As the couple deplaned, Evan said, "If you will wait until I call Harrington, I'll get us a cab and take you over to your commuter."

"That would be great, Evan. Thank you."

Once inside the gate, the couple readily located a bank of phones where Evan was able to place his call to his driver.

CHAPTER 8

It was nearly 7:15 p.m. when the black Lincoln Towncar pulled up in front of the terminal. Jessica's flight had taken off for Washington, D.C. only minutes before. Evan Judd stood staring out of the terminal when the car arrived. He hurried through the automatic doors as soon as he saw the car pull up in front of the building. When Harrington saw his boss, he immediately got out and hurried to open the door of the vehicle for him.

"Ev-nin' Mr. Judd. Let me take that, sir."

Harrington took the carry-on bag from Evan and placed it in the opened trunk of the car closing it as he completed the job. He returned to be certain his passenger was secure and closed the door for him. Harrington then got back into the car and looked into the rear view mirror. "Where to, Mr. Judd, sir?"

"Better take me to the office first, Harrington. I need to check on some things."

"Yes sir, Mr. Judd."

With that, the car sped off into the darkness. Evan decided he had better get in touch with Edna now that he was back in town. He hit number two on the speed dial.

She answered her phone. "Hello."

"Edna. Evan Judd. How are you?" he said to his long time confidant.

"Oh, Mr. Judd, are you alright?"

"Fine, Edna."

"Mr. Judd, I was so worried about you."

"I'm fine, now Edna. Listen. I just got back to town and I need to go into the office. I'm leaving the airport now. Can you meet me there?"

"Certainly, Mr. Judd."

"Good." He returned the car phone to its position.

Most of the heavy traffic had dissipated by the time the Towncar headed from the Island to mid Manhattan. They were pulling up in front of the building before Evan could get the thoughts of the last day or so together in his mind. In many ways, the whole thing just didn't seem real to him. But it was. Unfortunately, it was all too real.

The doorman at the Madison Avenue office building recognized the Lincoln as it pulled up in front. He went to the curb and opened the door. "Evening, Mr. Judd."

Evan climbed from the car without saying anything. He hurried into the building and onto the open elevator which took him to 74th floor. When the door opened onto his suite, it was brightly lighted. Edna Carlisle was already there waiting for him.

"I'm glad to see you, sir."

"Good to be here, Edna. What's been happening?"

"Well, Mr. Spector has been trying to reach you."

Evan could feel himself bristle at the mention of Spector's name. He was still very angry with him for deserting him. "What else?"

"You have had several calls from your wife as well as Evan, Jr., Sir."

"What did they want?"

"Well, Mrs. Judd called at least three times this afternoon. I told her I didn't know where you were. The last time she called in she got so mad at me that she accused me of covering for you. She was really very angry, Mr. Judd. She swore and slammed the receiver down..."

"I'm sorry, Edna. She's under a great deal of pressure lately. I'll call her now."

He went into his office and with much dread, picked up the phone. He knew how nasty her temper could be. He thought she appreciated his position. He dialed his home phone.

Mrs. Hoffsteader's voice was all business as she responded to the ringing telephone. "Judd residence."

"Mrs. Hoffsteader, this is Evan Judd. Is my wife there?" He twisted the telephone cord in nervous anticipation.

"Just a moment, sir. I'll get her."

In a few moments, Alice Judd's angry voice yelled into the phone. "Evan Judd, where the hell have you been? I've been trying to reach you for two days. Get your ass back home here." She obviously had been drinking. Her voice was much louder than usual, and there was the slightest slur to her words. "These damn kids are driving me crazy. You are going to have to deal with them yourself, you lousy, good-for-nothing son-of...."

"Now Alice, calm down....."

"Don't you dare tell me to calm down you miserable excuse for a husband. Who the hell do you think you are to drop a bomb like that on us and then leave us? You'd better get your miserable ass back ..." She slammed the receiver down in his ear without finishing the sentence.

He hated to deal with her when she got so unreasonable. He looked longingly out the window and decided not to go home. "I wish Jessica had stayed in town," he thought out loud.

"What's that, Mr. Judd." Edna Carlisle had come into his office and was standing in front of his desk as he faced the opposite direction staring out into the glittering lights of the Manhattan sky.

"Oh, Edna, I didn't hear you come in. I guess I was talking to myself."

"Did you reach Mrs. Judd?"

"Yes, I did. Why don't you get me that Marlton file, Edna, and we'll call it a night. I need to check on something. I'm not going to be long."

Edna Carlisle brought him the file. "No need for you to stay, Edna. Buzz down and tell Harrington I'll be down within the half hour. I'll lock up. See you tomorrow."

"As you wish, Sir. Goodnight."

"Goodnight, Edna."

Evan Judd opened the file and rechecked the figures he had on the Marlton agency. He was getting nervous again. He crunched a few numbers into his calculator, and decided enough was enough. He had to get himself calmed down. As he picked up the phone and pushed a button on the instrument, he spun around in his chair to take another look at his favorite view while the automatic dialer on his telephone dialed Tammi Lee Trottman's apartment.

A sexy female voice breathed into the phone. "Hello..."

"It's Evan, babe. I'll be there within the hour."

He returned the phone to the cradle without looking away from the window. He was a basket of emotions--sad, depressed and nervous all at once. He need physical release.

Slowly, he got up from his chair and walked toward the outer office, turning out lights as he closed the doors. As he stepped onto the elevator, his mind moved from Marlton to Tammi. Actually, the desires of his body directed his thinking. He could feel familiar stirrings in his groin. "How long has it been," he thought, since I've had a night with that babe?" His body responded as he remembered some of the exciting times he had had with her in the past. A night with Tammi, no strings attached, was just what he needed.

The apartment on 79th Street was comfortable. He had spent many a lustful night at this address. That was part of the bargain. He would pay the rent but she had to be available to him nights when he wanted her. She had willingly agreed. She was flattered to have a man of his stature and age interested in her. Also, she could not afford the rent and acting classes on her salary from Bloomingdale's. Although he had his own key, he signaled her from the lobby. She buzzed him up immediately.

As he raised his hand to knock at the door, she opened it and let him in. She was dressed in a very skimpy black teddy. Nothing else. Her cherry red finger nails and toe nails completed the outfit. She threw her arms around his neck and pressed her body against him as she gave him a passionate kiss.

He did not need to be aroused. He brushed her aside and headed directly for the bedroom, loosening his tie as he moved. She followed close behind him. She had candles lit around the room and his favorite songs of the fifties were playing in the background. He threw his jacket onto the chair and unbuckled his pants.

Tammi had slid into the bed ahead of him. She had learned to pose to excite him. Tonight was no disappointment. He could barely hold his aroused body away from her while he removed his underwear. He threw himself on the bed and rolled over onto her waiting body. As he pulled the straps away from her shoulders, her eager breasts leapt from confinement. There was no need to undo the bottom. She had noticed his eagerness and unfastened the snaps herself.

She did not have to help him as he found his way. For a few moments, his body pounded into her ruthlessly until he was spent. Soon, the physical act was finished and he had rolled over onto the satin sheet before Johnny Mathis had finished singing "Chances Are." He was sweating profusely, but his physical desperation had dissipated. He fell asleep immediately.

It was nearly 4:00 a.m. when Evan awoke from a sound sleep. The room was very dark. He was not sure where he was at first, but as his eyes became accustomed to the darkness, he recognized Tammi who was sleeping soundly beside him. This did not comfort him. To the contrary. Evan began to think of Jessica and in some strange way, these thoughts made him feel uncomfortable that he had used this other woman for his satisfaction. Suddenly, he became enormously uncomfortable. "What's wrong with me? Damn, don't tell me I am actually beginning to fall in love?" he questioned himself.

Evan could not go back to sleep. An hour passed, and he was still awake, filled with an ominous fear about the assignment ahead of him. He wished Jessica was here. He could talk with her about it. As he thought of her, he continued to experience an unfamiliar guilt about being in bed with someone else. He did not belong here.

Quietly, Evan got out of bed and began dressing. He did not want to awaken Tammi. He knew he had not been considerate of her but, hell, he needed some relief from the pressure. Before he left the room, he reached into his wallet and pulled out two one hundred dollar bills and left them on the stand next to the bed. He went into the living room and called a cab before he took the elevator to the street.

The cab delivered him to his Madison Avenue office building. It was too early for the doorman, but the security guard recognized him immediately and let him in. He took the elevator to his office.

Once inside, he reviewed the Marlton file for nearly two hours before he went into his private bath to shower and dress for the day. He always had a complete wardrobe in his office dressing room.

By the time Evan had completed his toilette and returned to his office with a fresh shirt and pants, Edna Carlisle had arrived and was bringing coffee to him in the bone China he had imported from Austria. She also had some fresh pastries which she placed on the coffee table in front of the leather couch.

"You are a lifesaver, Edna. What would I do without you?"

"I don't ever expect you to do without me, Mr. Judd," Edna Carlisle stated coyly over her shoulder as she quietly let herself out of the office closing the door behind her.

Evan wasn't very hungry, but he was dying for a hot cup of coffee. The smell teased his nostrils as he carefully poured the steaming liquid into the fragile China cup. Perhaps he would try a cheese Danish.

Evan Judd was pouring his second cup of coffee from the silver service when the intercom sounded. He set the pot down and went to his desk. "Yes, Edna?"

"There's a Ms. Powers on your line, Mr. Judd."

Evan immediately hit the button to take her call. "Jessica. I'm so glad to hear from you. Did you get home alright?"

"Yes, thanks Evan. I'm at my office now. Evan, I have to talk with you. I'm coming to New York."

"Sounds urgent..."

"It is."

"I'll send my car to the airport. What time does your fight get in?"

"I think it will be just as easy for me to catch the train from Union Station. I have some work to do anyway. I can bring my lap-top computer and do some of it on the train."

"Okay. What time will you be getting into New York?"

"I haven't checked the schedule yet. Why don't I call you when I get there?"

"Sounds great, Jessica. I'll wait for your call."

"Evan?"

"Yes, Jessica."

"Have you set up your meeting yet?"

"No, I was just getting to it when you called."

"Give me time to get there."

"I'm not sure I can put off setting a time..."

"Evan, you don't have to go through with this."

"Jessica, I have no choice."

"But I think you do."

"Jessica, I don't. You know..."

"Evan. That's what I want to discuss with you in person."

"Jessica, you know that I have to do this. I can't talk about this over the phone, put I must do this."

"Evan, I'm going to New Jersey with you."

"No, Jess. I can't have you risk..."

"Evan, I am going."

"Jess..."

"I must go with you Evan. Wait for me, please."

There was a click at the other end of the line and then a dial tone. Evan sat with the phone to his ear as he puzzled over the conversation he had just completed. She certainly was some woman. He wondered why she was so insistent. He wondered what she knew.

CHAPTER 9

Evan Judd spent the next several hours in his office working on figures for his purchase of the Marlton Agency. It was around two thirty when Edna walked into his office. "Excuse me, Mr. Judd."

Evan did not look up. "Yes Edna. What is it?"

"Mr. Judd, Mr. Spector wants to see you."

"I have nothing to say to him."

"But, Mr. Judd, sir, he says it is important."

"Evan looked up at his secretary. "Oh, he does, does he." Obviously still hurt and infuriated with Spector, Evan continued, "Just tell him I am busy."

"Busy?" Frank Spector came into the office.

"I thought we had finished our business," he sounded sarcastic and distant.

"Evan, Evan, please listen to me."

"Listen to you, you bastard, you are never available."

"Evan, I tried to provide you an attorney, but you would have nothing to do with him."

"I don't want one of your damn flunkies, Spector. When I have a problem, damn it, I want you."

"Evan. Calm down. Listen to me."

"Why should I?"

"Evan, we have known one another for a long time. Listen to me."

"What the hell do you think I pay you that outrageous retainer for anyway? Damn it, Frank, I needed..."

"Listen Evan, I can't put myself in a position of risk like you are determined to get yourself into. But I don't want to desert you either. Tell me what is going on."

Underneath it all, Evan was anxious to share his burden with his old friend and legal counsel. So it was not difficult for Frank Spector to encourage Evan to fill him in. When Evan had finished, Spector was sitting in his chair shaking his head in a negative response.

"Don't do it, Evan."

"Frank, haven't you heard what I said?"

"Yes, I heard what you said. I can't let you do it. Wire tapping is a criminal offense. Don't do it."

"Frank, Frank. Can't you see? There is no choice. I have to do it!"

"Damn it Evan, NO! DON'T DO IT."

They were both on their feet. "Will you help me?"

"Evan, I can't help you. You are talking about engaging in illegal, criminal activity. YOU SHOULD NOT DO IT."

"But Frank..."

"Get yourself another attorney, Evan. I won't do it. I can't risk it."

"Please Frank, I'm begging you."

"No Evan. I'm sorry. Goodbye."

Frank Spector turned away from Evan and left the office. Evan sat down heavily in his chair, the weight of the world on his shoulders.

He was sick to his stomach. Frank Spector's visit had confirmed how serious the situation was. He sat staring out the window just thinking for some time. "I'll get myself another attorney if I need one. Lazy good-for-nothing is just a playboy anyway. I can probably handle most of this myself."

Evan was furious. "I support the bastard and then when I really need him..." Insecurity swept over him once again. Not having an attorney was just not good policy and he knew it. Maybe....

Before Evan could decide what to do next, Edna Carlisle startled him by signaling him on the intercom.

"Yes, Edna."

"Ms. Powers."

"Jessica?"

"I'm at Penn Station now, Evan."

"Listen Jess, I have a couple more things to do here. Can you catch a cab to the Plaza. I have a room for you there. Just tell the desk to use the one in my name. I'll meet you there within the hour."

"Okay, Evan. I'll see you when you get there."

Evan hung up the phone and forced himself to finish the work at hand. It was nearly quarter to five when he pushed himself away from his desk and headed for the door. The buzzer signaled him on the intercom as he reached for the door knob. He opened the door and spoke directly to Edna. "What is it, Edna?"

He surprised her. "Oh, Mr. Judd. It's your son, Evan Jr. Says it's urgent."

I'll take it in my office, Edna. Thanks.

Evan returned to his desk. "What is it, son?"

"Dad, you have to get home right away. She's out of control! I don't know what to do with her. Somebody's got to..."

Evan cut him off. "Evan. Calm down and tell me what is happening."

"She's been drinking. Jesus. She's out of control. She's gone crazy!! You've got to come home now."

"I'm on my way."

"Oh God, she's throwing things. I don't know what to do! Dad, hurry!"

Evan hung up the phone and immediately headed for the door. Alice had had problems with drinking before. But from the tone of Evan Jr.'s voice, this was urgent.

The car was waiting when Evan emerged from the office building. The doorman held the door as he got into the car. "I've got to get home right away, Harrington."

"Yessir, Mr. Judd. Right away."

The car pulled from the curb immediately. There was no hurrying in this 5:15 p.m. traffic.

Evan reached for the phone. He dialed the Plaza Hotel.

"This is Evan Judd. Miss Jessica Powers should have arrived at the hotel by now. She's in my suite. Put me through to her."

"Thank you, Mr. Judd."

After two rings, Jessica picked up. "Hello"

"Jessica, Evan here."

"Evan. Are you down stairs?"

"No Jessica. I have an emergency at home. I am calling from my car."

"Oh."

"I have no idea how long this is going to take, but I will be back as soon as I can."

"Is there anything I can do to help?"

"No Jess. This is something personal I have to handle. I hope I will be able to get back to the city tonight. I'm sorry, Jessica."

"I'll see you later, then."

Evan responded with depressed resignation. "Yes, later."

"Goodbye, Evan."

"So long for now, Jess."

It was dusk and the head lamps on the Lincoln Towncar were on as it turned down Beach Road on the approach to the Judd home. They had been delayed a couple of times with major automobile accidents, but that was to be expected at this hour in the evening. Evan was anxious to get home but also dreading what he would have to face.

Throughout the years, Alice's drinking had increased gradually, but progressively. At first, she would never drink before evening cocktail hour, and certainly, never alone. Then, by the time their third child was in school, Alice would have a cocktail or two on occasion at lunch with the women at the club. But during the last five years or so, her drinking had become noticeably heavier. There had been times when Evan could smell alcohol on her breath in the morning, but that was rare. But then again, how often was he around her in the morning any more. On a couple of occasions, she had gotten quite rowdy at parties, and he had to bring her home. This would infuriate her and she would throw what ever she could find at him once they were in the house. Tonight must be one of those unfortunate nights and evidently, so far, Evan Jr. was taking the brunt of it.

The car began to pass the tall boxwood hedges which lined the either side of the road at the main entrance to the estate. The car reached the gate and turned into the long approach to the circle drive.

There were flashing lights in the distance in front of the house. Evan pulled himself forward on his seat in the rear of the car.

"What the..." his stunned voice could not seem to mouth the question.

"Looks like an ambulance, sir."

"Oh, Jesus."

"It looks like they are closing the doors now sir."

"Hurry, Harrington."

The emergency vehicle pulled away from the front door and headed out the other side as Harrington pulled under the portico. Evan was nearly out of the car before it stopped. Mrs. Hoffsteader, Cook and Evan Jr. starred after the ambulance. "What going on?" Evan asked breathlessly.

"It's Mother. She fell down the front staircase and hit her head into the railing."

"How bad....?"

"She's unconscious."

"Where are they taking her?"

Evan, Jr. starred into the darkness. "I never saw her like that before, Father. She went berserk. She was absolutely crazy. She was screaming and yelling and throwing things. Smashing stuff. It was awful."

"I'd better follow. Where did they take her? Memorial?"

Mrs. Hoffsteader who had been standing to the side responded. "Yes. They called ahead, Mr. Judd."

"Are you coming, EJ?"

Father and son jumped into the back seat of the Lincoln as Harrington hurried back into the driver's seat. The car pulled away from the front of the house leaving Mrs. Hoffsteader and Cook watching them as Harrington quickly maneuvered the car around the drive and back down the road.

When they arrived at Memorial Hospital, Harrington dropped his two passengers at the emergency entrance. They hurried on inside to the triage desk.

"The ambulance just brought my wife in here," Evan blurted out at the nurse behind the desk. "Alice Judd. Can you tell me where she is, please?"

"Oh, Mr. Judd. Yes. They are taking her into surgery right now."

The triage nurse pointed to a gurney which was hurriedly being wheeled down the hallway.

Evan and his son began to run down the hall after them. "Doctor! Doctor! My wife..."

A young man who looked to be even younger than Evan, Jr., dressed in a green surgery outfit slowed and turned to look at Evan. "She's bleeding pretty heavily, sir. We are going to find out where it is coming from. We don't know what the damage is exactly."

"My God...is she going to be alright?"

"Why don't you wait in the surgery waiting area. I'll see you as soon as we are out of surgery."

"But, is she conscious?"

"Please sir. We need to get into surgery right away. We don't know what is causing the bleeding."

"Yes, of course."

The two stood still in the hallway looking after the doctor and the emergency team as they hurried down the hallway and through the automatic doors into the surgery suite. After the doors had closed behind the medical team with Alice Judd, Evan and Evan Jr. made their way to the surgery waiting area.

It was nearly two hours before the surgeon came into the waiting area. As he approached, Evan got to his feet. "How is she? Is she going to be alright?"

"Please have a seat, Mr. Judd."

Evan sat down and Evan Jr. came back to the area to join them. The doctor pulled in a free standing chair and sat facing the father and son.

"The injuries your wife sustained, Mr. Judd, were primarily superficial. She was fortunate--this time. She had a gash in her head where she must have bumped into something sharp. We had to take several stitches. Of course, she has a major bump on her forehead as well. At first we thought there had been major internal damage. But, the substantial bleeding coming from her mouth was caused from where her teeth had penetrated the skin inside her mouth. In a couple of cases, we had to take stitches inside her mouth. She also has some cracked ribs, and we have taped them for now. Fortunately, the fall did no other internal damage. It is remarkable."

"Thank God."

"But, Mr. Judd. Your wife has a serious drinking problem. She had consumed a considerable amount of alcohol before the fall. I expect she had lost consciousness from the alcohol, not the blow to the head."

Evan sat quietly looking at the doctor. He had tried to talk with her about the drinking, Lord knows. But she had insisted she did not have a problem. She could stop any time she wanted.

"I am going to have to keep her here, Mr. Judd. She is going to need some medical attention with her ribs, and I want to watch to be absolutely certain there is no concussion. I also feel that she is going to experience some withdrawal symptoms when the alcohol wears off. Is this alright with you??"

"Yes! Of course, doctor. Of course."

"I would also like to have someone talk with her about her drinking when she sobers up, if you don't mind?"

"Mind?! Please do."

"Okay," the doctor had gotten to his feet and was holding out his hand to Evan. "I'd rather you not disturb her tonight. She is resting quietly now."

"Thank you doctor. Of course."

The doctor shook hands with Evan and Evan Jr. and was gone.

"I'm going to call a cab for you, son. I have business I need to attend to in the city."

"Right, Dad. Business in the city. Who has business at this hour? That's probably why she drinks."

"Evan!"

"You and your women. Now you are in trouble with the law... you're a criminal, for God's sake!"

"Evan! You have no right to judge me. I told you I would handle the FBI. There is a misunderstanding, perhaps. But I am not a criminal."

"Well, handle it then before you kill her!" He stormed off down the hall and out of sight.

Evan shook his head and sighed wearily. Then he went to the phone to call Harrington to bring the car around. No need to stick around here. He would head back to the city--and Jessica.

CHAPTER 10

It was well after midnight when Evan Judd walked into the Plaza Hotel. He had called Jessica from the car and told her what had happened. He hated to discuss his family with her, but she seemed open to anything he wanted to tell her. He went to the house phone and dialed her room.

"Yes?"

"Jessica, it's Evan. Are you still awake?"

"Yes, Evan. Please come up."

He went directly to the elevator and rode to the 17th floor alone. The hotel was reasonably quiet at this hour. He knocked at the door of room 1723. The door opened and there stood Jessica, even more beautiful then ever. He opened his arms and she was in them before either could speak. With a free arm, he shoved the door closed. He gently tilted her head up and instantly, they were locked in a passionate kiss, his hard body pressing urgently against her. He pulled her even closer as she began to respond to his passionate embrace.

Within moments, they were urgently pulling at each other's clothing. Evan threw his jacket and tie on the sofa as she led him swiftly into the bedroom. There he quickly slid the sheer light robe back from her shoulders as she undid his belt. His hand moved down her shoulders and arms as he gently dropped her short, silk nightgown to the floor. There bodies were completely entwined as they fell onto the soft white sheets.

They were both spent after their lovemaking and she fell quietly into a deep sleep as he continued to hold her in his arms throughout the night.

It was nearly seven when Evan awoke the following morning. Quietly, he got out of the bed and got dressed. He needed to get back to the office. He still had not made the necessary final arrangements to handle the Marlton deal. Before he left the suit, he wrote a quick note to Jessica telling her where he was going and that he would call. Before leaving the hotel, he stopped at the desk and made arrangements with the clerk to have a dozen red roses sent to the room. The bell captain opened the door to a waiting cab.

Evan was in the office before Edna got in so he slipped into his private bath area where he showered, shaved, and dressed in fresh clothing for the day. Edna Carlisle was bringing in a tray with his morning coffee and Danish when he stepped into the office.

"Good morning, Edna."

"Morning Mr. Judd. You are here early. Is everything alright?"

"Okay for now, Edna," he dismissed the question. He didn't have time to explain.

"Can I get you anything else?"

"That's all, Edna. Thank you."

She poured his coffee into the China cup and handed it to him. He reached down and picked up the morning paper as she left the room. He was still looking at the front page when she buzzed him. "Yes?"

"A Mr. Singer on the phone, sir."

Evan felt the knot in his stomach tighten. Henry Singer, Erlich's number one man in charge of Marlton. Oh...no...this was it. He had to do something," he thought as he punched the button.

"Henry! How nice to hear from you. I was hoping to talk with you this morning."

"Listen, Judd, I have a message from our mutual friend. Either you make the buy now or..."

"Henry, Henry, I was just about to call you myself and set up the deal. Sorry it took so long, but I had an emergency at home."

Thank God for finding an excuse--not that he didn't indeed have an emergency at home, but that had only come up last night.

"Well, our friend thinks maybe you lost interest and says either we finalize our deal or he'll get someone else to make the buy."

"No, no. You don't want to do that."

Damn. Was he sounding too anxious? He didn't want to do that. On the other hand, if he wanted to save his ass from the FBI, he'd better get this deal down on tape. Evan was beginning to sense panic.

"Henry. When can we get together and handle the transaction?"

"Tomorrow morning," Henry responded in his flat, secure voice.

"Tomorrow it is! The Hyatt?"

"Meet me here and we'll sign the papers. You deliver the money within the week."

"How about ten tomorrow morning?"

"Ten sharp!"

The phone went dead. Evan got up from his desk and went directly into his private bathroom where he vomited. He was scared. How the hell could he get through the next 24 hours?

It was nearly eleven before he felt together enough to give Jessica a call at the Plaza. She answered immediately. "Yes?"

"Jess?"

"I got your note and your flowers."

"Good, ah, Jess?"

"Evan, are you at the office?"

"Yes. I'm on my way over to the Plaza. I'll be there in 15 minutes. Then on to New Jersey."

"Okay. And Evan?"

"Yes?"

"Thanks for the flowers. They are beautiful."

As he remembered the night, the tension of the moment dissipated. He buzzed Edna. "Edna. Have Harrington bring the car around."

He went to his private bath and dressing area and picked up the suitcase that was always packed for unexpected, quick trips. He put on a fresh shirt and tie and splashed some expensive cologne on his face and neck. He ran a brush quickly through his hair as he checked his appearance out in the full length mirror. Before reaching for his jacket, he stuffed several fresh hundred dollar bills into his wallet. He was ready.

Harrington was waiting as he came out of the building. Evan spoke to him as he got into the car. "We're going to make a quick stop at the Plaza, Harrington, then we are heading for New Jersey."

"Very good, sir." Everything was always "very good" to Harrington. In fact, everything in Harrington's life had been good since Evan Judd hired him so many years ago. He didn't know where he would be if it had not been for his boss. There was nothing he wouldn't do for his boss.

"Wait for me Harrington. I won't be too long."

Evan entered the Plaza and went directly to Jessica's room. She opened the door and signaled for him to enter. Evan embraced and kissed her. She willingly responded.

"Jessica, I need to make the phone to call the FBI boys. They are waiting in Philadelphia. I told them I would call as soon as the deal was set." Evan had picked up the phone and was dialing the number given to him by Agent Cooper. Cooper had said to leave the message on the voice mail.

"This is Evan Judd. The deal is at 10:00 a.m. sharp tomorrow in Marlton. I'll be at the Cherry Hill Hyatt within three hours." He put the receiver down and stood starring at the phone for several seconds. Jessica moved closer and took is face in her hands as she spoke. "Are you alright?"

"Oh God, Jess, sure as hell, Erlich's boys are going to know. Jess, I'm scared, really scared."

"Evan, you don't have to go through with this."

"Jessica, I do. You know I do. I don't want to go to jail. Jessica, I would die in prison. I don't want to die in prison."

"Evan, listen to me."

"Jessica, I have to do it. I have to go now. They will be waiting for me." Evan headed for the door. Jessica tried to hold him, but he pulled away. "Evan, wait, I AM going with you."

"Jessica it is too dangerous. I don't want you to come."

"I'M GOING WITH YOU." She grabbed her oversized bag and threw the strap over her shoulder. He didn't have time to argue with her.

The Lincoln Towncar sped south on Interstate 95. Jessica Powers was sitting in the rear seat next to Evan Judd. Although he was certain his mission was dangerous, he was comforted, in a strange way, to have her at his side.

Jessica watched this man that she had become attached to as he stared out the side window. Obviously, he was determined to go through with this deal that he believed would keep him from prison. It seemed equally obvious to her that he was realistic in his fear for his life. She thought carefully before speaking. "Evan, I have some information that I feel you need to know."

He looked at her. "What's that?"

"When I said you didn't have to go through with this, I was basing my advice on some information I was just beginning to uncover. I have been doing some investigating of my own and I think you need to know what I found out."

"Jessica, there's no need to try to talk me out of this. I was at the meeting in New Orleans. I'm not going to prison."

"Please Evan, let me finish. You're not the only person who has ever gotten pulled into FBI investigations by prison threats." Evan looked at Jessica suspiciously, but reluctantly remained quiet. She continued. "The Justice Department gets its funding from Congress. Congress will provide funding when the FBI resolves cases. So, in order to solve cases, the FBI engages private citizens, like you, hooks them on simple fraud charges, and gets them to work for the Department at their own expense while, in effect, working for the FBI."

"No Jessica, no. Why would they do that? They have funds. They have agents who are trained. I can't buy that, Jessica."

"Evan, I believe there is something to this, but I haven't had enough time to check it out thoroughly yet. But, I still think you could refuse."

"Sure. And go to prison. No thanks. I have to do this. Please Jessica, try to understand. I need your support, not your second guessing what I am doing."

"Evan, I DO understand. Believe me. I share your fear. I can't stand the thought of anything happening to you."

Evan takes Jessica's hand in his and kisses it. "Jessica darling. I love you."

Jessica melted into Evan Judd's arms and responded eagerly to his gentle kiss. The two remained entwined in a loving embrace as the car sped south on the New Jersey Turnpike. It was 2:37 p.m. when Harrington pulled up in front of the Cherry Hill Hyatt. Evan started to get out of the car then closed the door. He reached into his pocket and pulled out a role of money. He handed some bills to Jessica. "I think it will be smarter if you get your own room. This will cover it."

"I agree about the room, but I can't take..."

"Take it Jess, please." He got out of the car and looked back at her. "Harrington, drive Ms. Powers around for a while. Give me ample time to get checked in then drop her off back here." She nodded in agreement.

Evan had been in his room for nearly a half an hour when there was a knock at his door. "Who's there?"

"Open up, Judd."

Evan recognized the low raspy voice of Agent Cooper. He disengaged the dead bolt and chain lock. Agents Cooper and Swift entered the room and quickly closed the door behind themselves.

"Okay, Judd. Where's the equipment? Let's give it a test before your meeting tomorrow."

Evan was flabbergasted. "I don't have any equipment! I thought you were bringing it."

"Judd, do you ever use your head?" It was more of a rhetorical question. "You're the one wearing the wire. Wouldn't you be the one to get it?"

"But I never wore one before."

"So?"

"I don't know anything about wearing a wire. I..."

"Enough, enough already. Damn it, Judd, do we have to do everything? You'd think when someone's saving your ass from prison, you'd take on some responsibility. Cooperate. Gordon, have we got anyone in the area who can fix us up on short notice?"

Evan was feeling panic mixed with false guilt. "I'm sorry, I didn't know..."

"Shut the hell up, Judd. Let the man think."

Gordon Swift responded to his partner's inquiry. "How about our old friend, what's-his-name, the radio sales distributor in Morrestown who sells those radio transceivers?"

"Oh yeah, what's his name, Charlie, Charles, ah shit, what's his name? Damn, I almost had it." Cooper puzzles..."Chuck Johnson!"

"That's it. Chuck Johnson. He's got to have a battery operated wireless mike."

Cooper eyed the phone and headed for it. "Let's see if we can get in touch with him."

Cooper dialed a series of numbers. "Joe, see if you can get me a number for Chuck Johnson, the radio sales distributor in Morrestown, New Jersey."

The party at the other end of the phone responded. "Do you want me to call you back?"

"No, no. I'll hold on. I need it right away."

Cooper looked at his watch and then at Agent Swift and finally at Evan Judd. He studied his fingers as he waited. "What's that? Wait a sec." Cooper snapped his fingers and pointed at a pen and notepaper on the desk nearby. "Judd. Get me a pen and something to write on, would ya?"

Evan obeyed. He didn't like the role of underling that he was being forced to play, but he wasn't about to argue--out loud, anyway. Inside his head a seething voice responded automatically to Cooper's demand, "Get it yourself, you son-of-a- ....Who the hell do you think you are? Don't you realize who you are ordering around?" But Evan never said a word as he handed Cooper the pen and paper.

"Okay, Joe. Shoot. No, I don't need the area code. Yup. 783-9933. Got it." Cooper hung up the phone. "This better work, Judd. If we can't get this wire on you before the meeting, you might just as well bag it and head for prison."

Agent Swift moved toward Cooper. "Give me the number, Ian. Let me see if I can get a hold of him."

Agent Swift dialed the number. The silence in the room was deafening as the trio waited for someone to answer at the other end of the telephone wire. "Chuck Johnson, please," Gordon Swift spoke politely into the phone.

Swift held the phone so that Cooper and Judd could hear the voice at the other end of the line. "This is Chuck Johnson. Can I help you?"

"Chuck, this is Agent Swift with the FBI. I need a favor. We have a man who needs to be outfitted with a battery operated wireless mike. Can you help him out?"

"What does he need?"

"He's going to be wearing it, so he needs a compact transmitter unit with a small lapel-mike. You got something like that?"

"How about range? How far does he need to transmit?"

"Oh, about a quarter of a mile. And, it's static-free."

"Yeah, I have something that will work."

"Good. Johnson, we have an emergency. We need it right away. You gonna be there?" Swift did not wait for Johnson to reply. "He'll be there within a half an hour."

"Sure."

"Great. What are you getting for a unit like that?"

"It just came out a month ago. There's quite a demand. We've been getting twelve-fifty. For you, make it a thousand even."

"Deal. We'll be there shortly. You still at the same place?"

"Same."

"Good. See you in a few minutes."

Swift hung up the phone and looked at Evan "You've got some cash on you, I hope."

"Sure," replied Evan. "How much do I need?"

"He's going to let you have it for a thousand."

"For a wire?" Evan was stunned.

"Let's get a move on," pushed Cooper. "We'd better take our car. You never know when someone might be watching."

Evan followed the two agents from his room to their car.

With traffic at this time of day, it took thirty-five minutes to drive to the little shop in Moorestown. Cooper parked the car behind the little shop on Main Street. No one would have known the shop was there if they hadn't been familiar with it. Actually, you had to go to the rear of the building to climb the stairs that went to the second floor where Johnson's shop was.

Judd was between Cooper and Swift as the trio climbed the stairs. Cooper opened the door at the top of the stairs and the three men entered. Johnson was just inside working on some equipment. As the men entered, he held out his hand to Cooper, then to Swift. Finally, he held out his hand to Evan.

"This is the fellow who will be needing the wire," Swift said to Johnson not offering any name.

"I think you are going to like this one. How far do you want to transmit?" Johnson asked again.

"We want it to go about a quarter of a mile. No static."

"No problem. This little number will work like a charm. Here." Johnson handed the small, slim, black housing of the unit to Evan. "Pretty nice, eh?"

Evan looked back to Agent Swift quizzically. "Is this okay?"

Swift was smiling, a first as far as Evan could determine.

"It's a real beauty, Johnson. Perfect wouldn't you say, Cooper?"

"I'd say. Pay the man," Cooper barked at Judd in a raspy voice. "Let's get a move on."

Evan took ten one hundred dollar bills from his wallet and handed them to Johnson. Before he could get his wallet back in his chest pocket, Cooper and Swift were on their way out the door. Johnson thanked the trio as Evan turned and walked out behind Agent Swift.

On the way back to the Hyatt, Swift reached under the front seat of the car and pulled out a package. "Here," he said as he turned to the back seat where Evan Judd was clutching the small brown bag Johnson had given him as he nervously looked out at the passing scenery.

"What's this?" he asked Agent Swift as he reached for the large mailing envelope being offered to him.

"It's some tape and stuff we're going to need in the morning. We're going to have to wrap it close to your body so nobody will guess you are wearing it."

Evan held both packages on his lap as the car continued south on Route 73 from Morrestown. The car approached the intersection at Route 50 when Cooper spoke for the first time since they left Johnson's shop. He was leaning forward, stretching his neck looking for on-coming traffic. "I hate these Traffic circles. The next time you plan on buying an agency, Judd, I hope the hell you pick a place without these damn circles and jug handles."

Evan Judd almost smiled as he thought, "So there is something that bothers king cool. Good. I hope he's sweating."

The car headed west on Route 50 to the Hyatt where Cooper and Swift dropped Judd off at the main entrance. Agent Swift looked straight ahead as he spoke, "We'll see you in the morning, Judd." Evan went inside and immediately took the elevator to his room.

As soon as he got to his room, Evan had the operator ring Jessica. "Can you come up for a drink? I'm in Suite 673. I've had some visitors already."

"I was wondering what happened to you. I'll be right there."

Evan had been watching out the peep hole and opened the door to his suite before Jessica could knock. He hurried her inside and quickly shut and chain-locked the door. He had found the mini bar well stocked and had selected a small bottle of white wine for her and Tanqueray gin for himself. The drinks were on the coffee table in front of the sofa. "Tell me what happened, Evan. It was the FBI agents I take it," Jessica nervously blurted out. "What did they say?"

Evan took a quick sip from his martini and set it back on the table. "Swift and Cooper came right to my room--just knocked on the door. They knew I was here. I don't know if they were watching, or what..."

Jessica listened intently. He continued, "They took me out to buy the apparatus I'm gonna have to wear tomorrow. It's over there." Evan pointed to the two packages on the desk.

Jessica's gaze went directly to the packages and back to Evan. "Can I see?"

Evan went over to the desk and pulled the slim black box from the bag. He walked back over to the sofa handed it to her. He retained and examined the small lapel mike and wire. "This thing is so small, I find it hard to believe it will pick up everything we say."

"Let me see that," Jessica said as she held her hand out toward Evan. "Oh, this will work just fine." She plugged the cord into the small black box. "I guess you will strap it to your body so no one will be able to see that you are wearing it."

"Swift gave me this. Said it was the stuff they were going to use to hook-up the device in the morning."

Jessica returned the transmitter and mike to the bag. "You don't have to do this."

"I do, Jessica. I have to do this."

CHAPTER 11

EVAN HAD NOT SLEPT well. He had paced the floor most of the night. "Where the hell are they?" he thought as he walked over to the desk and picked up the wireless microphone and envelope Gordon Swift had given him. Damn, I can't put this thing on myself," he mumbled as he looked it all over again.

Nervously, he glanced at his watch for nearly the hundredth time during the last fifteen minutes. It was three minutes before nine and not a word. He was wearing just his undershirt for now. No point of putting on a shirt and tie until the wire was in place. As soon as he picked up the phone to call Jessica, there was a knock at the door. He put the phone down and hurried to the door. Quickly he released the deadbolt and removed the chain lock. Without looking through the peephole, he opened the door and began speaking. "Where the hell have..."

A short, pudgy man in a cheap summer suit pushed by Evan and was on his way into the room. "Get inside, quick."

Evan was frightened, "Who the hell are you?"

"Listen to me, Judd. You don't have to go through with this. It's against the law. You are putting your ass on the line if you go through with this," the strange man pleaded in an urgent voice.

"Get out of my room. I don't know what you are talking about."

"You have a choice. I'm warning you."

"Who the hell are you?"

"Are you listening to me?"

"I don't know what you are talking about."

"I'm warning you."

"Get out!"

"Don't do it!"

"I'm calling security."

The strange man brushed by Evan and was out the door as fast has he had come in. Evan quickly closed the door behind him and leaned on it in to catch his breath. Before he could get to the phone, there was another knock at the door. Evan hurried to the door and yanked it open, "I told you I would call..."

Cooper and Swift pushed into the room. "Judd, have you lost your friggin mind?"

Agent Swift quickly closed the door and secured it with the dead bolt and chain. Cooper continued, "Damn it, Judd, you have got to be careful. You could get all of us killed. What in the hell were you thinking of?"

"I, ah, I guess I was just getting nervous." Judd thought better of telling the FBI Agents what had just happened. Obviously, in some strange way, the man was trying to protect him no matter how ill advised. He was rattled about it, but it was also getting late, and he knew he could not afford to miss this appointment.

"For Christ's sake, Judd, you've got to be careful. Do you understand?"

"I understand."

"Good."

"Where's the wire?" inquired Swift. "We'd better get moving."

"Right here." Evan handed Swift the package.

Cooper barked, "Get your shirt off Judd. How the hell do you expect us to hide this bugger?" Again, more of a rhetorical question than anything else.

Cooper and Swift set to work and within five minutes, everything was in place. "Now put on your clothes," Cooper ordered. "Never know you were wearing anything but skin under there."

Evan put on his undershirt, his white shirt and tie.

The two men headed for the door. Gordon Swift turned back and looked at Evan. "Now remember, you have to draw them out. Try to make verbal sense of everything that is going down so that we can understand just what's happening. Do you know what I mean?"

"I think so," Evan responded nervously.

"We're gonna go get set up now. You just keep your appointment."

Cooper and Swift were gone. Evan felt the box under his shirt through the tape they had used to conceal the device. He moved toward the mirror to look critically at himself, especially for tell-tale signs of the equipment on his body, his fingers traced the wire from the box just below his waist to the small microphone in the hollow of his neck just under his necktie. He could hardly take a deep breath. He looked intently in the mirror at the face which was staring back at him.

"How the hell could this have ever happen to you?" he thought out loud. "You were just trying to take care of your family. Anybody would have done the same thing." He shook his head in mocking disbelief as he walked away from the mirror.

Evan checked his watch for the last time before leaving the room. It was close to nine forty. He walked over to the chair and picked up his suit jacket and put it on. He returned to the mirror for one final look. As he took a deep breath, he addressed the man in the mirror once again. "You can do this. No one's gonna know you are wearing a recording device. No one." As he drew one last deep breath with resolve and finality, he went to the desk and picked up his briefcase then headed out the door of his hotel room.

Harrington was waiting at the main entrance to the hotel as instructed. "Morning Mr. Judd, sir."

"Morning, Harrington. Let's get to the Marlton Agency. It's just down Route 70."

"Yessir. I know right where it is."

The car headed east on Route 70 to the rapidly growing Marlton area. Under normal circumstances, he could see the enormous potential for the business in the area. The highway was busy even at this hour. But, as relevant as it could have been, it really wasn't important to the moment. Evan Judd looked solemnly out the window of the Lincoln Towncar. His mind was beginning to project the conversation that was to take place within the half hour. "Henry, how are you?" No, that was too familiar. He didn't want the FBI listening audience to think he really was well acquainted. "Good to see you, Mr. Singer." *Crap.* Who the hell gives a damn about the salutation. Evan tried not to think at all, a most unlikely challenge.

It was exactly 10:00 a.m. when Evan Judd walked into the insurance office. There was a young, vivacious receptionist sitting at the front desk. "May I help you?"

"Evan Judd. I have an appointment..."

"Oh, yes sir." She got to her feet and stepped out from behind the desk. "Right through here, Mr. Judd. Mr. Singer is expecting you." She led Evan to the office in the rear of the suite of offices and signaled for him to enter the one where Henry Singer and Erlich's representative were waiting. Any other time, Evan Judd would have been more interested in what was under the very short, tight, black skirt held four feet from the floor by two very shapely legs.

"Come in, Judd. You remember Harold Turner. He represents our mutual friend."

Evan smiled slightly and extended his right hand to Turner. "Good to see you." Turner reluctantly extended his arm, his verbal response was inaudible.

Evan remembered his assignment. "So you are working for J. P. Erlich," Evan sounded awkward and unnecessary even to himself. Turner ignored the attempt at conversation. Evan's heart began to beat faster. Had he sounded too obvious?

Henry Singer sat behind an old steel office desk. Turner stood just to the side of Singer who was opening the file which was in the center of his desk. Singer spoke, "Okay, Judd, here are the papers."

Before reading the papers, Evan made yet another effort on behalf on the FBI tape. "Now this is for the usual forty-nine percent? Mr. Erlich will keep fifty-one?"

"You know the deal, Judd. Why are you asking so many questions?"

"No reason, Henry. No reason. Just making small talk."

If ever there was an understatement, that certainly was. Evan could feel the tightness in his stomach building as he began reading the contract to himself. He knew basically what to expect. It was the same as the other buys had been. His eyes moved swiftly down the page and quickly on to the second page. Singer and Turner watched as he began the second page which contained the financial arrangements. Evan Judd looked up abruptly from the page. "What's this?"

"What's what?" Singer sounded indifferent.

"What's this two million dollar figure? I though we had established a million eight would cover the reserves?"

"So, now the boss has decided that we need a couple hundred thousand extra. Sort of a bonus if you want to call it that. The boss says you are getting a real deal as it is. This is a very profitable agency. He wants the extra two hundred thousand up front along with the usual hundred at contract signing."

"Up front?"

"Today. The contract signing money."

"I don't carry an extra two hundred thousand around on me. What the hell does he mean by this?"

"He doesn't mean anything. He just feels that the agency is better than most and he wants a couple hundred more, that's all."

Evan was beginning to sweat again. He didn't know what to do. If he was on his own, he would have walked out with a cross-up like this. But, his deal with the FBI was to make a buyout. This was the buyout that was going to keep him out of prison.

Harold Turner persisted for Singer, "You got a problem with this Judd?"

Evan tried to smooth over his obvious nervousness. "No, no problem, I guess. It's just unexpected. I had our usual $100,000 with me and would deliver the million seven next week. I'm just not prepared...."

Again Turner spoke, "You want this business or not? The boss's got plenty of other fish."

Evan had become very insecure. The pressure was mounting. He wanted to bolt. "Now, now Harold. Of course I want the business. I just don't have the cash on me. I only have a hundred thou with me." He tapped the briefcase he kept at his side. "But I can get the dough. You guys know that. You know I'm good for it, Henry."

Meanwhile, around the corner in the parking lot of the diner, Agents Cooper and Swift sat in the rear of the blue van that contained the recording equipment. With them was Agent Russo who was a specialist in radio operations. Cooper spoke, "Stay with it Judd.

Don't blow the deal. Agree with the bastards. Give 'em anything they want."

"Listen," urged Gordon Swift. "I think he is regrouping."

They listened as Evan continued the transaction. "Atta boy, Judd. Remember our little deal. Stay with 'em."

Evan continued. "Well, everything else seems to be in order. I'll just sign this right here and I'll be the proud, ah part-owner shall we say, of a MOST profitable AND EXPENSIVE insurance agency." He forced a weak and awkward chuckle as he signed the document in order to dismiss any insecurity he might have demonstrated to Singer and Turner.

"Okay boys, this is going to have to do it for now." Evan put the briefcase he was carrying on the desk in front of Singer. "I'm going to have to get back to New York and get the rest of the money."

Turner was obviously uncomfortable that the deal was not complete. "How soon are you gonna be able to get the cash?"

Evan tried to be casual. "I'll have it by tomorrow. I just have to get back to my bank in New York. No big deal."

Evan got to his feet as did Singer who addressed the situation. "Okay, Judd. Get the rest of the money. We'll keep the hundred you brought. You'll have the rest of it for us tomorrow. What time?"

"I'll have it in my hands before noon. Then, I'll have to have my driver bring me back here. Sometime tomorrow afternoon?"

"No later," Turner interjected.

Evan went to the door and began to open it. Suddenly he remembered his instructions from Swift and Cooper. Again, he clumsily attempted to spell out the situation for the tape.

"That's right. I'm going to go back to New York and get the additional two hundred thousand dollars contract money. I am leaving you one hundred thousand dollars now and I am going to get two hundred thousand more which will mean a grand total of two million dollars for forty nine per cent interest in the agency."

Singer and Turner just stood staring at Evan. No one made any effort to confirm what he had said. His last words hung in the air and an awkward silence prevailed. The moment seemed to last forever. Finally, Evan began to open the door to let himself out. "I'll see you boys tomorrow."

As Evan left the Marlton office, he became panicky about getting the equipment off his body. He was soaked in perspiration and began to wonder if, in fact, he could get an electrical shock--paralysis, death. People die with electrical current in bath tubs. "Christ, I must be losing my mind," Evan shook his head in disbelief at his bazaar thinking and got into his car.

"Are we going back to the hotel, Mr. Judd, sir?" Harrington asked as the car rounded the traffic circle and headed west on Route 70.

"Yes, Harrington. Let's stop at the hotel and then we have to head north to New York."

Harrington delivered his passenger to the hotel. Evan wondered if Swift and Cooper were following him. He looked around the entrance area of the hotel as he got out of the car. He did not see a vehicle pull in behind them. "I shouldn't be too long, Harrington. Why don't you park the car and get yourself some lunch in the coffee shop while I take care of a few things."

Evan Judd went back to his room to take the wire off and call Jessica. If the Agents were tailing him, they would be able to pick him up there. Evan went into the room and quickly dialed her room. "Jess, I'm back."

"Evan. I'm so relieved. Are you alright?"

"Yes. I'm okay. But," he was wrestling with his shirt as he talked, "I have to get back to New York right away."

"Why?"

"Erlich wants an extra $200,000 for the deal. He wants it right away. So I have to get back and get the money. Then, I have to deliver it to Singer."

"Why the extra money?"

"I don't know. They said it is because it is such a high producer. A bonus."

"I see. Everything else go okay?"

"I guess. I haven't seen anybody yet."

"Evan, I'm going to have to head back to Washington. You have my numbers. Why don't you give me a call as soon as you can?"

"Don't you want to come back to New York with me?" Evan felt a sense of emptiness at the thought of not having her near.

"I just think it will work better for you. Besides, I have to make some attempt to look like I'm doing my job. I can't afford to get fired," she said to lighten the tension and provide a logical explanation for her decision. Underneath, she felt he could maneuver safer without her with him.

Reluctantly, Evan agreed with Jessica. Suddenly there was a loud knock on Evan's hotel room door. "Someone's here. I gotta go."

Evan put the phone down and hurried to the door. He peeked through the privacy hole. It was Swift and Cooper. He quickly undid the deadbolt and chain. They hurried inside.

Cooper spoke. "Okay. So you got half the deal done. Now, you get back to New York and get the money. We'll wait right here in your room. You stop off here on your way back to the agency tomorrow. You can leave the wire right here now and we'll hook it up when you get back with the money."

"Did you get everything? Was it what you wanted?"

Gordon Swift responded to Evan's anxious query. "It was okay. We need to get tomorrow's exchange. Now, let's get the wire off and you get moving. You can't afford to screw it up now."

Evan removed his sweaty white shirt and undershirt. Swift undid the tape they had used to attached it to his body. Evan's skin was red and irritated.

"You got another shirt, Judd?"

"Yeah. There's one in the closet in my bag."

He went to the closet and pulled his fresh clothing from the leather wardrobe. He went into the bathroom where he washed up before the long trip back to New York.

When Evan came back into the sitting room, Swift and Cooper had made themselves comfortable with refreshments from the mini bar. "Guess I'll be going, then."

"Right, Judd," replied Agent Cooper who was stretched out on the sofa with his feet resting on the coffee table eating a bag of macadamia nuts and watching TV.

"Better stop at the desk and tell them you won't be checking out for a couple of days," ordered Agent Swift.

"Right," replied Evan trying as usual to please. Evan went to the door and let himself out. As soon as Evan was gone, Gordon Swift spoke to Ian Cooper. "Well, I guess we better check in with headquarters and tell 'em what's up."

"Relax, Swift. They don't have to know just yet. We got us a nice room, plenty to drink.....Why don't you call room service and order us some lunch. What the hell, we'll just take in a little R & R and put it on Judd's tab."

Gordon Swift picked up the phone. "Whatdaya feel like having for lunch?"

CHAPTER 12

TRAFFIC WAS HEAVY ON the New Jersey Turnpike as the Lincoln Towncar carrying Evan Judd sped north. It was too late to go to the bank, so Evan directed Harrington to continue on to Connecticut. As inappropriate as it might seem considering some of his behaviors, his sense of duty and family told him he should see how Alice was doing.

It took nearly four hours to drive from Cherry Hill to the Greenwich suburbs. It was 7:30 p.m. when Harrington pulled the limousine up in front of the hospital entrance. He put the car in park with the flashers engaged, and began to get out of the car.

"Stay with the car, Harrington," Evan Judd quietly directed his driver as he began to get out of the car. "Wait for me here in front of the hospital. It's late, and I doubt I will be long."

"Will do, Mr. Judd, sir."

Evan was glad to get out of the car. Although he had plenty of room and comfort, he hated to be in a car for so long a period of time. After a quick stop at the men's room, he went directly to the patient information desk. "I am Evan Judd. What room is my wife in?"

"Your wife is in Room 521, Mr. Judd. You may take those elevators right over there and go to the fifth floor. When you get off on the fifth floor, turn right and go just beyond the nurses station. You should have no trouble finding her."

Evan followed the directions to the fifth floor. He stopped at the nurse's station to inquire about her condition. "I'm Evan Judd. Can you tell me how my wife is doing?"

"Oh, Mr. Judd. Yes. Your wife was given a sedative about a half an hour ago. I'm afraid she has been rather difficult to manage. The doctor felt he needed to give her something to quiet her down so that she could get a good night's rest."

"I see."

"She has not slept much since they brought her onto this floor, I'm afraid. You may look in on her, but I expect she may asleep by now. Your son hired a private nurse to stay with her," continued the nurse on duty.

"Good."

"They're in the second room to your right. Right over there," she pointed.

"Thank you."

Evan made his way to the room and went in. There was a nurse sitting near the bed. As he entered the room, she got to her feet and approached him. "I'm Evan Judd," he whispered.

"Oh Mr. Judd. She is asleep. She was very tired. She has not been resting well."

Evan stayed at the foot of the bed looking at Alice. She looked a lot like her mother, he thought. "When had she aged so much?" he wondered to himself.

"I don't want to bother her. Please sit down. I am leaving. I just wanted to see how she was doing." Evan was backing toward the door.

The nurse looked after him. "I'll tell her you were here."

"Yes, please do that." Evan turned and quickly left the room. He hurried onto the elevator before anyone could speak to him. Seeing her had depressed him. He hurried out the front door of the hospital and stood waiting for Harrington who had seen him as soon as he walked out the door. As soon as the car stopped, Evan pulled open the door to the Lincoln and got in the car. "Let's go home, Harrington."

"Very good, sir."

Mrs. Hoffsteader was the only one at home that evening. She prepared a light meal for Evan and, of course, something for Harrington.

She did not speak of Alice Judd. One good thing you could count on with Mrs. Hoffsteader--she didn't engage in small talk. Evan was particularly glad of that tonight. He did not want to think about Alice or the problems of his family. He had enough to contend with for the time being. He was exhausted and planned to retire early.

It was shortly after nine in the morning when Evan arrived at his Madison Avenue office. "Edna, get me Bill Burke."

Bill Burke was Evan Judd's banker. "Evan! How are you? What can I do for you?"

"Bill, I'm going to be taking some more money out of my account. I need to have another $200,000 in cash. I'll be over to pick it up within the hour. Would you be good enough to be sure it's ready? I have some urgent business."

"Sure thing, Evan. It will be waiting for you. Just come to my office."

"Thanks Bill."

"No problem, Evan."

Evan took a sip of his hot coffee before making his next call. He wanted to see if Alice had a better night last night. He had been carrying the telephone number for the hospital so he dialed it directly.

A familiar voice answered the phone. "Hello?"

"Evan. This is your father. How is your mother doing?"

"How do you expect she is doing?"

"I stopped by last night to see her, but they had just given her a sedative."

"I doubt she would have seen you anyway."

"Put her on the line."

"She doesn't want to talk with you."

"I don't understand. Let me speak with her."

"She doesn't want to speak with you, father."

"Evan. What's going on?" Evan was intuitively beginning to sense that there was more to the story than Evan Jr. was saying.

Evan Jr. was quiet for a moment, then he spoke. "I called Granddad Brandon."

"Yes."

"He wanted to know why mother was so upset. So I told him. It's all your fault, Father. I told Granddad that you are a crook and that you are in trouble with the FBI."

"Evan!!! Damn it all, Evan. You shouldn't have told him that."

"Well, father, you are."

"Damn it, Evan...."

"Granddaddy is sending his attorney to talk with Mother."

"Evan, I told you I would handle this. What have you done?"

"I can't talk anymore. The doctor is here."

"Evan...."

There was a click at the other end of the line and a dial tone soon followed.

Evan Judd was distraught. He put the phone down and put his hands over his face and let out an anguished sigh. "Oh God help us." He pounded the desk. He hadn't ever wanted Brandon Whitley to know anything about his trouble with the FBI. "Oh Lord." Brandon had hated him for getting his daughter pregnant. He had never forgiven Evan Judd. Things weren't bad enough already....Now with Brandon in the picture, things were bound to get worse. The intercom signal sounded and pulled Evan from his thoughts. He put the phone on speaker and responded, "What is it Edna?"

"A Mr. Singer and a Mr. Turner are here to see you, Mr. Judd. I know they don't have an appointment, but they insist you will want to see them."

"What the hell are they doing here?" Evan responded without thinking.

Edna did not respond.

"Ah," Evan looked nervously around his office, "well, ah, ah, send them in." Evan got to his feet and unnecessarily continued to anxiously survey his office for some kind of revealing clues. But, of course, there were none.

The door opened and Singer and Turner were in his office.

"What are you doing here?" Evan asked the two men.

Singer answered, "Harold, here, thought we should save you the trip to New Jersey."

"How thoughtful of you," Evan responds sarcastically.

"Ya got the money?" Turner pushed.

"Not yet." Evan Judd's stomach begins to tighten as he remembers Gordon Swift and Ian Cooper waiting for him at the Hyatt in Cherry Hill. Nervously, he looked at his wristwatch.

"Is there a problem, Judd?" Turner persists.

"I told you guys that I would bring you the money. It's in the bank. I don't have it yet. I was just about to go over and pick it up."

"We'll go with you," Turner pressed.

Evan felt his stomach churn. He was very uptight now. What choice did he have? If he didn't go back to Marlton to close the deal, he was in trouble with the FBI. If he didn't turn the money over to J. P. Erlich's men here in Manhattan, they could get suspicious. That could be dangerous. Very dangerous.

Evan pressed the intercom button. "Edna, have Harrington bring the car around. We're going to the bank."

Singer and Turner took seats in the rear of the Lincoln Towncar along with Evan Judd. Evan was clearly uncomfortable with this arrangement, but reluctant to make any objections. There was something foreboding about this whole arrangement. Harrington had been moving through the heavy early morning traffic of Manhattan with the skill of a driver who had had many years experience. As is often the case in New York City, the traffic came to a complete standstill.

Unable to tolerate the lack of conversation between himself and his uninvited guests, Evan began to speak. "Now, once you fellows have the three hundred thousand dollars contract signing money, I trust I have the usual week to deliver the remaining million seven hundred thousand."

Turner peered out the window of the car totally involved in street action. "Yup."

Singer watched Turner and followed his lead. "That's right, Judd."

"Now, I was planning to deliver it to the Marlton Agency. Is that what you want?"

Turner kept watching the people on the street. The two were completely silent for what Evan considered a long period of time. He tried again. "Do you want me to bring the rest of the money to New Jersey, or what?"

Turner turned his head slowly in the direction of Evan Judd. He appeared not pleased by Judd's insistence. "I like the City. I wanna come back. I'll check it out with the boss."

Again, Singer adds his two cents, "We'll let you know, Judd."

The car began to move forward, and the eyes of the passengers focused on various scenes of city life. It was not long before Harrington pulled the car up in front of the Chase Manhattan Bank. Evan waited for Harrington to come around and let him out of the car. He wanted his passengers to notice that he was indeed used to being served. He wanted to impress upon them that he was an important person--used to the finer things in life.

"I'll be only a few minutes, Harrington. Just circle and I should be back out shortly."

Evan went into the bank. He went directly to Bill Burke's office. His secretary sat just outside the corner office. "Good morning, Mr. Judd. Mr. Burke said you would be by. Let me tell him you are here."

Burke's secretary picked up the phone, "Mr. Judd is here, Mr. Burke."

As she put the phone down, she look back at Evan and smiled, "You may go right in, sir."

"Thank you," replied Evan as he moved passed her and on into Bill Burke's office.

Burke was on his feet and heading toward the door as Evan entered, "Good to see you, Evan. I have the money right here."

Burke returned to his desk and picked up a large, thick, brown, manila envelope. "You'll find it all there, Evan. I double checked it myself."

Evan sat his briefcase on Burke's desk and opened it. He took the envelope from the banker and placed in his briefcase without opening it. After he had closed the case, he reached forward and shook hands with his long-time banker. "I appreciate this Bill. I'm going to be withdrawing a million seven either Thursday or Friday next week. I'll let you know."

"Bought yourself another agency, Evan?"

"Yeah. Looks like a good one. I'll be in touch soon."

With that, Evan turned and left Bill Burke's office and headed for his car. Harrington spotted him as soon as he came out the door and maneuvered the car to the bank entrance. Evan did not wait for Harrington this time. He opened the door and got in.

"Okay, boys. I have the money," Evan said quietly to the men as he closed the door to the vehicle.

"Let's have it," ordered Turner.

"Right here?" responded a shocked Evan Judd who was used to deals going down behind closed doors.

"You got a problem with that?" Turner fired back.

"No, no. It's just that...well, I thought..."

Singer interrupted, "Do you have the money, Judd?"

"You saw me go into the bank."

"I didn't ask that."

"But..."

"Do you have the money?"

"Yes. Yes. Of course I have the money."

"Well, hand it over."

Angrily, Evan Judd opened his briefcase and took out the thick brown envelope. He didn't like the idea of being bullied by these thugs. This was not his style. "Who the hell did they think they were?" he fumed silently. On the outside, his usual charm seemed to prevail naturally. "I don't see the hurry."

"We're already a day late. Tell your driver to drop us at Penn Station."

"You guys took the train?"

"Did we say we took the train?"

"It's just..."

"Damn it, Judd! Would you shut the hell up and do what you are told?" Harold Turner's question was really a demand.

Evan ordered Harrington to drive to Penn Station. He said no more. He was humiliated that this scum-bag could order him around.

When Erlich's men were safely dropped at Penn Station, Harrington spoke to his boss, "Quite a pair."

"You have to put up with a lot to conduct business, Harrington. Let's go back to the office." Evan Judd was beginning to get quite anxious about how Swift and Cooper were going to take the news about the transaction being finished for now.

"Get me the Cherry Hill Hyatt," he said in a subdued tone as he hurried passed Edna Carlisle.

"I have the desk clerk on the phone, Mr. Judd."

"Give me Evan Judd's room." He could hear the phone ring.

"Yes?" Evan recognized the voice at the other end of the line as being that of Gordon Swift.

"This is Evan Judd. Is this Swift?"

"Yeah Judd. Where are you?"

"I'm in my office."

"Shouldn't you be on the road by now?"

"Swift, something has happened."

"Whatdaya mean something has happened?"

"They have the money?"

"What?"

"They have the rest of the money?"

"What are you talking about, Judd?"

"Singer and Turner came to New York."

"Wait. I don't understand."

"They came to New York and got the contract money."

"Holy shit, Judd. You were supposed to bring the money here. That was the deal."

"I know, I know. But they came here."

"Why did you have them come there? You knew we were here."

"I didn't have them come here. They just did. There was nothing else I could do, so I let them have the money."

"Hold on."

Evan could hear that Swift had put his hand over the phone and was talking to someone, Cooper, no doubt, in the background.

There was some noise and Cooper was on the line. "Judd?"

"Yes?"

"How the hell did this happen?"

"Like I said, they just came to my office this morning. I didn't know they were coming. The just did."

"Son-of-a-...damn! This screws everything up. Our deal is off."

The knot in Evan Judd's stomach tightened. He thought he would wretch right there. He was beginning to panic. "It's not my fault. I didn't know what else to do. I was afraid if I didn't go through with it, they'd catch on. Please, let's work something else out."

"You blew it, Judd. We've been trying to save your ass, and you blew it."

"No, no. We can work something out on the major funds."

"Like what?"

"I have to think."

"He has to think. Judd, if you could think, we wouldn't be in Cherry Hill, New Jersey and you handing money over to some crooks in New York City."

"Look, it wasn't my fault but I know I can work something out. Give me the weekend to get my thoughts together, will ya?"

"Wait a sec, Judd."

Evan could hear Cooper talking to Swift in the background, but he couldn't make out what they were saying. He could feel his blood pressure rising.

"Judd, call us in Washington first thing Monday morning."

"Oh that's--thank you, thanks so much, sir. I know I can work something out."

"You damn well better!"

The line went dead. Evan hurried to his washroom and heaved. When he was finished, he washed his face in cold water. He looked into the mirror and was sickened by what he saw. He didn't want to acknowledge this scared, pathetic, trembling creature he saw starring back at him. He looked away and dried himself off. He went to the bar and fixed himself a very dry Tanqueray martini.

He seemed to feel a little better after the drink, so he fixed himself a second and went back to his desk and picked up the phone. He dialed Jessica's office number.

"Jessica Powers," said the voice at the other end of the wire.

"Jessica. Evan here."

"Evan, how are you?"

"Not so good, Jess."

"What's the problem?"

"Can you come up for the weekend? Things have changed and I need desperately to talk some things over with you."

"Sure. Have you handled the business in New Jersey?"

"I'm not going to New Jersey. Things have changed. I need to talk with you. When can you be here?"

CHAPTER 13

Feeling somewhat relieved to know that Jessica would be with
him for the weekend, Evan set out to deal with the business at hand.
Since the FBI had entered the picture, he hardly had time to do any of
his regular work.

He had no difficulty reserving one of the executive suites at the
Plaza. He felt confident that Jessica would be willing to share the
facility with him. He then had Edna make dinner reservations at Bice`
for sometime between 8 and 9 p.m. With these immediate concerns
addressed, he dedicated the rest of afternoon to the regular necessities
of running his insurance agencies.

Evan was heavily involved with his work when Edna Carlisle came
into his office. "I was wondering if there was anything else I could do
for you Mr. Judd?" she inquired.

"Oh no, Edna. My goodness I didn't realize it had gotten so
late. You did tell Harrington that I wouldn't be needing him this
weekend?"

"Yes sir."

"You run along Edna."

"Now if there's anything you might need, I'd be happy to stay...it's
just that I had plans to meet a friend for dinner this evening...."

"I won't be needing anything. Thank you, Edna. Have a good
time."

"Good night, Mr. Judd."

"Good night, Edna."

Evan stretched and looked at his watch. He decided he had earned himself a drink. He had been working pretty hard. Then he suddenly remembered he had not had anything substantial to eat all day. He decided it might be wise if he stuck with a soft drink for now. He wanted to be in good shape when Jessica arrived. He went to his small refrigerator, put some ice in a glass and poured himself a soft drink. He went back to work.

It was nearly 7:45 when his private line rang. "Hello?"

"Evan, I'm at Penn Station."

"Let me catch a cab and I'll be right there."

Evan put the phone down, grabbed his jacket and hurried out the door. The building was virtually empty and he met only the cleaning people as he headed for the elevator to take him to the lobby. Outside the building, he hailed a cab.

The cab took him to Penn Station. "Wait for me. I'll be right out," he said to the driver as he hopped from the cab and went into the building. He had no difficulty locating Jessica. He took her bag in one hand and her hand in the other. "I can't tell you how glad I am to see you, Jessica Powers."

"And, I you!"

He hurried her to the waiting cab. "Take us to Bice` please driver. Are you hungry, Jess?"

"Starved."

"Me too."

The city traffic was reasonably light. They were at the restaurant within 15 minutes. Evan paid the cabbie and the doorman opened the door for the couple. "Could you hold this for us until after we have dinner?" Evan checked the bag with the coat check.

The maitre-de took the couple to the table. "I'm dying to know what happened today," Jessica whispered as they were seated.

"May I get you a drink," inquired the wine steward.

"Wine, Jess?"

She nodded.

"A white wine for the lady and a martini on the rocks for me," Evan ordered. Never a need to specify brands at this fine eating establishment, they knew he liked the best.

"Very good, sir."

Evan reached over and took Jessica's hand in his. "I'm so glad you're here. I need you so much."

She smiled shyly at him.

The usual attention was bestowed upon them for the first several minutes of their arrival. When the drinks arrived, Evan toasted Jessica and a good weekend. Then he began to tell her about the extraordinary events of the day.

Jessica listened intently. When he finished, she sat quiet for a moment. Then seeing the fear building in his face, she offered, "Evan, I know we can work this out. I just know it. We have the whole weekend and I have some ideas already."

"Oh Jess, do you?"

"Evan Judd, indeed I do. Let us enjoy this magnificent place and dinner. We have plenty of time to put this together."

Evan and Jessica finished their dinners several hours later and took a cab back to the Plaza. "Jessica," said Evan as he held her hand in his in the rear seat of the cab, "I have booked the executive suite. I did not get two rooms. Do you mind?"

She smiled as she turned and looked into his eyes, "Mind? I'm relieved."

He put his arm around her and pulled her to him. They were engaged in a passionate kiss as the cab pulled up in front of the hotel. The cabbie looked in his mirror. The couple did not seem to realize that they had arrived at their destination. He cleared his throat, "Excuse me, ahem, excuse me folks. Weee're hee..ere."

Jessica and Evan were embarrassed when they realized that the driver was starring at them in his mirror. Embarrassed by being caught, she pulled quickly away as Evan reached into his pocket for the money to pay the cab fare.

"Keep the change, buddy."

The cab driver seemed pleased by the rather generous tip.

"Thank YOU, sir! Have a good one, he sang after them. The doorman was holding the door as they went into the hotel and took the elevator to the suite he had reserved.

It was difficult for Evan to keep his hands off of her as they crossed the lobby and waited for the elevator. They held hands and stood very close in an all but empty elevator until they reached their floor. The bellman had accompanied them carrying Jessica's bag. Evan had sent his things over earlier.

He opened the door and turned on the lights for them. "Will there be anything else, sir?"

"Thank you, no, that will be all." Evan tipped the bellman and he quietly left the suite.

Evan lifted Jessica in his arms and carried her to the bedroom. They did not discuss the problems of the day.

Evan awakened first. He laid on his elbow for some time just looking at Jessica before he got out of bed. It was after nine when he got up. He went to the phone in the sitting room to call room service to order them a champagne breakfast. As he placed the phone back in the cradle, he felt a hand on his shoulder. "Darling, did I wake you?" He was obviously delighted she was awake.

"No Evan. I can't remember sleeping this late in a long time."

"I've ordered us some breakfast."

"So I heard."

By the time room service arrived, Evan had gotten nervous and was beginning to pace the floor. As soon as the waiter had left the room, Jessica addressed the situation. "Evan, why don't we have some breakfast, get dressed and head for Central Park where we can perhaps walk and discuss the problem. I can see you are having a difficult time sitting still. I know we can pull some ideas together once we have some nourishment," she gently pleaded.

"Good idea, Jess."

There was a light breeze as they walked along hand-in-hand through the park. No one would have guessed that there were serious concerns on their minds. Not unless, of course, you saw the deeply worried expression on Evan Judd's face. "I know I'm going to end up in prison, Jess. Cooper already said I blew it."

An attentive and concerned Jessica responded, "But, you still have a chance to make it up. All we have to do is to figure out how. The way I see it, we should be able to arrange to have the FBI Agents tape record as long as we can have them near enough to pick up your microphone."

"But, if I don't know where the exchange is going to take place...?"

"Ah, but you will. All we have to do is make certain that Erlich's thugs don't take you by surprise."

"Oh Jessica, I don't know."

"Now Evan, what other choices do you have?"

Evan thought for a moment, "None, I guess."

"Okay. Let's take a look at the facts," Jessica's education as a journalist gave her the training to work things out with detail and logic. "You have until Tuesday to complete the buyout, correct? Didn't you say you had five days from the signing of the contract?"

"Yes."

"So Tuesday is the day?"

"Right."

"Now, we know you will be wearing the wire. What we have to be sure of is that Singer and Turner don't take you by surprise somewhere like they did yesterday."

"There's no way we can do that."

"But, I think we can. Can't you make arrangements to have the money delivered to your office?"

"Well, I guess, I don't know, Jessica. I never..."

"Didn't you say you had known the banker, what's his name...?"

"Burke, Bill Burke."

"Haven't you known him for a number of years?"

"Well, yes, Bill and I go back a long way."

"Evan, I am sure if you just asked as a favor to you, he has a bonded security guard who he could send with the money."

"I expect. But how will that help?"

"Well, then you know they can't catch you off guard. It would mean they won't catch you in the car or on the way into the bank. You will be in your office, the money will be in your office, now all we have to do is arrange for your buddies with the FBI to be somewhere in your office." She raised her eyebrows in a sarcastic way when she identified Cooper and Swift as Evan's buddies.

"Yeah, but what if they want me to bring the money to Marlton?"

"I don't see that as a problem. You know they have a mobile unit..."

"That's true."

"So, all we have to do is set up a recording unit somewhere out of sight in your office. You have a private room and bath adjacent to your private office, you said."

"That's true."

"I have a friend at the paper who could help us set it up. I am sure you will impress the FBI boys if they need to use it."

"Oh Jessica, do you really think it can work?"

"Evan, you have to try."

"Let me give my friend, Jamie, a call."

Evan and Jessica hurried along until they came to a public phone where Jessica placed the call to the paper. "If he's not in today, they will give me his home phone."

"Washington Post, how may I direct your call?"

"This is Jessica Powers. Is Jamie Fisher in today?"

"I believe he is Ms. Powers. Let me check."

Jessica held the phone and waited as the operator tried to locate Jamie. Evan watched her anxiously.

"Ms. Powers, I'll put you through to Mr. Fisher. Hold on please."

"Fisher."

"Jamie. It's Jessica Powers."

"Jess!"

"Jamie, I need your help."

"Sure, Jess, what do you need?"

"Jamie, first, this is confidential. I don't want anyone to know what I am asking you."

"Sure..."

"I need you to tell me how to set up a recording device that will pick up a wire someone is wearing."

"Jess, you'd better be careful. Don't get yourself in trouble."

"I won't Jamie. Now tell me..."

"What are you up to, Jessica Powers?"

"Jamieeeeeee, please!"

"Okay, okay, already."

Jamie proceeded as requested and Jessica quickly wrote down what Jamie told her. "So you are saying that any electronics' store will have these parts?"

"Sure. They are all pretty standard equipment."

"And, one more thing before I hang up, Jamie. Can I have your home number in case I run into a problem?"

"You bet, Jessica. It's 875-4321. But I am going to be here until late today."

"875-4321. Great Jamie. Appreciate your help. Thanks!"

"No problem, Jess."

Jessica smiled exuberantly at Evan. "This will do it. No more worrying for awhile, promise?"

"Promise. Jessica Powers, you are amazing. How about some lunch? Tavern on the Green is right over there."

As soon as they had finished lunch, Evan and Jessica took a cab to an electronics' boutique on Broadway. It took them less than fifteen minutes to find everything they needed and pay for it. Soon they were on their way back to Evan's office where they began hooking up the equipment.

It was early evening when Evan and Jessica were satisfied that everything was in order for what could be the possible taping of the Marlton deal. They caught a cab back to the Plaza and went to their room to bathe and dress for dinner. Jessica had just finished her shower and was wearing only a towel when Evan brought her a martini. They triumphantly toasted the success of the day and took a sip from their glasses. As they began to relax from the intense responsibilities of the afternoon, passion began to stir in each of them simultaneously. Evan took the drink from Jessica and set it beside his on the stand next to the bed. She was in his arms before he could finish saying how much he loved her. As he continued to speak, she put her lips over his and they kissed urgently. As she pushed her body closer and tighter against his, her towel fell to the floor. His hands caressed her. They fell to the bed and made love to each other as neither had ever dared to do before. They were more intense, more committed.

It was well after nine in the evening before the urgency of their passion was quelled. Jessica spoke gently to Evan, "I don't know about you Evan Judd, but if you expect me to continue making love at this pace, I am going to need some sustenance. I starving."

"Me too. Do you still want to go out for dinner? Or would you rather I call room service and have them deliver an intimate dinner for two?"

"I'm definitely in favor of the latter."

Evan put on a robe and went to the phone in the sitting room while Jessica headed for the shower. She was drying herself off with a towel when he came up behind her. He gently turned her toward him. She dropped the towel as she undid his robe. With his free hand, he turned the water on. He lifted her gently in his arms and stepped into the shower. The water fell softly over them as they embraced. Her lips found his and food did not seem important any more. They had become one with each other once again.

Evan placed a phone call to the hospital to check on his wife. She refused to speak to him and the nurse said it would be best not to push it. She advised him that Alice was having severe withdrawal symptoms.

He spent Sunday with Jessica. They stayed in their suite at the Plaza for the better part of the day just talking and getting to know each other better.

Jessica had an article she was writing and wanted to use the time on the train to Washington to finish it. So, Evan put her on the train late in the afternoon. He decided to spend the night in the city. When he left Penn Station, he took the cab back to his office just to have another look at the equipment he and Jessica had set up.

He carefully checked the operation out once again, and was reassured that it would work if he needed it. Convinced that all was in order, he went back to the Plaza, ordered up a light supper and went to bed early. He felt relaxed enough to get a good night's sleep. The opportunity as well as the state of mind were both rare these days.

CHAPTER 14

EDNA CARLISLE WAS SURPRISED to find Evan Judd in his office when she arrived early Monday morning. She had not been aware of any of the activities of the weekend, nor would she be if Evan was unable to set up the deal. He did not want to involve her in this unless he had to. Consequently, he decided to handle all the preliminary calls himself.

Shortly after nine a.m., Evan called Cooper and Swift at the Washington office and explained what he hoped to do. Gordon Swift could see no problem with the plan so he agreed that he and Cooper would be willing to record the meeting using the equipment he had installed--providing Judd could get Singer and Turner to come to New York, of course.

That was the tricky part. Evan was nervous about making this arrangement. He couldn't appear too eager, yet he had to maintain control. He and Jessica had discussed that psychology when they talked it through over the weekend. In fact, they had pretty much rehearsed a couple of scenarios. Now it was time to place the call.

Evan dialed the Marlton agency and got the receptionist. "Good morning, this is Evan Judd. Let me speak with Henry Singer, please."

"I'm sorry, Mr. Judd. Mr. Singer is not here yet." Can I have him call you when he gets in?"

Damn! Evan thought. He let out a nervous breath and responded, "Please do."

"As soon as he gets here, I'll give him your message."

"Thank you."

Evan hung up the phone and got up from his desk. "Damn it. Why couldn't he have been there?" Now Evan would have to wait for the call and this inconclusiveness made him nervous."

The intercom buzzed. Evan went back to his desk and quickly picked up the phone. "Yes?"

"Ms. Powers on two."

"Jessica."

"Evan, how is it going? Did you reach Swift and Cooper?"

"Yes, and they are okay with our plan. But I just called Singer and he isn't in yet. Now I don't know what to do about the bank."

"Why don't you call the bank and make arrangements for them to deliver--oh, yes, I see. If you have to go to New Jersey, you will have to pick up the money."

"That's right. I'd have to pick up the money today."

"Wait a minute, Evan. I think I have the answer to the money. Why don't you make arrangements to have the money delivered to your office first thing in the morning either way. Now if Singer wants the meeting in New Jersey, then all you have to do is make it late in the day. He's not going to argue with you at this stage."

"I suppose you are right, Jessica."

"I'm sure, Evan. You can't afford to let them take you by surprise. You must force them to meet you either in your office or in the Marlton office. Anywhere else, you can't be sure of the recording."

"I'll call Bill Burke right now, Jess."

"I'll talk with you soon, Evan."

"I love you Jess."

"Me too."

Evan dialed Bill Burke and his secretary put him right through. "Bill, I need a favor."

"Sure thing, Evan."

"Bill, remember I told you I would be withdrawing the money to buy the new agency?"

"Yes."

"Well, I need to withdraw one million, seven hundred tomorrow."

"Okay. We'll have it for you."

"Bill, could you have it delivered to my office? It's important."

"Well Evan, I ah, er, I expect we could do that."

"Great! I really appreciate this Bill, and you know how I express my appreciation..."

"Now, Evan, I, ah, ah, there won't be any, ah need..."

"Nonsense, Bill. You scratch my back--I scratch yours."

"You know I'd do it anyway, Evan."

"Can you have it here first thing?"

"You bet."

"Thanks Bill."

"Don't mention it Evan--and I mean that literally."

"Don't worry."

Both men laughed and hung up the phone.

Evan felt relieved to some extent. Now all he had to do was to wait for Henry Singer to call.

It was nearly eleven thirty before the call came in from Singer. "Got your message, Judd. Got the money?"

"Henry, I'll have it by tomorrow. I was hoping you boys might want to come up here and pick it up. I'll make it worth your while."

"Well, Evan, I don't know."

"I will throw in two special incentives for you and old Harold if you want to come on up and spend the night?"

"Hold on a sec."

Evan could hear Singer put his hand over the mouth piece and talk to someone else. "Turner must be with old Henry," Evan thought. Henry appeared to be a conservative, all business type guy. But Evan had heard he had a weakness for kinky sex.

"We could do that."

"Good. I'll get you rooms at the Waldorf.

"Okay. We should be there no later than, mmm, say seven."

"Then, I'll see you here in my office around eleven, let's say."

"Eleven, tomorrow."

Evan hung up the phone and leaned back in his chair. He released an audible sigh of relief before he remembered what he had promised.

"Shit." He dropped his feet to the floor. "I gotta get those broads for the boys," he thought out loud.

His mind began to work quickly. "Tammi! She owes me." He had been paying her rent for damn near five years, now. She and her girlfriend, what the hell was her name? Dora. Dora would do anything for a couple of hundred bucks."

Evan dialed Tammi's number. A sleepy voice at the other end of the line answered. "Hel-lo?"

"Tammi, love. It's Evan. I need a favor."

"Evan. How are you baby? I ain't seen ya for a while. I miss you. Ya comin over?"

"I can't right now. I need a favor."

"Sure."

"This is very important, Tammi."

She was becoming more alert. "Anything, baby. What do you want?"

"I have a couple of guys coming into town that need entertaining. I want you and your friend, Dora, to meet them at the Waldorf tonight."

"Sure."

"This is very important, Tammi. You can't let me down."

"Baby, I ain't never let you down, have I?"

"Good girl. There names are Henry Singer and Harold Turner. Treat them good, and there is a bonus in it for you."

"You got it, baby."

"Give them anything they want, ya hear?"

"Sure thing, love."

Evan immediately booked the two rooms and guaranteed them for late arrival. When he had those arrangements completed, he hung up the phone and tipped back in his black leather swivel chair and smiled. He had done it. "I'm a damn genius," he thought. "This is going down without a hitch."

For one moment, Evan Judd was not nervous, not filled with the usual anxiety. He even forgot for a moment, a least, the very real possibility that he could land in jail. With far more confidence, he picked up the phone and called the FBI.

Swift and Cooper agreed to meet him at the office by eight the following morning. He phoned Jessica to let her know he was in charge. All was going well.

Again, he stayed over at the Plaza Hotel only this night, he didn't sleep as well. He tried watching television, but he could not keep his mind from drifting back to the events that were forthcoming in the morning.

Evan was in the office at 6:30 a.m. Tuesday morning. He wanted to be certain nothing went wrong. At exactly seven, Gordon Swift and Ian Cooper magically arrived at his office door and wanted to check out the equipment in his office.

"It all looks good to me," said Swift.

"Let's test it," Cooper said less assured. "I'll see if I can record you and Judd. We'd sure as hell hate to lose this one. This is our last chance for this deal."

Ian Cooper set himself up in Evan's private suite while Evan and Gordon Swift conversed for a few minutes about nothing in particular. "Okay, everything seems in order."

When Edna came in a short while later, Evan called her into his office to apprise her of the entire situation. Cooper and Swift stood by as Evan explained what was about to take place. Her confidence was naturally assured.

"Do you suppose you could get us some coffee, Ms. Carlisle?" asked an unusually polite Cooper.

"Certainly, Agent Cooper. Will there be anything else, Mr. Judd?"

"No, just what I told you--the money then the boys from Marlton. Absolutely no one else until this business is taken care of. No one. Do whatever it takes."

"Yes sir."

By 10:30 the security men from the bank had arrived with their delivery. Evan tipped them handsomely, and they left without a hitch. Now, the only thing left was Singer and Turner.

Cooper and Swift were safely tucked away in Evan's inner sanctum. Evan began pacing the floor of his office. The time passed slowly. Evan kept constant tabs on the minutes by checking watch with the time on the wall clock. As the clock approached eleven, Evan could feel every muscle in his stomach tighten. He was beginning to feel sick from nerves again.

Eleven came and went. "Where the hell are they?" he thought as he continued to walk back and forth in his office. Eleven-twenty. Eleven-twenty-five. He could hardly breathe he was so nervous.

Suddenly the intercom sounded scaring him half to death.

"Mr. Singer and Mr. Turner are here," Edna said stiffly.

"Send them in, please," Evan said formally. He hurried to sit down at his desk so that he could look as casual as possible when the men came into the office. He signaled for them to have a seat in front of the desk so that they would be near the microphone as they transacted the business at hand.

"I trust you gentlemen had a satisfactory night. Let's get down to business," pushed Evan.

Evan began the transaction trying to remember to spell everything out as he went along. "Now before I hand over the one million seven remaining of the two million total, do you have the rest of the papers, Harold?"

Harold Singer reached into his brief case and pulled out a file. "Okay, here is the client list. I think you will find everything in order."

Evan took the papers but noticed that Turner was getting rather fidgety. He appeared to be losing interest as he looked around the room. Suddenly, Turner was on his feet heading for the door to Evan's private suite. With his hand on the doorknob, he inquired, "You got a john in there?"

Singer who had been in Evan's office before knew this to be true. "Sure he has, Harold. Just go ahead in that door. You'll find it."

Evan's heart began racing and perspiration immediately began to form over his upper lip as Turner opened the door to Evan's private suite where Swift and Cooper were recording the transaction.

Evan's mind was racing, "Son of a ..., I never should have set this up. I should have seen this coming."

Meanwhile, Henry Singer continued, "Here is the set of keys that will get you into the files. Judd, are you with me?"

"Yeah, yes, Henry. I'm with ya." Evan forced himself to look back to Singer. By now, Turner was out of his sight.

Singer continued with the details, "So by Friday, you will have your own office manager in place."

Again, Evan Judd does not respond.

"Judd, what the hell's wrong with you?"

Evan tried desperately to refocus his attention on the business at hand, but he was ready to bolt. He didn't dare look back to the door, yet he could think of nothing else. His mind was racing. He couldn't contain his thoughts, "What the hell is he doing in there? What the hell takes a guy so long to take a piss?"

Evan forced himself to respond to Singer. "Ah, nothing, Henry. I, ah, I was, ah..."

"You were what?"

"Thinking. That's all. Just thinking about the guy I was going to put down there," he recovered.

"You want to get yourself a good lawyer to handle these cases. I got a couple of names when you get to that. You don't want just anyone in that area. Those cops are something. Got their own kangaroo courts and all."

"Sure, Henry, I'd like your recommendations."

"Well, I guess that's it. Just give me the money, and we'll be on our way."

"Here it is." Evan slides two large briefcases across the desk at Singer.

"What the hell is Turner doing in there, anyway?" asks an impatient Singer.

Just then, they hear a flush of the toilet and some running water. Within a few seconds, Harold Turner is standing inside the opened door.

"Come on Turner. Grab one of these cases and let's get moving."

Turner advanced to the desk and picked up the briefcase as Singer had directed.

Singer looked toward Evan. "Have your man there by Friday morning. I've got a well deserved vacation due me."

"Are you the one taking the money out of the country this time?" inquires Evan expressly for the tape.

"Me and old Harold here are the chosen ones."

And they were gone. Evan reached for his handkerchief as he fell back into his chair. Suddenly he was drained. He turned in his chair to look out the window at his coveted view as he wiped the sweat from his face.

He had been so relieved when Singer and Turner left that he was startled when Agents Swift and Cooper reappeared in his office.

Swift spoke. "We got it all, Judd."

"I was so afraid he would see you," replied Evan. Where did you go?"

"Don't forget, we knew he was coming. We were listening to every word," responded Cooper.

"We ducked out of his line of sight, but we didn't have time to move any of the equipment," Swift added.

A grin actually came to Agent Cooper's face as he shook his head, "He never stuck his head out of the can."

"Not a hitch, this time. Good job, Judd," said Gordon Swift.

Feeling relieved, but still quite shaky, Evan hospitably offered the agents a drink so that he could have one and calm his own nerves. "Can I offer you a drink?"

"We got to get going. We're heading back to New Orleans," responded Swift.

"We could use a ride to the airport," hinted Cooper.

"I'll get my car. Harrington will take you." Evan was on the intercom, "Edna, have Harrington bring the car around. Agents Swift and Cooper need a ride to the airport.

"Do you need anything else?" Evan inquired feeling rather magnanimous as he put down the phone.

"That will do it for now," Cooper said patting his jacket pocket. "We need to get these tapes to headquarters." On their way out the door, Swift turned back to Evan, "We'll be in touch. Don't go any place where we can't reach you."

They were gone and Evan headed directly to his bar. He had earned himself a double martini.

After lunch, Evan settled down to business. Now that he had bought the Marlton Agency, he would have to get one of his best men to manage it. He needed to put someone in charge who could work a high producer like Marlton. "If I have to pay the price," he thought to himself, "I want the profit." He would not entertain the idea that his own financial success was coming to a close.

He was engaged in working out the final details of getting his best manager to take over when Edna buzzed him on the intercom. "Yes, Edna," he said in almost a cheerful voice.

"Your housekeeper is on the phone."

"Mrs. Hoffsteader?" he asked incredulously. Mrs. Hoffsteader rarely, if ever, called him at the office.

"Yes, Mr. Judd. She's on line one."

"Mrs. Hoffsteader?" Evan inquired into the phone.

Mrs. Hoffsteader's no nonsense voice answered. "Mr. Judd, sir, you know I don't like to bother you at the office."

"That's perfectly alright, Mrs. Hoffsteader," he reassured her. "What is it?"

"I think maybe you might want to come home," she stated flat out. No explanation.

Evan was shocked. "Why's that?"

"Mr. Judd, I feel maybe you ought to see for yourself."

"See what, Mrs. Hoffsteader?"

"I'm not really at liberty to say, sir, but I do think you ought to come home."

"Mrs. Hoffsteader, can't you give me an idea what's going on? Why do you think I need to be there?"

"Mr. Judd, you know I mind my own business. I don't but in where I don't belong."

"Mrs. Hoffsteader, I know that. You have always been an outstanding housekeeper."

"Well, I never took sides, and I'm not starting now. But you need to come home, Mr. Judd. You really need to get home right away."

Mrs. Hoffsteader had hung up the phone. She had sounded extremely distraught which was a first for her. She would not allow herself to show emotion. "What the hell could be going on there?" he wondered. He'd better call Jessica and postpone their rendezvous. They had planned that she would to come to the City for a late dinner and Evan was going to fill her in on the events of the day. He dialed her number at the Post.

"Jessica. It's Evan."

"Evan, I just about to pack up and get out of here. I need to go home, change and pick up a few things before I catch the 4:17. I was hoping to get in a little early and surprise you. I'm about caught up here for the moment."

"Jess, I have to cancel. The strangest thing just happened."

"Not more trouble, I hope."

"Well, to tell the truth, I really don't know. Certainly not the same thing we have been going through for the last few days, but Mrs. Hoffsteader, my housekeeper, just called and told me I had better get home."

"Why, Evan? What's going on?"

"She wouldn't say over the phone, but she was most insistent. So, I am going to head out to Greenwich right now. I'll call you as soon as I can, Jess. Mrs. Hoffsteader has been a very sensible and reliable person over the years. If she thinks I need to be there, then there must be something important going on."

"By all means, Evan, go. Let me know."

"I will Jess."

The ride to Connecticut seemed to take forever. A tank-wagon truck had over-turned spilling fuel all over the highway. Traffic was tied up until the vehicle was righted and the spill safely cleared. Evan was frustrated. On the one hand, he knew he had to go, but on the other, seeing Jessica tonight was what had kept him going through the ordeal of the last couple of days. She breathed new life into what had become a sorry existence for him. She made him feel special, desirable. Hell, half way intelligent even. She was interested in him for himself not for his money or what he could do for her.

It was dusk as the car pulled in under the portico to the house. Before Harrington had stopped the car, Mrs. Hoffsteader, who had been watching out the window for her boss, opened the front door. Evan did not stand on the usual formality of having Harrington open the door for him. He was anxious to see what was going on. He climbed out of the car immediately and spoke to his long-time housekeeper. "What's the problem here?"

Mrs. Hoffsteader held the front door wide open for him to enter. "Just come in and see for yourself. Look, Mr. Judd, just look inside here."

Evan hurried inside. The house was empty. All of the furniture was gone. Slowly Evan began to walk from room to room. Everything was gone. Even the walls were bare--stripped of the expensive paintings that had been hanging on them. He climbed the stairs to the second floor. Very slowly, he walked through each room in disbelief. The entire second floor was empty as well.

He felt as if he had been hit by a cement truck. Slowly, he descended the circular staircase to the foyer where Mrs. Hoffsteader stood watching him. "What happened?" he inquired of his long-time employee? "My God, what happened?"

"Well sir, Mr. Evan Jr. came in early this morning with a big moving truck and several men. They just started emptying the house." She reached for a hanky which she always kept in her apron pocket and began to wipe her nose. Her eyes glistened with tears which uncharacteristically were about to spill down her cheeks at any moment.

Evan just stared at her as she continued. "When I asked him what he was doing, he said these were his mother's things, and he was putting them in storage. That's where she wanted them. So then I asked him where Mrs. Judd was. I thought she was still at the hospital. But he said his Granddaddy had made arrangements for her to go up to Albany. He said they were going to live with him for awhile."

By now the tears were running down her face. Evan could not find words to respond. Finally, he went to the staircase and sat down on a stair. He put his head in his hands. Neither he or his housekeeper spoke. There was really nothing to say.

Evan was at his desk early the following morning. His devastation had moved to anger. "Here I have devoted my entire life to this family, and this is the thanks I get." Late last night, he had gotten a hold of Alice's father, Brandon Whitley. Not surprisingly, his father-in-law blamed Evan for Alice's drinking problem as well as every other problem he could think of. He had ended the conversation by telling Evan to leave his daughter alone. Evan had also tried to reach Frank Spector, but, as had become the case, he was out of town. He would have to reach him today to see what he needed to do. Alice's behavior, as far as emptying the house, had caught him totally off guard. But, he had enough good sense to know that he did need his lawyer at this point.

Edna brought him a pot of hot, fresh coffee. "Can I get you something else, Mr. Judd?"

"Edna, I've got to track down Frank Spector. The sooner we get started on it the better. My wife has taken all of my things and left."

"My God, sir. Everything?"

"Everything, Edna. I believe her father's influence directed her actions."

"Oh my God, sir. I'm sorry. I never..."

"I know, Edna."

"Is there anything I can do, sir?"

"Just get me my lawyer, Edna. I tried late last night, but he was out of town."

"Right away, sir."

Edna hurried out of the office.

Within the hour, Edna had determined that Frank Spector was unavailable to Evan Judd under any circumstance. "His office said that Mr. Spector had left the name of someone who would be available to you. Do you want to get him on the line?"

"Damn it! I don't want one of Spector's flunkies...."

"Do you want me to contact one of our company attorneys, Mr. Judd?"

"No, no, Edna. Let me think for a few minutes."

Evan was heartsick. He felt cold and alone. "After all I have done for them...." He sat staring out the window onto the city. The view might have been one of the best in New York City, but nothing seemed to matter to him right now. He was drained.

The sound of the intercom buzzing jolted him out of his reverie. "Ms. Powers is on your private line, sir."

"Hello Jessica."

"Evan, you sound ill. What's wrong?"

"She took everything and left."

"What are you talking about?"

"My wife. Alice moved out of the house and took everything we had spent our lifetime accumulating. My art, all of my collections, everything."

"Where did she go?"

"Her father's behind it all. I called him last night. He wouldn't let me talk with her. He told me to leave them alone and hung up on me."

"I'm so sorry Evan."

"Well, Jess, I knew the marriage was in trouble. I told you that. But I never expected her to take everything. Never! I have some expensive collections...I, I just don't know what to do next. My lawyer won't talk to me. He wants to stick me with some...."

"I have a friend who is a darn good lawyer if you are interested."

"Maybe that's a good idea. My own attorney doesn't seem to give a damn any more."

"I'll have Bill Forest contact you. Evan, I'm so sorry this had to happen."

"I know, Jess."

"Evan, I hate to abandon you, but the reason I called is that something is going on in New Orleans and I have got to get back there."

"What's happening?"

"We are not sure, but our contact says that they are bringing in some other agency guys and possibly some of Erlich's men. It could be big and I need to be there just in case."

"When are you leaving?"

"I'm on my way to National Airport right now."

"Will you be staying at the Latin Arms?"

"Yes."

"I'll call you."

"Take care of yourself, Evan. I'll get in touch with my friend. He'll call you."

"Thanks, Jessica."

"So long, Evan."

It was late that afternoon when Bill Forest called Evan. He advised him to immediately close out his joint bank accounts in Greenwich. With information he received from Evan, he was going to draw-up papers which would protect the estate. They decided that he should prepare separation papers in the event that Evan wanted to pursue a divorce.

CHAPTER 15

Dick Youngblood had not been with Evan much more than three years, but he seemed to have a flair for the business. Better yet, he was hungry. Evan decided that he would be the best man for the job at the newly acquired New Jersey Agency. He didn't understand the operation well enough to be in a position to betray his boss if summoned by the FBI, but he was greedy enough to follow orders to reach the top. Youngblood was coming to the New York office so that he could offer him the position as branch manager of Marlton.

Edna led Youngblood into the boss's office. "Mr. Judd. Good to see you, sir."

"Dick, please sit down. I have a proposition for you."

"Yes sir."

"Dick, I have just acquired a new agency in Marlton, New Jersey, and I would like you to manage it for me. It will mean a substantial raise, but it will require a lot of attention from you. Whatdaya say?"

"Yes sir. I appreciate the opportunity, sir. I am sure I can handle it."

"So am I, Dick. Now, there is a catch. I need you to take over right away. Is there any problem with that?" inquired Evan knowing full well that Youngblood would not refuse.

"No sir. When do I start?"

"I thought I'd have Harrington drive us down today. I have a couple of things I need to handle, but I will be ready within the hour.

Let me get Edna, and she will find you some coffee and a comfortable place to wait."

He signaled Edna. "Edna, would you get Mr. Youngblood some coffee and make him comfortable? Then, get Harrington to bring the car around in about an hour. We are going to head down to the new Marlton Agency. Mr. Youngblood has agreed to manage it for us."

"Very good, sir. I'll take care of it."

As soon as Youngblood had left the office, Evan continued to try to get through to the bank manager in Greenwich where he had his joint checking and savings accounts. The other accounts which he kept in New York were safe, but Bill Forest had said that he needed to close the joint accounts immediately. Unfortunately, the branch he dealt with had recently changed managers, and he did not know the new manager personally.

The intercom interrupted him. "Yes Edna?"

"A Mr. Forest on line two."

"Bill, I am not having any success with the bank in Greenwich and I am going to have to head for New Jersey."

"Well, Evan, all I can say is that you need to close those joint accounts as soon as possible. If your wife has an attorney, I know he will be advising her to withdraw the money."

"Well, I may have to chance it. I have got to get my new man in as manager in Marlton today. I have no choice as far as that is concerned."

"Do what you have to Evan. I called to let you know that the papers will be ready by Friday."

The Lincoln Towncar headed south on the Jersey Turnpike just before noon. Evan Judd and Dick Youngblood worked on the details of managing this particular agency. By the time Harrington exited the Interstate at Cherry Hill, Youngblood had received full instructions. All they had to do now was to physically go in and take over. Harrington pulled the car into the small parking lot when they reached Marlton and left his passengers off at the door while he found a place to park the limousine.

The perky receptionist who had greeted Evan last week was at her desk when they arrived. "Mr. Judd," she sang in a high pitched voice. "How are you?" she inquired in an overly friendly manner. "And, who is this handsome gent you have brought with you?"

"Is Henry here?" Evan cut her off at the pass.

"I'm sure he is, Mr. Judd."

"We'll just find our way to his office."

"But.....I wanted to..."

Ordinarily, Evan would have given her the attention she was demanding, but not today. He was all business, and he had business to attend to. They found Henry in the process of putting the last of his things in a briefcase.

"It's all yours, Judd. I thought you'd never get here."

"Henry, this is Dick Youngblood. He's agreed to manage the office here in Marlton."

"Good to meet you, Youngblood," Singer perfunctorily offered his hand. "It's a good business. It will keep you pretty busy, let me tell you."

"I'm sure I can handle it," a confident Dick Youngblood replied.

"Well, I've left everything you will need. You have a boss that knows what he is doing, so I guess I'll be moving along."

The three shook hands and Henry Singer was on his way out the door. Dick Youngblood stood still waiting for approval to move. "There's your desk. Why don't you try it out?" Evan said smiling at the eager young man.

The men took a few hours to familiarize themselves with what all had been left for them at the office. Evan used his keys and opened the files for them to take a look inside. By the time they were satisfied that they could work out any kinks, it had gotten to be nearly 9:00 p.m. Evan decided to stay over at the Cherry Hill Hyatt, so he called and made reservations for the three of them. They decided that Dick would stay for the day on Friday to check out the staff and be certain all was going as well as it seemed. That weekend, he would begin the process of finding a place to live permanently. Meanwhile, Evan left him with a substantial advance so that he could purchase anything he needed personally in order to make the move.

Friday morning early, Harrington drove Evan back to Connecticut. They went directly to the bank where Evan discovered that both accounts had been cleaned-out. Alice had taken everything. An angry, dejected Evan Judd returned to the empty family estate for the weekend, a very lonely weekend.

Actually, it was a disaster. Mrs. Hoffsteader had gone to stay with her sister since no one was at the Judd estate. Evan had told her it would be okay, but the house was so empty that he wished she had stayed. He and Harrington ate their meals out, but Evan was not anxious to run into anyone he knew so he did not go to the club or any of his other favorite haunts.

Evan tried but he had not been able to catch Jessica in her room at the Latin Arms all weekend. He had been depressed, and therefore, not tried all that often either. Nor, did he feel like leaving a message for her to return his call.

By Sunday evening, Evan could not take the emptiness anymore, so he had Harrington drive him back to New York where he spent the night in the office. The pull-out couch was not the most comfortable bed in the world, but he didn't feel like interacting with anyone either. He was at his desk when the phone rang at 7:00 A.M. on Monday morning.

It was Gordon Swift calling from New Orleans. "Judd, is that you?"

"Yeah, who's this?"

"It's Swift, Gordon Swift. Where the hell have you been? I've been trying to reach you since Thursday."

"I never got any messages?"

"No, I didn't want to leave any messages. I didn't want anybody to know that I was calling you. But I wanted to warn you, things could get ugly for you."

"Whatdaya mean?"

"One of the other guys we brought in spilled his guts, and they think you have been in on the same kind of deal, too. So you are probably going to be implicated. But you have been…ah well, cooperative, and I wanted to give you warning that they are probably gonna want to bring you in again. You had better be prepared."

"Why are you telling me this?"

"Like I said, you have been cooperative. I think you deserve a break. But, listen, you can't let on that I called you."

"No, no, I won't."

"Sit tight, now. That's about all you can do. Expect an official call probably some time today."

"What should I do?"

"Not much you can do. Like I said, one of your counterparts has spilled his guts, so they are nailing him to the wall."

"But, I can't go to prison. Oh sweet Jesus, I'd never survive prison."

"I don't know for sure, Judd, but, remember, the only thing they have brought up against you is possible mail fraud."

"Would I go to prison for that?"

"I don't know. Depends pretty much on the judge. Hey, listen, I gotta go. Remember, I didn't call. Good luck, Judd."

Evan stood in the office with the phone to his ear listening to a dial tone. He was too stunned to hang up. Finally, he put the phone down. He was beginning to feel a familiar knot in his stomach. He sought relief from the building tension by stepping into his private shower and letting the hot water run over him.

After his shower, he dressed and got ready for the day. Edna was in by 8:30 and brought him his morning coffee and newspaper. It was shortly before 9:00 when she buzzed him to announce, "Agent Cooper on line one."

Evan held the phone for a moment trying to calm himself down before he plugged into the line with Cooper. "Cooper, how are you? What can I do for you today," Evan chirped in his friendliest voice. If there was something you needed to say about Evan Judd it was that he could charm the skin off a snake.

"Judd, you need to get yourself to New Orleans pronto. We are going to need you."

"But I thought...ah, wasn't the tape...ah"

"Something has come up. We need you."

"Well, if I must. I'll try to get a flight in the morning..."

"No, you had better get on a flight first thing."

"This afternoon?"

"Drop what you are doing, and head for the airport, is what I mean."

"But..."

"Judd, just do it. Hang up the phone and head for the airport."

Cooper cut off from the connection. Evan was getting panicky. Frank Spector had warned him. He decided he would not waste what little time he had getting put off by Spector's office. He pulled Bill Forest's number from his top desk drawer and began to dial.

"Forest, Abrams, and Hunter," the receptionist answered the phone.

"This is Evan Judd calling for Bill Forest."

"One moment, Mr. Judd, I'll see if he is available."

"This is urgent. Could you please tell him that?"

"Yes sir. I'll tell him."

Evan could hardly breathe. He was scared. Really, really scared.

"Evan, what can I do for you?"

"Bill, I am in a real bind. I need your help desperately."

"What is it, Evan?"

"Bill, it's a long story, but I'm involved in an FBI investigation. Now, I know I engaged you because of my personal life, but, Bill, I really need an attorney to help me with this FBI business. Can I get you to meet me in New Orleans right away?"

"Well, Evan, this is really short notice, but..."

"Bill, I wouldn't do this if it wasn't critical. I may have to go to prison and I need representation. Will you help me?"

"I...I..."

"Bill, I'm begging you. Will you do it?"

"Evan, I have a case in court in one hour. But I will send my partner, Michael Hunter ahead. I don't know how long I will be tied up in court. It could take several days. But Mike is a good lawyer and I know he is in a position where he could adjust his schedule right now. He just finished a big case last week."

"Great. I have to get to the airport and get the first plane to New Orleans."

"What should I tell Mike to do?"

"Have him catch the first flight to New Orleans and go to the Latin Arms Hotel. That is where I will be staying."

"Okay, Evan, I'll tell him."

"Thanks Bill. Really. I mean it."

"It's okay, Evan. Glad to do it."

Evan tried calling Jessica on his way to the airport. He had little hope that he would ever catch her in her room, but he had to try.

"Hello?"

"Jessica, my God is that you?"

"Evan?"

"Yes, it's me."

"Evan, are you okay?"

"Jessica, I'm on my way to Kennedy International."

"Evan, you aren't coming down here, are you?"

"Yes, as a matter of fact, I am. I have to catch the first available flight. I am on standby."

"Oh, no, Evan. You don't want to come now."

"But, Jess, I have to."

"Why Evan? This is not the place for you to be right now."

"Cooper called early this morning and said I had to come."

"Oh Evan. Things seem to be coming to a head here."

"Jess, do you know Michael Hunter?"

"Yes. Why?"

"I just called Bill Forest to see if he would come with me but he has to be in court. So he is sending Hunter."

"Good. Is Bill coming later?"

"As he said, he has a case in court. I guess it depends on what happens."

"I think you ought to plan...well let's see when you get here. I don't suppose you know when that will be?"

"No, Jess. The airlines said that it didn't look good for me getting on this first flight, but perhaps the next one mid-afternoon."

"I have to go out now, but I will try to be back in the hotel by early evening, Evan. I'll look for you."

"I miss you."

"And I you, Evan."

"See you tonight, Jessica."

"Goodbye Evan."

Evan managed to get a seat on the 2:47 p.m. flight to New Orleans. It was still very hot and humid when he landed and caught a cab to the hotel.

The phone in his room was ringing when Evan stepped out of the shower. He grabbed a towel and hurried to answer it. "Hello?"

"Evan, it's Jessica. I stopped at the desk on my way in and they told me that you had checked in. How are you?"

"Cooler, since my shower. I forgot how hot it is here. And you, Jess?"

"Oh, I'm okay, Evan. There's a lot going on..."

"Like what?"

"Maybe we should get together."

"Of course."

"I want to take a shower and get changed. Why don't we meet in about an hour."

"Good. What room are you in?"

"534."

"I'll be down in about an hour."

Evan hung up the phone and dried himself off. Everything was so damp he felt he could hear the mold growing on the walls. Before shaving, he decided it might be a good idea to check to see if Hunter had gotten in. He was beginning to feel the knot in his stomach tighten more intensely now that he was here in New Orleans. A conditioned reflex. "Has a Mr. Michael Hunter checked in yet?"

"No sir. No one by that name has registered."

"Thank you." Evan hung up the phone and found his watch. It was nearly eight o'clock. "I hope he was able to get on a plane this afternoon," he thought to himself.

Evan returned to the bathroom mirror and continued shaving. The shrill sound of the telephone ringing startled him. He nicked the edge of his ear as he jumped. "I'm a basket-case," he thought to himself. "Everything is under control for now," he consoled himself as he took a deep breath and picked up the phone.

The party at the other end of the line did not wait for him to speak. "Judd?" the demanding voice at the other end of the wire inquired.

"Yes?" answered Evan, blood from the cut on his ear was beginning to trickle slowly down his wet neck.

"You know who this is," the deep voice said dryly. "Just listen."

Evan Judd stood at attention in his under shorts as the man at the other end of the line spoke.

"The government boys are closing in on our business. I don't want you blabbing anything about our deals, if you know what's good for you. You know I have the means to keep you quiet. Right now, they are only talking about charging you with mail fraud. I want you to plead guilty to this misdemeanor and bow out of the rest. Understand?"

"But...I don't..ah..I don't want..."

"Did you hear me, Judd?"

"Yes, but..."

"Judd! If you know what's good for you, you will forget any buts."

"I don't want to go to..."

"Listen, Judd. That's the deal. Accept the pending charges and bow out. Keep quiet about the rest or I will see that you are kept quiet permanently. Do you hear me?"

"I hear you."

"Good."

The phone went dead as Evan Judd continued to stand at attention in just his underwear in the dark, damp hotel room. The smell of mildew stung his nostrils as he tried to take a breath. His legs were weak and his arms were trembling as he dropped the phone back on the hook. Bright, red blood was tricked slowly down his chest and onto his belly.

CHAPTER 16

JESSICA COULDN'T IMAGINE WHAT was keeping Evan. He was usually early when he made a date with her. She needed to tell him about what had been going on in New Orleans since she had arrived. Some of the information could become critical and she wanted him to be aware of what had happened. She had cultivated a contact on the inside of the Justice Department, Nancy Newton. Nancy had a grudge against all insurance companies and was pleased to do what she could to crucify, (especially in the media), anyone connected with insurance fraud.

Nancy had told Jessica her story and it was gruesome. It seems she had been paying insurance premiums for years. Then, she had an automobile accident. She and her young son were in the car. Nancy ended up with a concussion, broken pelvis, a couple of fractured ribs along with some superficial cuts and bruises. The young child had sustained serious head and spinal injuries. They were hospitalized for weeks. Finally, she was released, but when she had tried to get money from the insurance company to pay the bills, the company would not pay saying that it was the fault of the other driver. Since the other company would not pay, she had to sue.

Meanwhile, the son's injuries had rendered him paralyzed from the neck down. The doctors at the hospital wanted to send him to another hospital for special therapy. If he was to ever walk again, this was his only chance. Timing was critical. But, the therapy required money which she did not have without the insurance money.

The insurance company tied the case up in the courts with legalities for years. There was postponement after postponement without a hearing. By the time the case did get to the courts, it was too late for her son. Costs had prevented her from providing him with the necessary physical therapy when the condition demanded it and his condition deteriorated. He needed constant care. He could do nothing for himself. The money she earned working for the FBI provided just enough for her to get by plus hire someone to stay with Jason while she was at work. Consequently, anything Nancy could tell Jessica that would make the public aware of the crookedness of the insurance business, she was more than willing to do.

"Where is he?" Jessica wondered as she looked at her watch which indicated that Evan was twenty minutes late. She had just picked up the phone to call his room when a knock at her door interrupted her. Jessica put the phone back on the hook and went to the door. "Who is it?"

"It's me, Evan."

Jessica removed the chain lock and opened the door to Evan. "My God, Evan, what has happened to you?" she whispered as she stepped back to let him in the room.

Evan Judd said nothing as he stepped inside, quickly closing the door behind him. His eyes were wide with terror and his face was chalky white.

"Evan, what's wrong? You are scaring me. What is it?" Jessica motioned him to the chair. "Here. Sit down."

Evan sat down in the chair and put his hands over his face. "Oh Jessica," he tried to catch his breath. "Oh Jess, I am going to have to go to prison." He was trembling.

"What are you talking about?"

Evan took his hands from his face as Jessica got on her knees in front of him and gently took his hands in hers. "I just got a telephone call."

"Yes? And?" she urged.

"It was from Erlich," Evan whispered.

"My God! What did he want?"

"He told me to accept the wrap for mail fraud."

"Oh, Evan, no. You can't. Not now. Not after all you have gone through. You have been working with the FBI. My God, that would mean prison for sure."

"I know, Jess. But I don't have a choice."

"Sure you do."

"No Jess. I don't."

"We have to talk with Mike--even Bill. But, you can't go to prison. I don't know what....." Jessica's voice broke.

"Please don't cry," Evan leaned forward and put his arms around Jessica to comfort her while tears welled up his eyes. Evan pulled her to him and they sat holding each other.

The solace they were seeking through their closeness was interrupted when the phone began ringing. Jessica got to her feet and went to the nightstand to answer it. "Jessica?"

"Yes?"

"Jessica, this is Mike Hunter. Bill told me you would be staying here."

"Michael. How good to hear from you."

"Jessica, I am trying to locate a friend of yours, an Evan Judd. Do you know where he is?"

"He's right here, Mike. Hold on."

Jessica put her hand over the mouthpiece as she spoke to Evan. "It's Mike Hunter for you."

Evan went to the phone. "Mr. Hunter. I have been waiting to hear from you. I need to talk with you right away. Where are you?"

"I checked into the Latin Arms about ten minutes ago and I am in my room. What do you say we meet at the bar in, what, five minutes?"

"Five minutes." Evan returned and hung up the phone.

"I'm going to meet Mike at the bar in five minutes. Do you want to come?"

"No, no, Evan. You and your attorney should meet by yourselves. I'll wait for you here."

The hotel bar was quiet. By the time Evan arrived, there were two couples sitting at the bar and a man at the far end. The lone man had to be Mike Hunter. Evan walked up to the stranger. "Mike Hunter?"

"Yes sir."

"I'm Evan Judd."

"Good to meet you, Evan. What do you say we get a couple of beers and sit over there?" Hunter indicated a table in a distant corner of the bar.

The two men picked up their drinks and headed toward the remote corner. "So, Evan, I understand you need some legal help."

"I sure do, Mike."

"Well, why don't you fill me in."

Attorney Hunter listened intently while Evan Judd relayed the story. He told him about the charge of mail fraud as well as wearing a wire for the FBI. It was nearly ten thirty when Evan finished telling Hunter what had been going on.

When he had finished, they called Jessica and went out for a late supper. It was 1:30 a.m. when they returned to the hotel. The trio rode the elevator to their respective floors, and before getting off at his floor, Hunter told Evan to call him as soon as he heard from the FBI agents. Evan continued on with Jessica and walked her to her room.

"Would you like to come in?" she asked.

As much as he wanted to spend the night with her, he had concerns for her safety. He responded innocently, "No, I had better get some sleep before we have to go back to headquarters. They probably will be calling me early tomorrow. I need to be well rested to handle those boys." He took her in his arms and gave her a tender kiss and said goodnight.

Hunter took a shower and went to bed but could not sleep. He was troubled by the way Evan Judd was being manipulated by the FBI. He tossed and turned all night and decided to get in touch will Bill Forest first thing in the morning. He needed to brush up on the legalities of what was going on.

Three floors up, Evan Judd went directly to bed and fell into a deep, exhausted sleep. The ringing of the phone awakened him before his alarm went off the following morning. It startled him and set off an all too familiar panic. Gripped in fear, he picked up the phone. "Yes?"

"Judd. This is Swift. I want to warn you. No monkey business. The boss is beginning to put the scam together. My advice to you is cooperate. Tell him what he wants to know, and it may just keep you out of prison."

"Why are you warning me?" Evan inquired nervously.

"Because I think basically you're a pretty good guy. Got in over your head a little, maybe. You've cooperated with me and Cooper and I think we can continue to work together."

"What are they going to ask me?"

"I don't know, but cooperate. I gotta go. I shouldn't be calling you."

The line went dead. Evan sat in the dark room shaking. Sweat was beginning to trickle down his sides. He hung up the phone and hurried into the bathroom to throw some cold water on his face. As he dried off, he caught a glimpse of himself in the mirror. "Why?" he thought. "Why is this happening to me? I never did anything to hurt anyone. I was just earning a living."

The alarm in the bedroom started ringing pulling Evan into the reality of the moment. He put down the towel and returned to the bedroom to shut it off. Before going into the shower, he picked up the phone and called Hunter. "Mike?"

"Yes."

"Evan Judd. I just got another interesting call from Gordon Swift."

"Official?"

"No. A friendly warning."

"I'm not sure of his game. What did he say?"

"Just to cooperate."

"Did you ask him why he was warning you?"

"Yeah. He said he knew I was a good guy. Just got in over my head."

"Sure."

"He likes me, Mike."

"I don't know..."

"I cooperated. He likes that."

"Well, maybe..."

"I'm going to shower and dress now. There could be an official call any time."

"Call me as soon as you hear from them."

"I will." Evan put the phone down and headed for the shower.

By eight-thirty, Jessica could not contain herself another moment. She had gotten a call from her source, Nancy Newton, a few minutes earlier telling her that something was up. Evidently, they had learned something from one of their witnesses. She called Evan's room. "Evan?"

"Jess?"

"Yes. Have you heard anything?"

"Just Swift. He called real early. I'm waiting for the official call now."

"I'll be right up to wait with you. Have you had coffee?"

"No."

"I'll bring us some." Jessica returned the phone to the hook and went to the hotel coffee shop where she bought two cups of hot black coffee and took them to Evan Judd's room.

"Jess. I can't stand this waiting." He let her into the room.

"I know Evan. It is very difficult." She removed the lid from the styrofoam cup and handed it to him.

"Thanks," he said as he took a sip from the cup.

"I had a call from my source this morning," Jessica began as she threw the lids in the waste paper basket. "She told me she would meet me later today. She is sure 'something is up,' as she put it."

"Swift, too. He warned me to cooperate."

The phone rang interrupting them. Evan carefully picked up the receiver. "Yes?" he said quietly into the phone.

"It's Cooper. We need you here at headquarters. Get a cab. No cars are available this morning."

Evan looked as if he had been sentenced to death as he looked away from the phone and the line went dead. He felt weak as he sat down on the edge of the bed and looked helplessly at Jessica.

"What is it, Evan?"

"Evan!"

"Coo..Coop...Cooper."

"What did he say?"

"Evan, talk to me. What did Cooper say?"

"He said to take a cab to headquarters."

"Okay. You can do that. Let's call Mike."

"Okay." Evan hurried into the bathroom. His stomach could not hold the coffee.

When he came out of the bathroom, Jessica had Mike Hunter on the phone. "Here Evan. It's Mike."

"Mike. It's time to go to headquarters."

"I'll meet you in the lobby, Evan."

Jessica helped Evan with his jacket and straightened his tie. The couple then headed for the lobby to meet Michael Hunter.

"Good morning, Jessica, Evan." Hunter looked serious.

Jessica nodded and Evan stuck his hand out to him.

"I called Bill early this morning and told him what is going on here. He's going into the office early this morning to check on something and then he will catch the first flight available for New Orleans. His case has been delayed. I think we have some serious problems here."

Evan looked grim as he listened to Hunter.

"Bill is the man with the expertise in this type of representation. Now, what's happening here today?"

"We have to take a cab to headquarters," Evan responded in a flat, heavy voice.

"Okay. Let's do it."

"Jess, aren't you coming?" Evan looked back as Jessica stood still in the center of the lobby.

"No, no. You two go along. I have some work to do here. I'm expecting a call. I'll see if I can catch up with you later. You're in good hands, Evan."

The summer heat nearly knocked them over as they walked out the door of the hotel. It was unbearable and not a cab in sight. The doorman sat on a small seat outside the door. "You lookin for a cab?"

"Yes."

"Got one coming 'round in justa a minute. Hold on." He wiped the perspiration from his face with a huge white handkerchief. "Gonna be another hot one."

It seemed forever, but finally a cab appeared in front of the hotel. Evan and Mike got in.

"Where to?"

Evan told the driver the address of FBI headquarters and the driver pulled slowly away from the curb. "Could we have some air conditioning?" Evan inquired.

"Oh, sorry gentlemen. Been so hot here lately it busted and I ain't had time to get it worked on. Won't be's bad when we gets movin'."

Mike Hunter kept his eyes on the streets as the cab left the hotel and headed for FBI headquarters. Evan was consumed by his misery and fear. He was having difficulty catching his breath. Mike helped him as he squirmed out of his jacket and loosened his tie. The trip seemed to take forever.

The cabbie pulled up in front of the familiar government building and Evan pulled out his wallet and paid the driver. Familiar with the building and the routine, Evan silently led the way to the appropriate waiting area. Ian Cooper and Gordon Swift seemed to appear from nowhere as soon as they entered the door to the main floor that housed the FBI.

Cooper spoke, "Who's this?"

"This is my attorney, Michael Hunter. Mike this is Agent Cooper and Agent Swift."

They shook hands before Cooper continued. "Listen, we have had a slight change in our schedule. The boss is tied up with a key...er, a, ah with someone. You guys can wait in the waiting area."

They walked back into the interior of the huge room. "Judd, you know where the waiting area is. Why don't you just wait over there and we will come and get you as soon as the boss is ready."

It really wasn't a question. Evan nodded the direction to Mike and they continued on to the waiting area on the far side of the office while Agents Cooper and Swift disappeared into the sea of desks and people.

Meanwhile, back at the Latin Arms, Jessica Powers had been working on her article. She had several pieces of information she needed to check out through the Post's research department back home. It was about one o'clock when she decided to stop her work and go to the coffee shop in the Latin Arms for some lunch. She was just finishing her salad when she recognized a familiar voice call her name. She turned in the direction of the voice and came face to face with Bill Forest.

"Bill. How good to see you. Please join me."

Bill Forest approached Jessica and gave her a kiss on the cheek. "Jessica. How are you?"

"I'm so glad you are here, Bill. Mike told us this morning that he had contacted you but we weren't sure just when you would get here."

"It all worked out. First, the case I was working on got postponed. Then, I got lucky and I found the information I was looking for and was able to get on the first flight for New Orleans."

"My friend really needs your help, Bill. This is crazy what the FBI is putting him through."

"Where is he now? Where's Mike?"

"The FBI called this morning and told Evan to get over to headquarters this morning. Mike went with him. I've not heard from them since they left."

"Do you think we could meet them at headquarters?"

"Well, Bill, I'm not sure that's a good idea. We can't call them ahead, and they could very well be on there way back to the hotel. Besides, I'm not sure the Justice Department boys would be receptive to us barging in."

"That's true. I just wasn't familiar with the set up. I thought perhaps they might be outside of a complex of offices, or a building or..."

"Oh no. From everything Evan has told me, I gather they keep him pretty close at hand. I am familiar with the building, and from his descriptions, they have him within eye shot all the time. Again, they may be on there way back here anyway."

"Yes, you are probably right."

"Have you had lunch?"

"No, actually, I haven't. I was just beginning to realize how hungry I am."

"Well let's order you some lunch and then get you checked into the hotel. Evan and Mike may walk in any time now."

That didn't happen. Evan Judd and Mike Hunter continued to set in the FBI waiting area for the entire day. Every hour and a half or two, either Agent Cooper, Swift or Russo would stop by the area and tell them it would be a while longer. At quarter of six, Agent Cooper returned for one last word. "Looks like they aren't going to get to you until tomorrow, Judd. Be back here by eight-thirty." Cooper turned and was gone before Evan or Mike could respond.

Over eight long hours of waiting, and Evan Judd was showing signs of severe psychological stress. He remained terrified of going to prison, certainly, but the waiting game was really wearing him down. They left the hot stuffy waiting room and headed out of the building into the oppressive humid air of early evening in New Orleans. When they arrived back at the hotel, Jessica and Bill Forest were waiting for them in the lobby.

Mike addressed his partner. "Bill, this has been one hell of a day. I'm glad to see you. You know Evan Judd."

Bill Forest held out his hand, "Evan, how are you?"

"I could be a lot better," he replied solemnly.

"Evan, why don't get yourself a nice cool shower while Mike fills me in. Then we'll talk."

"I'll meet you in the bar as soon as I'm changed," responded Evan.

"If you gentlemen will excuse me, I know you have work to do." Jessica excused herself and walked with Evan to the elevator.

"Pretty rough?" Jessica looked lovingly at Evan.

"Yeah."

"Are you going to be alright, Evan?"

"Sure Jess. I'm just getting very tired of this stupid game of theirs."

"Did they interrogate you?"

"We waited. ALL DAY we waited."

"No questioning?"

"No questioning."

"Oh Evan."

"I can't take it Jess! I just can't take any more of this."

"Evan, I have known Bill Forest for several years. He's a good man. He'll help you."

When the elevator stopped on her floor, she gave Evan a quick hug and got off. "It will be alright."

Twenty minutes later, Evan Judd joined his lawyers in the bar. It was quiet and they decided they could discuss the case at a table in the far corner without being overheard.

Bill Forest spoke first. "Evan, Mike has filled me in on what has been going on with you and the FBI over the passed several months. In essence, what they are doing is making use of a little known law called *Federal Code.*"

"I don't understand." Evan looked perplexed as he tried to figure out what Bill Forest was getting at.

"Didn't you tell Mike that the FBI told you that they could charge you with mail fraud?"

"Yes, but they won't as long as I cooperate with them, they said."

"Exactly. According to Rule 35, subsection (b) of the Federal Code, they can keep you working for them at your expense until Doomsday if they want."

"I don't know. No." Judd shook his head. "I thought just this once."

"Did they say that?"

"Well no, but..."

"I did some research this morning. When Mike called, I remembered another case, not the same, but enough similarities to give me reason to believe that you are in for a long haul here."

"I couldn't stand to continue this much longer."

"You don't have to."

"But, I don't want to go to prison."

"It's a miserable choice, but they are going to bleed you dry if you continue with them. I haven't heard of anyone who ever came out of this kind of deal ahead."

Evan Judd fell quiet as he pondered the situation. He was not feeling well at all. The events of the past few months, his business, the marriage and this FBI investigation were taking their toll on his health. He didn't know how he could keep it up. But, what choice did he have?

"If you gentlemen will excuse me, I think I'll call it a night. I'm not feeling very well."

"Certainly Evan." Mike Hunter got to his feet and offered his right hand to Evan. "Bill is going to go with you tomorrow morning. I am returning to D.C. so I'll say so long for now."

"Thanks for coming Mike. I really appreciated having you with me today."

"That's quite alright, Evan. I'll be seeing you."

"Goodbye, Mike. See you a little before eight, Bill."

Evan Judd and Bill Forest took a cab to FBI headquarters and arrived at Evan's appointed time. Shortly after nine, Agents Swift and Cooper came for Evan Judd. "Judd, we are ready for you," Cooper said in a dry voice.

"Ah...Agent Cooper, Agent Swift, this is my attorney, Bill Forest."

"What's he here for?" Cooper barked.

"I just thought..."

"You don't need an attorney, Judd. You are just helping us with an investigation."

"But I'd like him to be with me."

"You really don't need a lawyer," Gordon Swift responded.

Cooper looked at Bill Forest. "Why don't you just wait right here, Forest? Mr. Judd won't be long."

"I think Mr. Judd would like me to accompany him. Is there a problem with that?"

"No. It's just unnecessary. The boss hates to have too many people at these preliminaries."

"Just the same, it is important to my client that I be with him."

"Well, I suppose. This way." A reluctant Agent Cooper led the way to the now familiar conference room in the back.

The room was empty as Cooper and Swift ushered the men in. "Sit anywhere, gentlemen."

As soon as Evan and Bill sat on one side of the long conference table, Cooper and Swift sat opposite them. In about five minutes, Agent Russo came to the door and stuck his head in. "I'll go get Maloney."

It took nearly twenty minutes for Russo to return with Maloney. Maloney was a big man, about six feet, three with graying hair. He was not overweight, but had a large, imposing frame. "Gentlemen. I'm Chief Investigator Maloney."

Maloney sat at the head of the table and began opening a file he had carried in with him. He said nothing for several moments.

Evan fidgeted nervously in his chair while Bill Forest kept his eyes on Chief Maloney. Swift and Cooper sat tall in their seats as they waited for the Chief Investigator to continue.

"According to my men, you have been cooperating in our investigation, Mr. Judd. They have been pleased with your cooperation and have suggested that you would be willing to help us continue our investigation of Erlich."

The sound of the name Erlich being spoken out loud in this FBI conference room sent chills down Evan Judd's spine on this hot day.

"We need to have someone go out to Syracuse, New York and make arrangements to purchase a hot agency he is trying to unload there. Russo has all of the details on this particular deal. I'll have him fill you in."

Maloney got to his feet. "Thanks for coming, gentlemen." He was gone from the conference room before anyone had an opportunity to speak.

Evan leaned into Bill Forest. "I don't usually do business in Western New York."

"Shhh. We'll talk later."

The four sat silently for nearly half an hour. Cooper and Swift watched Evan and Bill the entire time. Evan could hardly handle the mounting pressure when Joe Russo hurried into the room. "Sorry to keep you men waiting. Now let's get right down to business."

Russo sat on the opposite side of the table a couple of seats away from Cooper and Swift. "Okay, here's the address of the agency we want you to buy. Actually, it's in Cicero. We know that he's ready to unload it, Judd, and we want you to do whatever it is you need to do to make the deal. Agents Cooper and Swift will be with you all the way. Handle it like you did the last."

Evan Judd looked at his attorney. Bill Forest spoke, "We'll get back to you. Is that all?"

"That's it." Russo closed his file and pushed the sheet of paper with the agency address on it across the table at Evan. "Here."

The three agents got to their feet and immediately left the room. Cooper looked back over his shoulder as he was about to go out the conference room door, "You got our number here, Judd. Call us when you are set."

Evan Judd and Bill Forest got to their feet and headed for the door. "Let's get out of here, Evan."

Chapter 17

It was afternoon by the time Evan Judd and Bill Forest got back to the Latin Arms. It was clear to both men that Evan had reached impasse with the FBI. He was in a dangerous bind on both sides. If he was to continue working for the FBI, he could easily become suspect to Erlich and his organization which was life-threatening to say the least. If he did not, he would have to face charges and probably go to prison. Bill felt that Evan Judd had no choice but to face the charges brought against him.

Evan Judd remained panic stricken with the thought of going to prison. "But if I do this--just one more assignment, then, maybe, I'll be off the hook."

"Secretly taping is against the law. Evan, I can't let you do this."

"I don't know what to do Bill. I think they will let me go if I cooperate this time."

"Don't you see, Evan? They aren't ever going to let you go. Not ever!" The attorney was becoming exasperated. "As long as they can get you to work for them, at your expense, they will. It's wrong, but they have been getting away with it for years."

"Actually, money is becoming tight. The divorce, the Marlton deal, I'm not as liquid as I would like." His voice trailed off as consequences of the last several months began to impact him.

"What do you say we pack-up and get out of this hell-hole?" Bill Forest knew there really was no point in staying in New Orleans any longer. They needed to be back in their own element to work this out. He was also beginning to feel a little sorry for his client who seemed to have fallen in over his head. He was far from innocent, but there was something decent about him underneath it all.

"Yeah, Bill. I guess I know you are right. Let me tell Jessica we are leaving."

Evan went to the desk phone in the lobby and dialed Jessica's room. She answered on the first ring. "Jessica Powers."

"Jess, it's Evan."

"How did it go?"

"Not good. They gave me another assignment. Bill says not to go through with it. We're heading back north."

"Where are you?"

"We are in the lobby."

"When is your flight?"

"Bill is on the phone right now making arrangements."

"Will I see you before you leave?"

"I'm on my way up to my room to get my bag now. I'll stop on my way up."

They hung up and Evan turned to see what arrangements Bill had been able to make. "We are booked on the 5:30 flight to New York. We will have just enough time to get our things and head out to the airport."

"I'm going to stop off at Jessica's room and say goodbye."

"Let's get moving."

Bill Forest and Evan Judd reviewed the situation from beginning to end as the plane carried them back to New York. By the time they arrived at Kennedy International, Bill had pretty well convinced Evan that it was counter productive to continue working, or "cooperating" with the government, as they so advantageously put it. "Honestly Evan, it is pointless to continue," Bill had said. In reality, he knew the entire scam had been useless for his client from the very beginning. It was time to face formal charges. There would never be an end to his so-called assignments with the FBI. They had him over a barrel and they knew it. They agreed that Evan was to call Cooper in the morning and tell him he would not do the Syracuse assignment.

Harrington was waiting at the gate for his boss when the two men deplaned. Evan Judd was moved at the sight of his faithful employee. "Harrington, I told Edna not to send you."

"Yes sir, Mr. Judd. She told me. But I thought you wouldn't mind."

Evan appreciated the kindnesses from his long-time employee. For so many years, Harrington had always been there for him. Now, during this difficult time, neither he nor Edna were going to let him down. But Evan was beginning to sense that he would not be in a position to keep them in his employ much longer. His time was running out.

"Let me give you a lift to catch your next flight, Bill."

"I appreciate that, Evan."

The three men headed out of the terminal and to the waiting car. Harrington drove them to LaGuardia.

"Call me after you reach Cooper, Evan," Bill Forest said as he climbed out of the car.

"I'll do that, Bill."

Bill Forest disappeared into the airport as Harrington pulled away and headed for Manhattan. Evan Judd sat quietly in the back seat of the car. He felt overwhelmed with loneliness.

"Where to, Mr. Judd?" Harrington asked his boss as he looked at him in his rear view mirror. He was not the same vital man he had known for so many years.

"I guess I'll be spending the night in my office, Harrington. Just drop me there."

"Yes sir, Mr. Judd." Harrington was filled with pity for this man who had befriended him so many years ago. He wished he could help him, but as Edna said, "We can just continue to be there when he needs us." Edna could see the problems mounting. She was not exactly sure how bad it was. However, she did tell Harrington not to say a word but be prepared for the worst.

Night had fallen over the city as the car pulled up in front of the familiar Madison Avenue building. Harrington got out of the car and helped his boss with the bag. "Thanks Harrington. I can handle it from here."

Evan Judd walked slowly into the building and took the elevator to his office on the 74th floor. When the elevator opened, he got off and stood for a moment taking in this familiar sight which had represented his growing empire. "I never did anything to hurt anyone," he thought to himself. "I just needed to take care of my family. And now, they have deserted me." He walked slowly to his office and turned on the soft, indirect, overhead lighting. He dropped his bag on the sofa which was just inside the door against the wall. Then he walked slowly to the far end of the room and stood behind his desk looking out the window which provided him with his envious view of Manhattan. With its millions of lights turned on, it was, indeed, a breathtaking sight.

There were thousands upon thousands of people out there in that city, but he felt as alone as he did when he was that 13 year old boy arriving from England. His mother's cousin, Marion, was gone. Her husband, Earl, was never really interested in him anyway, so he had lost track of him as well as Earl Junior. Evie had moved to the West coast soon after high school, and he had not spoken with her for several years. He had not seen his sister for about three years now. She was married and very much involved with her grown family and grandchildren.

Now, his own family had deserted him and gone with Alice's father. And, if that weren't bad enough, his best friend and attorney, Frank Spector, had bailed out on him at the beginning of this whole mess. He sat down wearily in his chair and stared out at the lights as his mind drifted back over his life and how it had brought him to today and this sorry state of affairs.

When the racing season at Saratoga ended in August that summer of 1957, young Evan and Alice said their sad good-byes. They made arrangements so that they could contact each other by phone every couple of weeks. Alice was quite sick that fall, and her parents took her to several doctors before they found out that she was five months pregnant. At first, her parents were devastated. After the initial shock passed, Brandon Whitley became very, very angry. He demanded that Evan marry his daughter in the church, immediately. He would have sooner killed Evan, but, the child had to have a father and, in the eyes of the church, his beautiful baby needed to be married to have this child.

So, in the middle of January, 1958, the couple was married by a priest in a small rectory next to the Catholic church on New Scotland Avenue in Albany, New York. Brandon Whitley set them up in a small apartment in Delmar and saw to it that Evan had a job in the insurance business.

Evan continued his high school education in night school, and Alice dropped out of school and learned how to keep house. Evan Jr. arrived early one morning during the spring of 1959. He was a colicky baby who cried a lot and, if it had not been for the Whitley religion, the marriage might well have ended that same year. Neither Alice or Evan was equipped to handle the demands of a baby or marriage.

But somehow, they persisted. Evan got his high school diploma and began to do very well in the insurance business. The extra money he began making helped and the marriage began to thrive. Evan, Jr. outgrew his colic and before long, they had enough money to move to a more comfortable apartment. Alice got pregnant again, and nine months later gave birth to their beautiful and healthy Julie. Evan moved on up the insurance business ladder.

It was around this time that he was put in contact with John Hughes at the Hudson River Insurance Agency. He remembered it was John who made the arrangements to hook him up with Erlich. He could remember the day he went to Troy and had lunch with John and Dick Seaman. It was Dick who warned him to be careful about putting anything illegal in the mail. "Sending anything questionable through United States Postal Service is risky business. At the very least, you could get nailed for mail fraud." The guy was successful. He had no reason to doubt him.

The phone ringing sometime later brought him back to the present with a jolt. "Hello?" His voice seemed to echo in the quiet of the empty office.

"I thought I might find you there."

"Jessica. I'm so glad you called."

"Are you okay, Evan."

"Yes. But I feel so terribly alone. I'm losing everything, Jess. Bill wants me to call Cooper and not continue, as he says, 'working for the FBI.' He says they will keep using me and I will still have charges to face in the end anyway. He feels the whole thing has been useless for me."

"Bill Forest is a good man, Evan. I think you have no choice but to listen to him. From the information I am getting on this end, I have to believe they are closing in here. Do what he says, Evan."

"When will you be coming back to Washington, Jess?"

"I can't leave now, Evan. There is too much going on here. But, I will be back as soon as I can."

"I wish you were here Jessica Powers. I love you so much."

"I love you, too, Evan. My life would be easier if I didn't, but I do. I'll talk with you soon."

"I miss you. So long, Jess."

"Goodbye for now, Evan."

Evan decided the best he could do was try to get some sleep. "Morning will be here all too soon," he thought wearily as he headed into the adjacent room. "It would be wise to have a few hours of sleep before I talk to Cooper. That challenge will need a clear, rested head."

It was shortly before nine in the morning when Edna Carlisle arrived. As was her routine, she checked her boss's office to be certain that everything was in order before beginning the day. When she entered, she noticed that the door to his private room was ajar. She carefully went inside to discover her boss asleep on the sofa. He was still wearing his white shirt and suit pants from the day before. "He doesn't look good," she thought as she stood looking at him trying to decide whether to wake him or let him sleep.

As if he sensed someone in the room, Evan opened his eyes. "Edna. What time is it?" he asked as he jumped to his feet.

"It's about ten minutes before nine, sir." replied Edna.

"I had no idea I would sleep at all, let alone this long. I need to shower and change. I have some important business I must attend to this morning."

"I'll get you some coffee while you are doing that, Mr. Judd."

Evan Judd quickly showered and dressed. When he came out of his inner suite, Edna had left coffee, Danish, and his newspaper on the sterling coffee service as usual. Once again, he was deeply moved by the attention of his devoted employee. He could not bare the thoughts of his world,(this world that he had worked so hard to cultivate), coming to an end. He decided he would not think of that for now. He would take care of the business at hand. He poured his coffee and went to his desk to place his call to Cooper.

As he sat behind the desk, he became so nervous he could hardly breathe. He noticed his hand was trembling as he tried to hold the cup of coffee. He picked up the phone and dialed the number. On the second ring, the voice at the other end responded, "Cooper." That was all.

"Agent Cooper, this is Evan Judd."

"Yeah, Judd," the brusque, condemnatory voice responded.

"Ah, Agent Cooper, I can't go on with the assignment in Syracuse," Evan could hardly get the words out, he was so nervous. He fidgeted with the cord to the phone.

"What the hell are you talking about, Judd?" an incredulous Cooper asked.

He consciously tried to breathe. "I'm sorry. I'm not going to be able to do the assignment you asked me to do. I'm sorry. Very sorry." Evan was shaking so badly he could hardly speak.

"Judd, I hope you are kidding."

"No, no sir, I'm not kidding. I can't take your next assignment."

"Are you sure?"

"I'm, I'm quite sure."

"Oh, damn it Judd." Cooper seemed to be softening.

"I'm sorry," Evan repeated.

"Judd, you've got to."

"No sir, I can't."

"Come on, Judd."

"No sir."

"I see." Cooper was quiet for a moment. "I was hoping you would continue. I hate to have the big boys press charges," Cooper seemed almost concerned.

"You know, I don't want that to happen either. Can't you just let it go?" Evan sounded almost pitiful.

"If it were up to me, Judd, I might. But I'm afraid it is out of my hands when you stop cooperating, you know, stop taking assignments. Then your case goes to the higher ups."

"But, maybe if you tell them I cooperated."

"It's out of my hands once you stop."

"I see."

"Are you sure Judd?" asked Cooper one last time. "Just do the Syracuse job."

"Sorry."

"Well, good luck, Judd."

"Thanks Cooper."

Evan put the phone down and leaned back in his chair. The relationship that had developed over the last several weeks was a strange one at best. For weeks now, Cooper and Swift had been threatening, manipulating him. Now that it was coming to a close, it was as if they cared about him.

Evan Judd was becoming a broken man. He could hardly think what to do next. Then he remembered Bill Forest. He had to call Bill. He picked up the phone and dialed Bill's Washington office.

"Forest, Abrams and Hunter," the voice at the other end sang.

"Give me Bill Forest. This is Evan Judd calling."

"One moment, Mr. Judd."

"Evan. Did you call?" inquired Forest.

"I did," responded Evan.

"And?" Bill pushed.

"And, said I would not take the Syracuse assignment. And you know what, Bill?" asked Evan.

"What?"

"He actually was disappointed. Cooper really cared about me, Bill. He wanted me to continue. He more or less said he would drop the charges against me if it was up to him."

"Is that it? Are they dropping the charges?"

"I don't know. He said it was out of his hands. It goes to higher ups."

"So now what?"

"I don't know, Bill. I just don't know."

Although he went through the motions of business as usual, the week was anything but. He sent his faithful driver, Harrington, on an extended vacation to visit family in Charlotte. Clearly, he didn't need a driver when he was virtually living in his office nowadays. He knew he had to get on with the separation, but he was waiting for the "other shoe to fall" so to speak, with the Justice Department. He knew, too, that along with the formality of the separation, came the end of life as he knew it. He loved his children, but they were deeply influenced by Alice and their Grandfather. It was not their fault. Perhaps he had not been available to them as much as he should have been over the years. "But, damn it, I had to provide for them," he consoled himself. "They had the best!"

Jessica Powers remained in New Orleans but was out on business most of the time. Consequently, she was not in her room to take each despondent phone call Evan placed. So, he spent most of the lonely weekend agonizing over potential plans that would effectively close down his business operation should the need soon arise. He talked with Bill Forest at home a couple of times to check some legalities. Calls to Forest served to insure his sanity as well. By Monday morning, he was ready to take his long-time employee, Edna Carlisle, into his confidence and make preparations to meet the situation head on.

When she arrived, she immediately went into Evan's office as she had done for so many years. "Good morning, Mr. Judd."

Touched by her "business as usual" routine, Evan found he had to clear the emotions welling up in his throat before he could confront her with his plans. "Ah hmm. Ah Edna, bring two cups with coffee this morning, if you would please."

"Yes sir. I'm sorry. I didn't know that you had an appointment this morning. There is no one on my calendar for you."

"No Edna. I would like for us to have coffee together this morning. There are many things I wish to discuss with you."

"Certainly sir. Right away."

Edna quickly prepared the coffee, and as she returned to his office, Evan was moving toward her indicating that they would be having their coffee informally in the sitting area.

Their meeting began awkwardly with mutual exchanges of appreciation for years of dedication on both sides. Then Evan shared the latest news concerning the expected charge which was to come from the FBI. "And so, Edna, I have no idea how this will all work out, but we need to prepare."

Edna Carlisle looked grim. She had shed a few inevitable tears. But it was not her custom to be overtly emotional in times of crisis. She was solid. Dependable. "I will have everything ready, Mr. Judd. You can be sure of it."

As their meeting was winding down, there was a knock at the door. Edna was exasperated. "I told that girl not to interrupt us under any circumstance. I don't know why I have kept Betty this long. You can be sure it won't be difficult for me to let this one go," she sputtered as she went to the door to respond to the persistent knocking.

Edna opened the door with much irritation and was instantly face to face with a burly looking man in his mid fifties. "What do YOU want?" she said in a shocked, yet irritated voice. "Who let you in here? How dare you stand knocking at this door."

"Are you Evan Judd?" the man looked passed Edna.

She was not deterred. "I beg your pardon."

Again he ignored her.

Surprised by the interruption, Evan found his voice and responded positively.

The stranger walked directly into the office. "This is for you." The stranger handed Evan the envelope, turned on his heel, and walked back past a stunned Edna Carlisle and beyond, out of sight.

Evan just stood there looking at the envelope in his hand for a moment. Edna Carlisle was obviously completely flabbergasted. "Mr. Judd. I'm sorry. He had no right to be in here."

"Edna. It's okay. Let's see what it is. We knew I had to hear from the Justice Department sometime soon. It might as well be now."

"But Mr. Judd, I feel responsible. She is my assistant. I hired her. I should have let her go months ago."

"Edna, Edna. It's not what we thought. It's from my wife's attorney."

Almost relieved by the unexpected summons and complaint, Evan headed automatically for his desk where he sat down to look at the papers. Edna followed and sat on the edge of her chair in front of his desk waiting for him to speak. After riffling through several sheets of paper, he spoke, "It's over Edna. The marriage is over. She wants everything."

"But what about you, Mr. Judd?"

"At this point, Edna, I don't know. I guess we look at first things first. She's got nearly everything now and I have to find out what's going to happen to me."

"But what about the house?"

"I don't know. Of course, she wants it. I guess I will have to get to that. But for now, it is important that we handle the business affairs. We've got to start letting the employees go. I figure I can give them a two-week severance, but I can't afford to keep paying them. So you are going to have to notify everyone today. That way, payroll will end by next Friday."

"I understand, Mr. Judd. I'll get right on it."

"Good. I'll start pulling papers for the shredder. We'll do that as soon as you are through notifying everyone."

Edna left the office and Evan acted as if he was about to start digging into the business records. Instead, he opened his top draw and started looking at the summons once again. He had been too emotionally unnerved to express the grief he felt with the loss of his family and everything he had worked so hard for. As he slowly turned in his chair toward the window overlooking the city, his shoulders shook as he could no longer hold back tears of deep sadness. He pulled the papers toward him as he quietly sobbed.

It was afternoon when Evan Judd realized he had not eaten all day. He slid into his suit jacket and headed for the door of his office. He stopped at Edna's desk to see how she was doing with her charge and advised her that he was going out for a bite to eat.

CHAPTER 18

IT WAS NEARLY AN hour later. Edna had completed the task of notifying all employees when Agents Swift and Cooper walked into her office. Swift spoke, "Ms. Carlisle, we need to speak to your boss."

"He's not here."

"Do you expect him back?"

Edna was clipped. "Sometime."

"Today?" Swift continued civilly.

"Probably. I don't know."

"We'd like to wait for him."

She gave them a sarcastic look, "I certainly can't stop you."

Cooper grabbed Swift's arm gently and pointed for him to go into Evan Judd's office. He spoke as they headed inside to wait, "Thank you, Ms. Carlisle."

After she determined they were out of earshot, Edna made half a dozen or so unsuccessful attempts to locate her boss but to no avail. She really had no idea where he had gone. Within twenty minutes, Evan Judd returned. Hearing the elevator bell ring, Edna was on her way to meet him at the elevator door as soon as he appeared.

In a whispered but frantic voice, she warned him, "Mr. Judd. They've come. They're here, they're here in your office. Waiting. Waiting for you. I didn't know what to do."

He had stopped and was leaning toward her, listening. Trying to make sense of what she was telling him. "Who Edna? Who is here?"

Evan's mind had been focus on thoughts of ending his thirty some odd year marriage.

"The FBI, Mr. Judd. The FBI!"

The color drained from his face as his body started to go limp. He felt sick and faint at the same time. "Oh God, Edna."

"Oh Mr. Judd. What shall we do?"

"Oh God, Edna, no. Tell me this is not happening."

Edna started to cry. Seeing his long-time employee and confidant breakdown provided Evan Judd with a real, even greater sense of fear for his own future. He mumbled, "It's alright, Edna. I'll see them," and continued moving toward his door. He was weak and his legs were shaking by the time he entered his own office. As he entered, both agents got to their feet. Cooper spoke first. "Judd, we have come to notify you that you have been indicted by the Grand Jury."

"Cooper wait," Agent Swift cut in on Cooper as he began to conduct there official business. "Mr. Judd, please. Why don't you have a seat. You don't look so well."

"Ah, yes, thank you. I, ah, feel a little weak."

"Please, have a seat right here." Gordon Swift indicated the chair in front of Evan's desk where he had been sitting.

Evan Judd sat pathetically in the chair as the two Agents tried to continue with their business.

Swift continued. "Mr. Judd, you pretty much know why we are here. As Cooper said, the Grand Jury has indicted you and a warrant has been issued for your arrest. A Federal Marshall was coming to pick you up. But we felt that, well, we wanted to come ourselves."

"You've been cooperative with us, so we felt that we'd rather handle it this way," Cooper interjected.

"You are to appear before the Federal Magistrate for arraignment tomorrow morning at 10:00 a.m.," Swift continued quietly.

Cooper handed him some papers. "Here, the address is 333 Constitution Avenue, N. W. It's right here," he pointed to the information on the document.

"Are you going to be okay?" Swift asked Evan. "Do you want us to get your secretary?"

"No, no," replied Evan in a barely audible voice, "I'm okay."

"We'll see you in court tomorrow then."

"Take care of yourself Judd. You don't look too good."

The two agents closed the door behind them leaving Evan sitting in the chair staring down at the carpet. He didn't move. As soon as the FBI agents were back on the elevator, Edna Carlisle, who had been monitoring the office the whole time, got to her feet and hurried inside. "Mr. Judd. Oh Mr. Judd, what happened?" she said as soon as she entered the office and continued toward her boss. When she got a look at the sorry shell of a man who had been so vital, she nearly gasped but caught herself. "Are you alright, Mr. Judd? Here, let me get you a nice glass of cold water."

Edna hurried into the inner office and ran the tap to cool the water and they reached to the ice maker to add some ice to the glass. She returned and squatted down in front of him. "Mr. Judd, here, drink this. Please, sir, have a sip of water."

As if he was coming out of a trance, Evan mumbled something that sounded like dying in prison, and then seemed to notice Edna. "Please sir. Drink this."

Evan took the glass from Edna and took a small sip. "One more, please, Mr. Judd. You look faint."

He took a couple more swallows of the liquid and returned the glass to Edna. "I'm okay, Edna. Thank you."

"Are you sure, Mr. Judd? Do you want me to call your doctor?"

"No Edna, I'm just very upset. I guess I never really believed it would happen."

The ringing of his private line interrupted their conversation. "Do you want me to answer that, Mr. Judd? Or should we just let it ring?"

"Let's answer it Edna. It could be my attorney."

Edna approached the phone with hesitation. "Mr. Judd's office," she answered cautiously.

"Miss Carlisle?" the voice at the other end of the line inquired.

"Yes," again with caution that someone would personally identify her.

"This is Jessica Powers. Is Evan there?"

Edna put her hand over the mouthpiece and whispered loudly to Evan, "It's Miss Powers. Do you want to speak with her?"

"Yes, of course, Edna. Give me the phone."

Edna used her best business manners. "Just a moment please." She handed the receiver to Evan as he got up from the chair and walked toward his desk.

"Jessica."

"Evan. I only have a moment before my plane takes off but I wanted to warn you. They have a warrant out for Erlich. A guy by the name of Weatherwax spilled his guts. The FBI knows the whole scam and they are trying to find Erlich now. It just happened this morning, and I am on my way back to Washington right now. It's all over here. I just wanted to warn you. Oh... they are calling my flight number. We are boarding right now."

"Jess, I'm being arraigned tomorrow."

There was complete silence then, "WHAT?"

"I'm being arraigned tomorrow."

"Dear God, Evan. I didn't know."

"Swift and Cooper just left."

"What happened?"

"They told me the Grand Jury had indicted me."

"I'm so sorry. Evan, there's my final call. I've got to go. I'll call you. Where will you be?"

"Here."

"Hang in there, Evan."

He heard the line disconnect and the dial tone engage before he put the phone back in the cradle. He stood looking at the phone for a few moments before he noticed Edna who had been sitting in the chair in front of him. She had learned what had happened as he spoke to Jessica. She wiped her eyes with a tissue and then looked up at him expectantly.

"Edna, we have work to do."

"Yes sir."

Evan made arrangements for the following day with Bill Forest as Edna executed the plans to destroy records and files. Fortunately, almost every employee had been notified in the morning and the immediate office was completely void of people. They had the rest of the afternoon and all night to clean out. It would take them that long.

By 4:30 a.m., Evan was getting into the rental car he had secured and began driving to Washington where he would meet his attorney and go on to court. To save time, they agreed it would be best to meet in one of the conference rooms in the Federal Building prior to arraignment. The trip was uneventful and although he stopped at one of the rest areas on Interstate 95 in Maryland for coffee to perk him up, he had no difficulty keeping awake. He was so wired he doubted that he would ever sleep again. When he reached the city, he dropped the car off at the rental agency and took a cab to the courthouse.

It was just quarter to ten when Evan walked up the steps of the Federal Courthouse. Bill Forest was waiting for him outside the door. They shook hands and went inside. "There is a conference room just down the hall we can use." The two men hurried down the hall and into the small room where they sat down at the table. Bill Forest leaned toward his client and, with concern in his voice, spoke to him. "Well Evan, I guess this is it. How are you doing?"

"I'm scared, Bill. Jessica called me and told me that Weatherwax had spilled his guts and that there is a warrant out on Erlich."

"Oh, that reminds me. Jessica called me at home early this morning to have me tell you that she would be here this morning. She said she couldn't get through to you last night to let you know. She called to ask me the time and place."

A spark of life returned to Evan's eyes. "I was hoping she would come."

"We have pretty much covered all that needs to be covered for now. They will use a standard format. You just answer the questions. If you have any concerns, ask me before your respond."

"Okay," Evan responded weakly.

"It's nearly five minutes to ten. We'd better get on down to the courtroom. All set?"

"Yup. All set."

"Good." The two men got up from their chairs and started walking down the long corridor to the courtroom. Just before they walked through the doors, Evan Judd grabbed Bill Forest's arm and pulled him back to the side of the double doors. Bill looked at Evan with great surprise, "We have to go in, now, Evan."

"I know, Bill. I just wanted to tell you something before we do."

"What is it Evan. We can't afford to be late and irritate the judge."

"I know. I just wanted to tell you that I'm *not guilty*."

"What?" an incredulous Bill Forest gasped.

"I'm not guilty of mail fraud."

Bill Forest pushed Evan away from the door and over to the side wall. "What are you talking about, Evan?" Bill spoke hurriedly in a hushed voice.

"I never committed mail fraud. I never mailed an illegal check or sent any money illegally in the U. S. mail."

"Jesus, Evan. Then you are not guilty?"

"No, I'm not."

"Then plead not guilty."

"I can't."

"Why?"

"Because they'll get me."

"Who?"

"Erlich."

"Damn it, Evan. I wish you had told me before."

"It wouldn't have made any difference."

Bill Forest shock his head in disbelief then looked at his watch. "Let's get in there. It's ten."

They just barely got to the front of the courtroom when the clerk began the proceedings. "All rise."

Bill Forest stood at attention beside his client as the clerk went through the formality of opening the arraignment and the Judge took the bench. When they were told to sit down, Bill leaned toward Evan and spoke into his ear. "If you are innocent, plead not guilty."

Evan starred straight ahead. The Federal Judge studied the papers before him. Finally he spoke. "Evan Judd? Are you present?"

Evan got to his feet and Bill stood beside him. "Yes, your honor."

"Good."

The judge was silent for a moment before he began. Evan's mind filled with surreal images as the judge commenced reading him his rights. "Evan Judd you have the right to remain silent," the judge began.

Evan's legs felt as if they were too weak to hold him by the time the judge got the end of his Miranda statement. How would he ever be able to continue on?

The judge continued," You are hereby charged with one count of mail fraud. Do you understand the charges?"

"I do, your honor."

"How so do you plead?"

The judge looked directly at Evan, waiting for an answer. The room was absolutely still and quiet. Evan Judd struggled for several moments to find his voice which then seemed to echo as he responded,

"Guilty your honor."

There was a stir of voices and movement in the courtroom when he responded. Then, after what seemed an eternity to Evan who felt his legs would no longer hold him, the judge said, "Please be seated."

"From the information which has been provided to me by the prosecution, I feel that the court will be able to schedule sentencing by tomorrow."

The judge looked toward the U. S. Attorney, "What is your position on releasing this criminal pending sentencing?"

The prosecutor was on his feet, "I recommend that the defendant be released on his own recognizance without bail pending sentencing, your honor."

"Mr. Judd, I feel that it would be expeditious for you to remain in the District until court resumes tomorrow morning at ten a.m. You are to let the court know of your whereabouts should you have to leave the city. Under no circumstances, are you to leave the country. Is that clear, Mr. Judd?"

"Yes sir."

"Then you are free to go about your business in the city as long as you continue to obey the laws. We will reconvene here tomorrow morning at ten a.m."

The judge pounded his gavel signaling the end of the proceeding. As soon as he was through the door to his chamber, the courtroom was alive with noise. During the hearing, Evan had been unaware that there were people there other than his attorney and the prosecutor and an assistant. He looked around to see who was there.

Agents Swift and Cooper. They seemed to be involved with several other people who must have been from the Justice Department as well. Evan asked Bill, "Who are all of those people with Cooper and Swift?"

"Well, some, of course, are FBI, but several of them are with the Department of Corrections. Between them, they will work out a recommendation for your sentencing."

Evan grabbed the edge of the desk as the reality of the prison term made impact on him. "Oh God, Bill, I don't know how I can survive."

"I don't know what to say to you Evan. You do remember that bombshell you dropped on me outside the courtroom?" Bill responded in a somewhat perturbed manner.

The two began to move toward the aisle to leave the courtroom so that they could talk privately. Just before Evan spotted Jessica in the next to the last row, he saw two men hurrying along the back wall toward the exit. For a moment, he though he recognized one of them, but as soon as he saw Jessica, he dismissed all other thoughts. She waived from the back. He hurried to her and they embraced momentarily.

Bill Forest joined them. In a strange way, he was relieved to see the person who had gotten him into this strange case in the first place. He gave her a friendly peck as he greeted her. "Jessica. Good to see you."

"Bill, I'm glad you are here."

The three made their way from the courtroom. Evan spoke first. "What now?"

"We've got to go upstairs and meet with the Correction Department for a pre-sentencing investigation. It could take the better part of the day. I'd like to speak with you for a few minutes before we meet with them."

Jessica got the cue. "I'm on my way back to the paper. Is there anything either of you would like me to do?"

"No Jessica. Thanks," responded Bill.

Evan looked desperately at Jessica, "Will I see you tonight?"

"Oh Evan, I'm not sure when. I'm on deadline now, but I will see you somehow." She looked at Bill, "Where do you plan to put him up?"

"I thought at the Hyatt near Capital Hill. It's convenient to my office."

"Good. I call you later, Evan."

"Okay, Jess."

She hurried out the door to the Federal Building as Evan and Bill went down the hall to the conference room where Bill prepared Evan for the events of the next several hours.

While far from grueling, the questioning was intense. "Do you have family?"

"Yes."

"Where are they now?"

Then he had to explain the personal dilemma he was in with a pending divorce. What about his children? Did he have relatives out of the country? This meant that the story of the untimely death of his parents which had long ago been put to rest had to once again be rejuvenated and rehashed. The next logical question in the chronology then would follow. Who took him in? Where are they now? And so on.

There were the person-specific questions: How was his health? Did he use drugs? Had he ever been convicted before? Again, there was a multitude of questions.

It was shortly after six in the evening when the Corrections Department investigation was finished. Bill Forest, of course, remained at Evan Judd 's side throughout the questioning. They were relieved to walk out of the building and take a breath of fresh air. "My car is just two blocks away. Why don't we walk. I'll drop you at the hotel on my way back to the office."

"Thanks Bill. Thanks for everything."

They drove quietly to the hotel where Bill dropped Evan at the front door. The doorman opened the door for Evan and he got out as Bill leaned over and spoke to his client, "I'll pick you up here tomorrow morning at nine-thirty."

"Okay, Bill. See you then."

Evan checked into the Hyatt and found a message from Jessica which asked that he give her a call when he got in. He did immediately. "Jessica?"

"Evan. How did it go?"

"It was a long day."

"Can I take you out for dinner?"

"Of course."

"I'll be there within fifteen minutes."

There reunion dinner was far from celebratory. They decided to remain at the hotel and have dinner in the restaurant up top. They were both very tired but wanted to be together. As they talked, Evan discussed with Jessica the guilty plea he had made and how opposed to it Bill had been. "Jess, I am scared, really scared of prison, but I know, I just know for certain that Erlich will get me if I don't. I guess I'd rather take my chances with prison than to risk losing my life on the outside."

"But Evan, they will soon find Erlich. He will be behind bars. Then he will no longer be a threat."

"Jess, he's a powerful man. He will get to me. I know he will-- whether he is on the outside or inside."

"I hate to see you go to jail. But to go to prison for something you didn't do is outrageous."

"Oh my God." Evan turned white as a sheet.

"Evan. You are frightening me. What is it? Are you alright?"

"Jessica. I just remembered who it was that I saw leaving the hearing today. I only got a very quick glimpse of him out of the corner of my eye just before I saw you."

"Who?"

"It was Harold Turner."

"Harold Turner? Are you sure?"

"Oh dear, God, Jessica. I know it was him. I'm sure."

"Evan. Please try to calm down."

"Oh Jessica. What would have happened if I hadn't pleaded guilty?"

"I don't know."

"He would have shot me right there, Jess. I know these people. He would have shot me on the spot."

"Let's get out of here, Evan."

Evan signaled the waiter who he brought them their check. He quickly paid it and they went back to his room. Once in the room, Evan still could not calm down. Jessica opened the mini bar and made them a drink. "Here." She handed him a brandy. "Please sit down and drink this. You'll feel better."

"Jessica, I don't know how I will get through the night."

"I'll stay with you. Just please try to calm down. Just try to relax for now. Sit right here."

Evan sat on the sofa beside her. He took a big gulp of his brandy. It began to warm him instantly. He took another sip and put his arm around her. He began to feel grateful for this strong beautiful woman at his side. They sat quietly for awhile. Eventually, the alcohol began to serve its purpose of calming his nervous system and loosening him up. He was beginning to breathe easier. He finished the brandy. "Can I get you another?" he asked as he walked over to the bar to refill his glass.

"I'm fine, thank you."

Evan returned to the sofa. The color was returning to his face and he was clearly more relaxed. He took a sip of his drink and placed the glass on the table in front of them. He turned to Jessica, "I don't know how to tell you how much you mean to me. I love you with all my heart. If it weren't for you..."

Jessica gently placed the tips of her fingers over his lips to prevent him from continuing. He kissed her fingers and wrapped his arm around her. As he held her arm and kissed the palm of her hand, he pulled her toward him. Their lips met for a brief moment before he moved his lips tenderly toward her ear. "I'll love you always, Jessica Powers," he whispered.

She pulled his head toward her mouth once again and they kissed passionately, longingly. She pressed her body against his. He unzipped her dress and eased it from her shoulders as his mouth covered hers. She returned his eagerness, willingly and passionately. There was no indication of awkwardness or shyness as they became consumed in each other. Their fervor and raw lust allowed them no time to slip over to the bed. They consummated their animal desires there on the small sofa. It was much later when they crawled onto the cool white sheets of the king-sized bed and fell sound asleep.

They awakened in each others arms just before dawn. Evan held Jessica and looked deeply and urgently into her eyes. It seemed inconceivable to both of them that their love for each other was so committed, so complete in and of itself. They seemed to have it all as long as they had each other.

"I'm going to slip back to my apartment and change. I need to stop by the paper before court. Will you be alright? Do you have a ride?"

"Yes. Bill is picking me up at nine-thirty. And, yes, I'll be alright." He gently stroked her hair, "Darling, having you has made a tremendous difference in my life. Last night I realized that with you, I could face anything."

He became more positive with each word. As he repeated "anything," the passion of his youth could once again be distinguished. "Jessica, had you been in my life earlier, all of this probably would not have even happened. But it did. Now I have to face it and, perhaps," he carefully tested her commitment, "move on with my life, and with you once this is finished."

Jessica could feel the excitement building in her as he spoke. "Oh Evan, I love you. We'll get through this. I am not going anywhere without you." They locked in an ardent, fiery embrace and soon became one again.

It was nearly eight by the time Jessica left the hotel and headed toward her apartment in the early morning rush hour. Somehow, this morning, traffic did not seem to bother her. Jessica Powers was deeply in love.

"All rise. All rise. Federal District Court is now in session. The Honorable Justice Harry P. Brown is presiding."

Justice Brown ambled into the courtroom as Evan Judd and his attorney stood at attention waiting to be seated. The Judge indicated that everyone should take a seat and they did.

Judge Brown addressed the court. "I have been provided with the recommendation of the Corrections Department," he tapped the folder in front of him, "and I have no problem accepting their recommendation."

The Judge looked out into the courtroom. "Evan Judd, are you present?"

"He is, your honor," Bill Forest was on his feet addressing the court for his client.

"And you are?"

"I represent Mr. Judd, your honor. I am his attorney, William Forest."

"I see. Is your client prepared to face the charges and sentencing for his crime, Mr. Forest?"

"He is, your honor."

"Would you please rise Mr. Judd?"

Evan got to his feet. The court became very still. Jessica Powers who was sitting in the row directly behind him closed her eyes for a moment as she pulled her notebook to her chest. The room remained quiet as the Judge looked at the notes. Finally, he spoke. "According to this, Mr. Judd, the Justice Department seems to feel that you are a pretty decent guy who got himself in over his head and engaged in some misguided activities among which, one such act was, in fact, illegal. For that crime, they feel you should pay. However, because you have attempted to redeem yourself in their eyes as well as in the eyes of the law, they recommend that minimum security is needed as far as prison. From what I have been able to determine, I concur with their recommendations."

"Mr. Judd, you have pleaded guilty to one count of mail fraud. Do you have anything further you wish to say?"

"Your honor, I am truly sorry for any wrong I have committed. I ask the court and society's forgiveness. I was young and foolish and meant no harm. I was trying to provide for my family. I am deeply sorry for breaking the law."

"I believe you, Mr. Judd, and obviously the Justice Department seems to lean favorably toward you." He cleared his throat and picked up the paper in front of him and continued. "Therefore, it is the recommendation of this court that you be incarcerated in the Federal Correctional Institution at Fairton for a term of three years and fined two hundred and fifty thousand dollars. Your term will commence immediately." He picked up his gavel and slammed it down on the bench. "Court dismissed."

As soon as the judge was out of sight, Evan turned to Jessica and they embraced. The courtroom was buzzing with talk. As Evan looked up from Jessica, he could see Agents Swift and Cooper approaching. His eyes looked beyond them as he noted two familiar faces at the far side of the courtroom. The bigger man who was now looking directly at him, reached his right hand to his forehead in a mock salute. It was Harold Turner. Turner nudged the man next to him who turned to look at Evan. "Son of a b... it was Oarlock's number one henchman." Evan's heart skipped a couple of beats as he identified the men. Oarlock was Erlich's boss. He had been correct in his analysis of the situation. They were big league. Had he not pleaded guilty, the end would not be far off.

The Federal Marshall cautiously approached Evan and his attorney. "Excuse me, Mr. Judd. My deputy and I will be taking you to prison in New Jersey. Let us know when you are ready."

"Well, Evan, I guess we better not aggravate the Federal Marshall. Jessica and I will follow you up to the prison just to be sure."

Evan was clearly grateful for Jessica and Bill. "I'm indebted." He turned and gave Jessica one last hug and turned to the Marshall. "I guess this is it, Marshall."

It was mid afternoon when the convoy arrived at the gate to the prison. The guard knew they were coming and waved them through. When they got to the main entrance, the Federal Marshall got out of the vehicle that was carrying his prisoner and went back to speak with Bill and Jessica. "You are going to have to wait until we get Mr. Judd through the formalities: search, finger-printing, and so forth."

"About how long will that take?"

"He should be through by six o'clock."

"We'll take a drive into town and have something to eat. We'll be back around six. Do we need a pass or something?"

"No just tell the guard you are coming back when you go out the gate."

"Thank you sir," Bill said to the Marshall. He made a U-turn in the drive and headed back to the main gate.

It was just after six when Bill and Jessica entered the small prison. Much to their surprise, Evan greeted them when they entered the reception area and led them back to his modest, but comfortable quarters.

CHAPTER 19

Prison was nothing at all like what Evan had expected. Actually, the facility provided him with many of the necessary creature comforts he would find necessary. His "cell," or living quarters, was actually an apartment complete with kitchenette, private bath, small but adequate bedroom and sitting area. He shared a common business area with several of the other "white collar" criminals. He, in fact, enjoyed the company of some rather sophisticated men.

With the help of Edna Carlisle, Evan closed down all of his interests in the insurance business. The FBI closed down the agency in Marlton and confiscated the records and files which, fortunately, were that of John Philip Erlich.

Alice Whitley Judd pursued the divorce. Evan did not oppose it. Their Connecticut estate was put on the market and all proceeds were to be divided equally among the children. Evan hadn't heard from them since he was in prison, but that was not surprising considering the circumstances. Also, he knew that Alice and her father would continue a campaign against him.

During the months that followed, Jessica visited Evan as much as was possible. She had several assignments which took her out of the country, but, every weekend that she was at home, she made the trip to New Jersey to visit him.

It was December, over a year later, when Jessica made one of these weekend runs to the prison. It had been nearly a month since she had seen Evan although she had talked with him by phone on several occasions during the interim. She was particularly excited to see him. She had some good news. It was dusk as she pulled up to the main security gate and waited for the guard to open it. As she began driving down the narrow road to the small facility, the lights from the one story building actually looked inviting. The irony of that thought did not escape her and she smiled to herself. In some ways, those inside the walls were actually better off than many folks who were on the outside. But, of course, they did not have their freedom and all who were incarcerated would trade anything for that.

She parked the car in the visitor's space and went inside the building. Along with her purse, she carried a large envelope which she presented at the desk for the guard to examine. He inquired about the envelope and she advised him of the contents. He smiled at her and nodded his approval as he passed the items back through the window. "He's waiting for you in the waiting area, Ms. Powers. He called down not more than five minutes ago to see if you had arrived." "Thanks, Smitty." Smitty buzzed Jessica through the steel gate. She headed for the reception area where Evan was waiting for her. She let herself in the door and hurried into his waiting arms.

"Jessica, darling, I'm so happy to see you. I have something for you. Let's go to my room."

Evan took Jessica's hand and led her quickly to the area where the individual units that housed the prisoners were. He was so excited that he was practically running down the hall pulling her with him. By the time they got to his unit, she was nearly out of breath. "Evan," she gasped, "I'm not in the kind of shape you are. What's the rush?"

Evan released her hand and hurried to the table where he picked up a large envelope and handed it to her. "What is this?" she inquired.

"Open it. Go ahead, open it."

Jessica opened the envelope and pulled out a thick legal document. There was a smaller enveloped tucked inside as well. "What's this?" she asked as she leafed through the paper.

"My parole hearing has been scheduled for December 23rd!"

"Oh Evan. I...I don't know what to say."

"Just be happy, Jess."

"Happy! I'm ecstatic." She threw her arms around him as he hugged her in return.

"Evan, why didn't you tell me?"

"I wanted to surprise you."

"You certainly did that. And, what is this?" Jessica realized she was still holding yet another, smaller envelope.

"My divorce is final, Jess. These are the final papers."

"Why didn't you tell me when I called?"

"I wanted to see your expression."

"How long have you known?"

"I found out about the hearing Thursday, and I knew you would be here today. The divorce papers came Monday."

"I can't get my thoughts together. I'm so excited. Oh, I know, I have something for you."

"What?"

"Here. Open it."

Evan took the big envelope from her and tore it open. "It's a newspaper," he said rather blankly.

"I know it's a newspaper. Go to the second section and read my story."

Evan followed her instructions and became completely engrossed in the article. After he finished reading the story, he put the paper down in disbelief. "It's all over. Oh Jessica, I can't believe the nightmare is nearly all over. He's dead. How did it happen?"

"Well, he had been hiding out of the country. The FBI found him and they were bringing him in. As you know he was a very powerful man. And, powerful people always have enemies. When they went to change planes in Miami, someone ran out and shot him. Of course, the place was crawling with agents and they were all over the guy who shot him."

"Who is he? You didn't say in your story."

"He was obviously is a hired gun. They have him locked away now. The FBI is trying now to figure out who it was that hired him. According to their speculation, there has to be someone in the picture who's a bigger fish than Erlich."

"My God, Jessica. I was lucky to get off the merry-go-round when I did. That whole time I was working for the FBI, I was in serious danger. And, I don't even want to mention the expense." Evan shook his head.

"It never would have ended, you know."

"And, when it came down to the wire, they wouldn't acknowledge I was working for them."

"That's the scam we tried to warn you about."

"I was so dumb. I could have died on the outside when all the time I was afraid of this." Evan acknowledged the comfortable accommodations and they both laughed with relief.

Although she had wanted to, Jessica was unable to return to the prison before the twenty-third, the date of the parole hearing. She wouldn't tell him exactly what she was working on, but she seemed to be consumed by her work. Evan missed her whenever he wasn't with her, but he spent all of his time preparing for this important hearing. He knew if he was well prepared, he would have a good chance of being released.

Jessica drove to New Jersey the night before to be certain that she would be there before the nine o'clock hearing. As she explained to Evan before she left, "The weather is clear now, but you can never be sure when it may snow at this time of year."

It had been an astute observation. When she got up early the next morning to drive over to the prison, heavy snow was beginning to fall.

The hearing was brief and, much to their delight, Evan was released effective immediately. She helped him gather his few personal belongings and they headed out of the prison. Jessica had found a quiet resort a few hours away where they would spend Christmas Eve and the holidays if things turned out the way they hoped. Meanwhile, they enjoyed the freedom of driving anywhere they wished. They lunched at leisure and when they arrived at the lodge, Evan picked her up and carried her over the threshold to their room. There could not have been a happier couple anywhere.

There were logs burning in the fireplace and a lighted Christmas tree stood in front of the sliding glass door. They took off there coats and Evan presented Jessica with a small package, very carefully wrapped in Christmas paper. "What's this?"

"Merry Christmas, darling."

Jessica opened the small box and gasped when she saw the beautiful diamond solitaire ring. Evan removed it from the box and slipped it onto her finger. "Jessica Powers, will you marry me?"

"Oh Evan, darling, of course I will marry you," Jessica replied, tears streaming from her eyes. He took her gently into his arms. They held each other and cried tears of joy.

That evening, they enjoyed a quiet but beautiful dinner in their room. They made love in front of the fireplace and fell asleep in each other arms.

They were awakened by a persistent knocking at the door, early next morning. "Who could that be?" Evan asked.

"I don't know. No one knows we are here."

Evan pulled on his shirt and pants and went to the door. "Who's there?"

"Telegram for Jessica Powers."

Evan opened the door. Jessica had put her robe on and was by his side. She took the envelope. "Sign here, please."

Jessica signed the receipt and began to hurriedly tear open the envelope. She quickly read the message.

Beaming from ear to ear, she handed Evan the paper. "This is what I have been working on during the last couple of months, darling."

Evan began reading the wire. The message read:

Senate sub-committee acknowledges irregularities in Justice Department activities/Accepts your challenge to investigate/Hearings to begin 2nd week in January/ Senate requests testimony from both you and Mr. Judd.

"I know you have learned your lesson, darling. But our country was founded upon justice. If our government is allowed to ignore the principles which have made us a great society, then we shall fail as individuals. We cannot tolerate unequal justice. There must be justice for all."

THE END